SIEGE PERILOUS

SIEGE PERILOUS

AND OTHER STORIES

BY

MAUD DIVER

"These things are life;
And life, some think, is worthy of the Muse"
MEREDITH

Short Story Index Reprint Series

BOOKS FOR LIBRARIES PRESS
FREEPORT, NEW YORK

First Published 1924
Reprinted 1970

STANDARD BOOK NUMBER:
8369-3527-6

LIBRARY OF CONGRESS CATALOG CARD NUMBER:
78-122694

PRINTED IN THE UNITED STATES OF AMERICA

AUTHOR'S NOTE

I HAVE only to say of these, my few, occasional short stories, that the three purely Indian ones ('Lakshmi,' 'The Gods of the East,' and 'Escape') are true in essence, taken from life; that my opening story, 'Light Marching Order,' is based on an actual incident in the second Afghan War. It was specially presented to me by one who knew, with leave to use it as I pleased; of course on the understanding that the Regiment was not 'given away.' I need only add that the incident, though true to fact, has been treated as fiction and that both characters concerned are purely imaginary.

Of my longest story, 'Siege Perilous,' I have frankly to admit a certain cousinship, as it were, between the principal characters and those of my last novel. The fact is, that the story was written first, by several years; and when the idea came to me of working out the same initial situation—or something like it—along different lines towards totally different issues, I had then no thought of collecting my shorter work in volume form. However, after due consideration, I am strongly advised, by those whose judgment I value, that the story as it stands is its own justification, and should be included with the rest. I can only hope that the majority of my readers will agree with that decision.

MAUD DIVER.

CONTENTS

		PAGE
I.	LIGHT MARCHING ORDER	3
II.	LAKSHMI	33
III.	THE GODS OF THE EAST	54
IV.	SIEGE PERILOUS	71
V.	SUNIA	151
VI.	COMPLETE SURRENDER	171
VII.	ESCAPE	207
VIII.	REQUITAL	231
IX.	AS OTHERS SEE US	263
X.	PRIVATE PITCHER	279
XI.	BOBS BAHÁDUR	293
XII.	'HE COMES!'	309

TO
MY HUSBAND

LIGHT MARCHING ORDER

LIGHT MARCHING ORDER

Impossible ? Ne me dites jamais cette bête de mot.
                                                    MIRABEAU.

I

DICK CHETWYND, said his brother officers, was in danger of becoming a crank.

But they did not say it in his hearing; for the cogent reason that the danger sprang from his superhuman zeal in respect of the Regiment; and Dick, for all his lively humour, was a red man. Sparks would fly. Moreover, to quarrel with his zeal were to impugn their own; and the Invincibles, collectively and severally, swore by the Regiment—the whole Regiment and nothing but the Regiment. The trouble with Dick was that, in addition to worshipping and swearing, he persistently worked himself off his legs in the service of the most exacting fetish on earth.

And the Colonel encouraged him. The Colonel, as the saying is, had his head screwed on the right way. His own zeal—though unimpeachable—was not of the practical variety. Wherefore, he had chosen for Adjutant the man who could best be relied on to keep his corps up to the mark with a minimum of supervision; who would, in fact, enable Colonel Fullerton Franks to live his own life untroubled by any irksome sense of neglecting his duty.

The Invincibles had been but a year in India and

were still in the stage of accommodating themselves to the tyranny of insects, dust, and personalities; to a sense of exile, far more acute in the Seventies, when India was not the playground of the tourist and the Member of Parliament ' out ' for theories. Not an officer among them, except the Senior Major, had seen a day's service. Their most arduous battles had been fought in the wilds of Hampshire and Wiltshire. Dick Chetwynd, for one, found nothing to quarrel with in a land that promised unlimited sport, and a reasonable chance of something better than playing at soldiers. He had blessed the Fate that sent them to a northerly station; and now, at the end of his first year, rejoiced openly, vain-gloriously, in the condition of his men. The whole corps was ' fit as a fiddle '; supple to handle; a complex instrument in perfect working order. And he yearned for a chance of the supreme test—active service. Rank Militarism? Chetwynd had never encountered the fatal word. Enough for him that fighting was the soldier's business; that men may die, but the Regiment is immortal. The more it is broken, the more it lives. In that simple faith he worked—confident of the issue. Nor was it long before the Amir of Afghanistan and a Viceroy of the ' forward ' school conspired between them to grant him the boon he craved.

For forty years, there had been little friction between India and her thorny buffer state. Since the victorious armies of Nott and Pollock marched down from Kabul to Ferozepore, the truce made with Dōst Mahomed had held good; but now there sat upon the throne one Yakub Khan—grandson of the great Amir, yet no more like his grandfather than Hamlet to Hercules.

And now, as then, the shadow of the Bear, rampant, loomed large on the political horizon.

A new Viceroy had lately arrived, with a new policy in his pocket ; a policy little likely to make for peace, as the sequel proved. Perturbed by Russian activity in Central Asia, his Excellency at Simla had graciously proposed to establish a British Resident at the Afghan capital. His Highness at Kabul—' after compliments '—had repudiated the proposal, without thanks ; and again—as in 1837—the crisis had been precipitated by the appearance of a rival Envoy on the scene.

Shortly before the Invincibles landed at Bombay, the Viceregal ultimatum had been issued, and three invading columns dispatched along the three main routes into Afghanistan. The spell of decades had been broken ; the masterly inactivity of the great John Lawrence discarded, for better—or worse.

Throughout that eventful winter, Chetwynd had followed, eagerly, enviously, every detail of those brilliant operations in the Kuram Valley that established the reputation of one of India's most distinguished soldiers and resulted in a British Resident being once more thrust upon a stiff-necked people at the point of the bayonet.

These things came to pass in June ; and in July the chosen Resident, with three fellow-countrymen and a detachment from the famous Corps of Guides for escort, betook himself to the Bala Hissar, the old grey fortress that towers above Kabul City.

The British troops retired within their own borders, but did not altogether disperse. At Peshawar and in the Kuram Valley they crouched, vigilant, like cats watching a half-stunned mouse.

For at Kabul there was small show of friendship; and men had not quite forgotten '42.

The Invincibles, meantime—flies on the wheel of an empire's destiny—had settled down to face their first hot weather, mitigated by the boon of two months' leave. Chetwynd—fearfully and wonderfully mottled with prickly heat and mosquito bites—abated not a jot of his cold-weather energy; but the irritability of his temper matched that of his skin, and his thirst was as the thirst of Thor when, at one draught, he diminished the waters of the sea.

Throughout those first months of initiation, the liveableness of life depended largely on the output of the regimental ice-pit and soda-water machine. Thanks to these and a few other mercies, the Invincibles came smiling through the worst that a Punjab 'hot weather' can do, and hailed the first of September as 'the beginning of the end.'

"Partridge shooting to-day in the old country," groaned the Senior Major. "Why the devil does a man ever desert England for this poisonous peninsula?"

"Give it a chance, Major," quoth Chetwynd, whose optimism was anathema to the Man of Grievances. "I'll wager you find better sport than partridge shooting round here, once the cold weather comes."

He spoke more truly than he guessed. Before September was a week old, there fell upon India, like a thunderbolt, the black news that those four Englishmen at Kabul, with their escort of seventy guides, had been killed to a man.

The patched-up peace had lasted a bare three months. A half-mutinous band of soldiers, clamouring for arrears of pay, had fired the train and set all Kabul in a blaze.

The British Residency—attacked desultorily at first by the malcontents—was soon in a state of siege. From eight in the morning till dusk, that little band of dauntless men and officers had held their own against thousands; while the prince, who had guaranteed their safety and honourable treatment, sent answer to their appeals for aid: " As God wills, I am making preparation."

By sunset there were neither Guides nor Englishmen in Kabul any more; but heaped around them lay six hundred dead and dying—proof of a defeat more gallant than victory.

Thus, for the second time, did Afghanistan scrawl upon the page of history her savage declaration of independence in letters of blood and fire. His Highness at Kabul had scored a point in characteristic fashion; but the privilege of the last word was not to be his.

Before sunset, on the very day that dread news reached Simla, the plan of campaign had been fixed, the leadership conferred on the hero of the Kuram Valley operations—one whose name was to be as imperishably linked with Afghanistan as the names of Pollock and Nott.

Next day every mess in the Punjab was abuzz with excitement; and when Brigade Orders appeared in a certain northerly station, Dick Chetwynd, of the Queen's Invincibles, knew that his hour had come.

There was no happier man in India that morning than this dapper, red-headed Adjutant, whose prayer had been answered, and whose faith in his corps stood scarcely second to his faith in God.

The troops were to move immediately in light

marching order, four pounds to a man. Chetwynd's hands were full and his heart jubilant as the heart of a schoolboy on the last day of 'term.' As a matter of course, all practical arrangements would be pretty well left in his hands. But he had yet to reckon with the idiosyncrasies of the 'great F. F.', whose readiness to die for his country did not include an equal readiness to forgo, indefinitely, the chief amelioration that made life worth living.

His marching orders to his invaluable Adjutant were brief and explicit.

"The General has cut things down pretty fine," said he. "But of course the soda-water machine goes with the Regiment."

Now a soda-water machine of the Seventies was, in the matter of size and bulk, first cousin to a grand piano.

"I—I beg your pardon, sir?" Chetwynd stammered, desperately, hoping he had not heard aright.

"I said we take the soda-water machine," Franks repeated with deliberate emphasis. "Fighting's thirsty work. I can't stomach whisky and water. Never could."

Still Chetwynd hesitated. "D'you really think we can manage it, sir?" he ventured; but a choleric spark flashed in the Colonel's eye.

"Damn it all, that's your affair. My officers don't question orders. You pride yourself on being a man of resource. Here's a first-rate chance to prove it."

Upon that doubtful consolation he departed; and Dick, with an audible groan, set his elbows on the table, and gripped his head in his hands.

"Light marching order—with a trifle of a grand-piano thrown in! Good God! It's a farce and a tragedy rolled into one!"

Then the humour of the thing smote him and he laughed aloud—laughed and laughed, there alone in the empty room, till the tears ran down his face.

Chetwynd came of Irish stock on his mother's side. He was not the man to make a mountain out of a soda-water machine. Besides, the Colonel's last remark had put him on his mettle. By some means he must contrive that the 'great F. F.'—known among his subalterns as 'Fortissimo'—should enjoy his full complement of 'pegs' in the wilds of Afghanistan, without imperilling the credit of the Regiment. Very well. It should be done.

He went about his work that morning brisk and alert as ever. No one dreamed that a grand piano was, so to speak, sitting on his chest: that while one half of his brain worked mechanically in its appointed grooves, the other half was engaged in distributing and redistributing countless sections of a certain machine; in working out reductions, possible and impossible, to keep the balance true.

The result proved successful beyond his wildest hopes; and on the appointed day, the Queen's Invincibles left the station in light marching order as the General had decreed. No flagrant superfluity of baggage could be detected in the transport column; nor did the men themselves know that each several load contained its own appointed fragment of the regimental soda-water machine.

II

A WEEK later found them encamped, with the whole Kabul Field Force, on three great plateaux, overlooking the Kuram Valley—metaphorically within a stone's throw of Afghanistan. An autumn nip in the air, and splashes of autumn gold on the wooded heights, spoke feelingly of Home; an illusion dispelled by the ordered mass of service tents, by scores and hundreds of tethered animals, audibly impatient for their evening meal, by the clatter and hum of six thousand armed men settling down for the night.

The intervening days had been filled with heat and thirst and flies innumerable; with the noise and dust of their incessant going; for the great little man they followed was not of those who let grass grow under foot, while they scratch their heads and consider the next move.

Only by making a clean sweep of the Peshawar district had he solved the crucial problem of transport and supplies. Even so, he was seriously hampered, and there were moments when Chetwynd marvelled blankly what would become of him should the General stumble on the discovery of that superfluous four camels' load cunningly dispersed throughout the baggage of a crack British Regiment.

So far, it had remained tucked away in the depths while the Colonel drank whisky and water to the betterment of his soul and the distraction of his palate :—but at any moment the cat might be out of the bag. And Chetwynd asked himself—what then ?

The question, it seemed, was superfluous : and as day followed day without mishap or revelation, he almost forgot to be anxious at all.

LIGHT MARCHING ORDER

At last came the long-delayed order to move on by detachments through the defile of a Thousand Trees, and up the Shutargurdan—the pass of the Camel's Neck—already occupied by troops who had wintered at Kuram.

Dick Chetwynd had read of Afghanistan's grim defiles in the tale of '42. Now he saw for himself the snow-fed torrents and naked rocks of dusky red sandstone, chiselled here into obelisks and pillars, there into dragon's teeth prophetic of the immemorial welcome in store for the intruder who defies their silent challenge. Though the defile itself was more open than most of its kind, an eerie spirit of melancholy seemed to brood over the place. Clouds hung low and grey, blotting out the higher hills. Scarcely a bird was to be seen; and there, where the Thousand Trees had once clothed the barren heights, remained only a dismal array of pine-stumps—dry bones of a departed glory.

It was the roughest march they had yet experienced; but the zeal and energy of their leader infected all ranks, and soon after dark the whole detachment had reached the plateau on the summit of the pass. Dead beat, every man of them, all they craved was food and sleep; but an entire camp must be pitched before they could come at either; and the Invincibles had grown skilled by now in the magic of briskly transforming shapeless bundles into a city of tents, the smallest imaginable, with bedding rolls and Spartan accessories to match.

Fullerton Franks, strolling through the camp in search of his Adjutant, found him near the mess tent that was being hauled and hammered into position.

"I've asked the Chief and his Staff to dine with

us to-night," he announced with unofficial geniality.
" Just cast a critical eye on the menu—will you ?—
and see that everything's up to the scratch. Wish
to God we could include 'pegs' in the programme ! "

The small man looked up at him with a twinkle
of amused understanding.

" All in good time, sir ! " said he ; and departed
on his errand.

He found Nur Bux, Knight Commander of the
Brick Oven, squatting among his cooking-pots, his
menu planned to the last item ; a dinner of six
courses—he recited them proudly in a mixture of
Hindustani and mangled French—fit for the *Burra
Lát* himself!

And it was so.

A native cook worth his salt may be trusted to
conjure a creditable meal from a pair of old boots,
a fresh-killed fowl, a tin of sardines, and a trifle
of Worcester sauce—that can be trusted to cover
a multitude of sins. But Nur Bux had material
more promising at command ; and the men who
sat down to eat that night were more hungry than
critical.

Chetwynd found himself next to the Chief's
A.D.C. ; and their talk, like that of the rest,
veered from present vicissitudes to future
possibilities.

" It's my belief," quoth the Aide, " that the
Amir Sahib is a proper skunk, and that we shall
be detained up in these parts a jolly sight longer
than we think for, which will make devotees of the
flesh-pots very sick. Camp fare's good enough to
fight and march on. But when it comes to marking
time——"

He paused and regarded the Adjutant of the
Invincibles with an unmistakable gleam in his eye.

"By the way, Chetwynd—talking of flesh-pots, there's a rumour in the air that we may hope for whisky pegs at Kabul—if we make ourselves agreeable to a certain regiment."

For the hundredth fraction of a minute Chetwynd was taken off his guard. But no start betrayed him; and his alert brain was equal to the occasion.

"Pegs at Kabul?" he echoed, raising innocent brows. "What the devil are you driving at?"

And the Aide, leaning closer, spoke under his breath.

"In plain language, my dear chap, your baggage is marked 'suspicious.'"

Dick was master of himself by this time. "What's wrong with our baggage?" he demanded, a note of challenge in his voice.

"That's precisely what the Chief wants to know! He's got wind from Simla that you've smuggled a soda-water machine in with your legitimate traps, and he's fairly fuming. Says he'll hold a drastic inspection of your transport department to-morrow morning."

Chetwynd drew in his lower lip.

"A pity the General should put himself to unnecessary trouble," he remarked coolly. "But that's his own affair. Thanks for letting me know."

And without giving his neighbour a chance to press the point, he quietly but decisively changed the subject.

The rest of dinner was purgatory for the man who knew that unless that thrice-accursed machine could, by some miracle, be spirited off the pass before dawn, the Regiment he served and worshipped would be made the laughing-stock of the force.

His real self seemed to sit apart, as in a dream, shuffling and discarding crazy schemes, each one crazier than the last ; while the outer shell of him ate and drank, and made all the correct facial contortions with imperturbable aplomb. The thrice-accursed must be a good four camels' load if it was an ounce ; and how the deuce could a hapless Adjutant, perched on a barren ridge, beg, borrow, or steal four camels at a few hours' notice in the dead of night, to say nothing of smuggling them past the pickets of ' Bobs Bahadur ' ?

It was a crazy situation ; but Dick was in no mood to relish the humour of it just then. Impatience consumed him. Would these men never cease their drinking and yarning, that he might escape and think to some purpose ?

A lull in the hubbub of voices promised release at last ; and upon the first plausible pretext he made his escape, while the source of his dilemma sat smoking with the General, in superb unconsciousness of the game afoot.

The first whiff of night air, keen and crisp, cleared his distracted brain. There must certainly be a village within reasonable distance ; and his very good friend, the regimental Munshi, could be trusted to raise camels from the vasty deep, if the credit of the *pultan*[1] required it of him.

But for once, Karim Bux, the resourceful, could only wag his beard. The Colonel Sahib was great and Chetwynd Sahib was his father and mother ; but would he be pleased to consider the fact that camels did not grow wild upon the hills of this God-forsaken country ; that the night was black as hell ; the path to the village a mere goat track, and the head man probably a *badmash*, who would

[1] Regiment.

sooner cut the throat of one Karim Bux than provide cattle for an infidel *feringhi*.

The Sahib, it appeared, had already considered these things; but they were as nothing to his urgent need.

" And among soldiers, as you very well know," said he, " an order is an order. The good name of the *pultan* hangs upon the departure of those camels by midnight. That is to say, they must be outside my tent within two hours; or, by the God who made us both, there will be a munshi's funeral to-morrow ! "

Karim Bux salaamed to the ground. " Of what avail to use bit and bridle upon the north wind ? The Sahib hath spoken. If I return empty-handed, your Honour may take the head of Karim Bux off his shoulders. *Bismillah* ! "

" And if you achieve this thing your services shall not be forgotten. Now go—and God speed you ! "

Thus encouraged, he went without more ado; and Chetwynd hurried off to interview the Quartermaster, the only other man who knew. His part it was to make sure that not a single section was overlooked, and that the loads, securely packed, be ready within an hour. That done, Dick returned to his Kabul tent and flung himself on his *resai*[1] to await the issue.

Tired though he was, his brain was too active for sleep. He heard his brother officers laughing and talking as they strolled back from mess. Thereafter silence—but for the restless shifting of picketed horses, the tread of sentries, the hacking cough of some luckless man from the plains, who was not appreciating the Afghan

[1] Cotton quilt.

climate. He consulted his watch every ten minutes or so, in the conviction that at least half an hour had elapsed.

Sounds grew fainter, and his thoughts had begun to ramble incoherently, when he was startled wide awake by a sonorous murmur between the tent-flaps.

"*Hazur*, we are here—I and the required camels. We await the pleasure of the Sahib."

Pleasure was a mild word for the sensations of that Sahib, as he sprang to his feet and charged through the flaps into the Munshi's arms. Yes, the camels were there. The unmistakable smell of them was sweeter to his nostrils just then than attar of roses; and he never again smelt camel without a vivid recollection of that moment.

Thereupon, all was swift and silent action. While their loads were being lashed into position, Dick had a private interview with the driver, whose doubts evaporated at sight of good rupees— a hundred and fifty, cash down, plus a written promise of a hundred and fifty more to be paid when the precious freight should be delivered to Chetwynd intact. The driver, gloating inwardly, was fain to admit that the Presence offered fair payment. At the house of his cousin, a coppersmith in Kabul City, he would await further instructions, and pray for the Sahib's welfare in this world and the next.

The Sahib's sole concern, just then, was for the welfare of those camels miraculously delivered into his hands. Karim Bux would manipulate them through the pickets; and, *inshallah*, all would be well.

On the stroke of midnight, Chetwynd stood alone outside his tent.

LIGHT MARCHING ORDER

Camels, driver, and munshi had been swallowed up by darkness. The incubus of weeks was gone; the credit of the Regiment secure. Once again he flung himself down; slept like the dead till *réveillé;* and awoke to the blessed realisation that a grand piano was no longer sitting on his chest.

Undismayed, he received the order for baggage inspection; undismayed, he watched the disembowelling of load after load, secure in the knowledge that the lynx-eyed General would discover no ghost of a non-regulation item in their depths.

Fullerton Franks, still blandly innocent of suspicion in the air, had merely remarked in passing, " No fear, I suppose, of those sections coming to light ? "

" No fear at all, sir, I've got 'em up my sleeve ! " had been Chetwynd's answer : and, for Franks, it was enough.

Leisurely and thoroughly the inspection progressed. Blank, and still more blank, was the amazement of the General, as it dawned on him that the unimpeachable authority at Simla must have had his leg pulled by some impertinent junior. And because he was a true soldier, his amazement was tinctured with relief.

Mule by mule the transport animals were reloaded. In the circumstances, nothing could be done; and Dick Chetwynd, bogey-ridden no longer, could throw himself whole-heartedly into the stirring campaign ahead.

Stirring and successful enough, it proved, to satisfy the most insatiable soldier of them all.

Within the week, a detachment of their modest force, under its wise, daring little chief, had met and routed the flower of the Afghan Army, captured all the guns brought out against them and swooped down on Kabul in masterly style. Though their numbers were insignificant, every regiment, British and Indian, came of fighting stock; and they swore by their leader as one man. No empty tribute, but faith born from knowledge of his works and ways. Thanks to his skill and untiring energy, they found themselves—five weeks after the outrage at Kabul—encamped under the lee of her high citadel, virtually masters of the situation.

III

THE twelfth of October was a day of very mingled feelings, in city and fortress and camp. On that day, all Kabul was assembled in its fort-palace, the Bala Hissar, there to hear a proclamation of victory, achieved by arms and confirmed by an absconding Amir—now a self-constituted 'guest' in the British Camp.

Through a brilliant avenue of Lancers and Highlanders, Sikhs, and Gurkhas, the General and Staff rode forth that morning. At the Peshawar Gate of the fortress, Horse Artillery guns boomed a Royal Salute, the Union Jack was unfurled above the archway, and in the garden of the Amir's palace Afghans thronged to hear a pronouncement all too mild in view of the offence. Not more than three leading Sirdars were put under arrest; a British General was appointed Military Governor of the city, till more stable arrangements could be made between the Indian Government and a new Amir, chosen from among the aspiring grandsons of Dōst Mahomed. Yakub Khan, on his own confession, aspired no longer. Rather would he be a grass-cutter in the British camp, than ruler of his turbulent people.

The formidable Afghan Army—having found the invaders' method of fighting little to its taste—had blown up its magazine and deserted the fortified cantonment on the plain. Therein—after drastic cleansings and fumigation—the British troops entrenched themselves. And there followed a great unpacking. Regimental messes were established—and Colonel Fullerton Franks bethought him of his long-delayed whisky peg.

Not till then did Chetwynd tell the tale of those unauthorised midnight proceedings on the Shutargurdan Pass; and the delighted Colonel clapped him on the shoulder.

"Here's your three hundred," said he, "and welcome! You're sure it's all safe in the city?"

Yes, it was all safe. Dick had disembowelled every load and counted every section, before the second hundred and fifty was paid. He had also managed to strike up an acquaintance with a friendly Afghan Sirdar, Hasan Khan, who would let their treasure be set up in a back courtyard of his town house, on condition that he should be allowed a share of the ' water made alive.'

"It'll prove a sound working scheme, I think, sir," Dick concluded, with a glow of justifiable pride. "We discover—or rather, our munshi discovers—by chance, that soda-water grows in Kabul City. We can quite well supply the hospital, plus the General and his Staff. Rather a lark, making the Chief accessory after the fact, so to speak, in spite of himself!"

At that the Colonel laughed aloud. "Upon my soul, young man, for sheer audacity you take the cake! Fix up any arrangements you please. Strikes me, I've blossomed out as a public benefactor! Quite a happy notion of mine bringing that machine along; though you must admit you didn't think so, at the time."

" No, sir, I didn't," Chetwynd confessed, smiling discreetly; and withdrew to crown his audacity by an arrangement—via the faithful Karim Bux— to supply Sherpur Cantonment with soda-water at very little more than canteen rates.

The working scheme proved as sound as heart could wish; that drastic inspection on the pass having quite set the General's mind at rest. How should the shrewdest suppose that a soda-water machine could be spirited off the Shutargurdan Pass in the dead of night? So much the better for Dick and his Colonel. So much the better for sick and wounded men in hospital. So much the better for the Chief himself, who enjoyed his ' peg ' as much as any officer of the force and earned it more strenuously than most.

He was not the man to be put off his guard by the deceptive quiet of those peaceful autumn days. Well he knew that, in Afghanistan, the end of harvest is the time of times for warfare on the slightest pretext: and no slight pretext was here. Well he knew, also, that, although thirty thousand British troops were in the field, he and his little force stood practically alone—hemmed in by hills that would soon be impassable till the spring. And knowing these things, he energised the more vigorously to complete and provision that unfinished cantonment against the day of trouble. Hap what might, he would not be starved into virtual surrender, like Elphinstone's pitiful army thirty-three years before.

The Afghan Sirdars, meantime, watched these proceedings in a puzzled, inimical silence. Retribution for the massacre of a peaceful Embassy, they had expected as a matter of course—retribution followed by prompt departure. But this ' pestilent, *zabbardusti* [1] little General Sahib ' seemed in no hurry at all. His suspicious zeal in the matter of provisions augured a prolonged visitation such as they had no mind to endure : and in Afghanistan there is always a convenient holy man to blow the spark of fanatical hate to a flame.

Such an one was the shrivelled, tottering high priest of Ghazni, Muskh-i-Alum, Fragrance of the Universe—a name befitting most of his kind, though the ribald infidel might express it in plainer terms. Ninety years old he was ; but the flame within burned fierce as ever : and very soon the General at Kabul knew him for the leading spirit of a national rising that was simply a question of time.

Husbandry was over for the year : and throughout those cool, quiet November days, herdsmen, landowners, discharged soldiers came flocking to the banner of the Prophet ; to loot and massacre the infidel Feringhi, as their fathers had done in the day of Mahomed Akbar Khan.

But these had another than Elphinstone to reckon with. The ' pestilent, *zabbardusti* ' one had no notion of sitting still inside his defences till their plans were complete. Whatever the odds against him, he would be the first to strike.

Early in December the storm broke, and there followed two weeks of sharp fighting for possession of the heights around Kabul—weeks that filled the heart of a certain Adjutant with secret pride in the men he had sworn at and loved and handled for years.

But neither gallantry, nor discipline, nor skill in the art of war could avail, for long, against

[1] High-handed.

the hordes that came pouring into Kabul Valley, from north and south and west, like torrents let loose in spring. By the middle of the month they amounted to anything between sixty and seventy thousand ; and in spite of the unconquerable spirit that pervaded all ranks, the General—wise as he was bold—decided to withdraw from all isolated positions, and avoid further useless sacrifice of life.

His field hospitals were already over full : and in one of them, among the recently wounded, lay the ' great F. F.', with a bullet in his thigh—a gift from an Afghan rifle during the last general engagement on the heights.

Though new to active service, and a man of many small weaknesses, Fullerton Franks had shown, throughout, a capacity for command and a cool intrepidity under fire that few would have given him credit for, six months ago. Now he lay stricken and in acute pain—he, the well-bred gourmet and messroom martinet—cursing the accuracy of Afghan marksmen, but with never a word of complaint or impatience on his lips. In war, the touchstone of character, these little surprises are not uncommon. And now, in his sorest need, there was no drop of soda-water to be had from the cherished machine that would probably be looted or destroyed by those who were sacking their own capital, with the unthinking frenzy of their race.

For a week that uncrushable little army remained in a state of siege, impatiently awaiting the combined attack that was to wipe it off the face of the earth.

And at dawn, on the 23rd, it came.

On the 22nd spies brought news of the intended

coup; the signal for action to be a beacon fire lighted on the heights of Asmai, above Sherpur, by the Fragrance of the Universe in person.

That night the old man—trembling with ague and fanatical zeal—had himself carried up the hill, where snow lay a foot deep: and there, in the bitter cold of a December dawn, he set the beacon aflare, pouring oil upon the flame with his own sacred hand. Sticks and oil burned merrily; and the wild signal, leaping aloft, flung pennons of light down to the snow-covered plain; down to that huge parallelogram of walls and bastions, where the infidel slept in supposed innocence of his approaching doom.

As a matter of fact, the infidel was very much aware.

Throughout the night, a strict watch had been kept within those walls. Every man was at his post; Chetwynd and Blundell shared a small tent in a ditch below one of the bastions, where the guns were ready. In the dark of earliest morning a gunner waked them; and, as they followed him up on to the tower, the flare of that huge beacon laughed in their faces, a welcome promise of action —at last!

"Thank the Lord, they mean business!" Chetwynd ejaculated piously under his breath.

No one on the bastion spoke above a whisper; and in the deep, expectant hush their quick ears caught the scrape of scaling-ladders dragged over frosty snow; the shuffling tramp of sandalled feet —thousands and thousands of them, hurrying across the open plain.

Then, as the grey east glimmered, a rifle shot rang out from Deh-i-Afghan; another from the King's garden; another, and again another, from villages on the south and east of Sherpur. Shadowy masses of men bearing huge ladders made a determined rush for the walls; and, at intervals, jets of flame flashed out.

For answer, the crackling laughter of carbines and the roar of howitzers announced that the 'surprise' was no surprise at all; and effectually checked the opening move. Within the zone of that leaden hail-storm men could not live, much less attempt to scale the walls.

And now—over against the south-eastern angle —there rose a shout that swelled to a tumultuous roar, as if the throats of half Afghanistan yelled defiance.

Here also counter-defiance greeted them in a deafening rattle of musketry from the Queen's Corps of Guides, well chosen by the General to defend his weakest point. But the Afghans, though smitten by volley on volley, came on again, and yet again. That awful composite roar and rattle swelled and sank and swelled anew; while other attacking parties howled in chorus.

Not until near noon was there any real sign of wavering. Then did the General—with a soldier's instinct for the right stroke at the right moment— let slip his Horse Artillery with most of his cavalry——

And the siege of Sherpur was at an end.

Fast and far rode the pursuers. Far and fast sped the pursued. By sunset that vast army— not less than a hundred thousand men—had been swept out of sight and hearing as if it had never been. Only the dead, lying unburied where they had fallen, remained for witness that the god of war had passed that way.

A victory indeed!

IV

CHRISTMAS again—and the Punjab! Bungalows again and mufti, and the sight and sound of English women, welcome exceedingly to men who had been cut off from them for more than a year.

After seven months of peaceful occupation, the second Afghan War had culminated, dramatically enough, in that daring dash from Kabul to retrieve the disaster of Maiwand and relieve an invested Kandahar. Within five days of receiving Viceregal sanction for his bold enterprise, the General and ten thousand picked troops were ready for any fate. There lay before them three hundred and twenty miles of hard, continuous marching through the fanatical Ghilzai country, cut off from communication with the world, from all hope of help, should disaster befall.

But the men trusted their General and the General trusted his men; a combination that puts failure out of question.

As many of his original regiments as were fit for this strenuous finale were included in his compact little force—Dick Chetwynd and his Invincibles among them. No possibility this time of smuggling in a ' grand piano ' even had the great Fortissimo given the word.

Dick had found his treasure intact, after the siege, safe sheltered under the roof of Hasan Khan. In the haste and excitement of departure, he had the happy inspiration of presenting it to the Chief as a trifling tribute of gratitude for services rendered; and had set out on that memorable 8th of August, feeling the lighter by four camels' load of responsibility—a free man at last!

He had undertaken to pull the thing through without ' giving away the Regiment ' : and he had done it ; but the firm resolve of his heart was : ' Never again : not for all the Colonels in creation ! '

For three weeks the General and his little force—marching, always marching, in the hottest month of the year—had vanished from human ken. In England and India the tension of suspense grew and grew, till it became almost unbearable. What then must it have been at Kandahar ? And still they marched and marched—footsore, thirst-tormented, stunned with lack of sleep. Nothing stayed their progress ; and enthusiasm grew out of the enterprise ; grew ' as a response to the unfailing spirit of the leader himself.'

In those three weeks he gave them but one clear day of rest ; and on August 31st, he marched them —dead beat, but triumphant—to the walls of the invested town. Next morning, after a sound night of sleep, they rose at dawn to fight the battle of Kandahar. And with that decisive victory the war came fittingly to an end.

Now, early on Christmas Eve, Captain, and Brevet-Major Richard Chetwynd, D.S.O., sat beside a cheerful log fire in his old bungalow, enjoying his *chota hazri*, previous to enjoying, still more, his morning ride.

If there were those who questioned the wisdom and justice of the second Afghan War, it was not in human nature that he should be reckoned among them. It had given him the best year of his life ; and seemed likely to prove the turning-point of his career.

There was also a girl—a wonderful girl—whose

LIGHT MARCHING ORDER

like had never been since the world began; a slender dark creature with violet-grey eyes.

Before leaving India, the spell had been upon him; and in a year of separation he had discovered that a man may arrive at worshipping a woman even as he has worshipped his regiment. Only last night he had confided that discovery to the Wonderful Girl, in fear and trembling; and behold, there was no reason to fear or tremble at all.

By way of confirmation, he was to fetch her that morning and take her for a ride. It was all very amazing and uplifting; and Dick had no quarrel, just then, with this best of all possible worlds. His beloved corps, though battered, had covered itself with distinction. The Colonel was at Home on sick leave; and there was a new soda-water machine in the regimental canteen. Some day he would tell that tale to the Wonderful Girl. For he was immensely proud of his own share in the transaction.

He found her ready for him; and in the rapture of that first greeting, confirmation was complete. Trotting leisurely down the Mall, absorbed in the only subject under the sun, Dick's eye was suddenly arrested by a man in a poshteen on a sorry-looking pony—an Afghan, beyond all doubt. As he drew near, Chetwynd knew him for a follower of Hasan Khan.

"What the dickens is *that* fellow doing in India?" he exclaimed in amazement; and very soon had his answer.

The Afghan, recognising him, cantered up and poured forth a tale of woe, that had brought him post haste from Kabul, in search of the little red Sahib who had given his master, at parting, a devil-machine that made water alive.

Now the Light of Nations, hearing of this thing, had denounced it as black magic, and had cast the owner into prison under sentence of death.

"Since that hour, Chetwynd Sahib," the man concluded, "I have ridden night and day to find your honoured regiment. And now, I beseech you, in God's name, make immediate arrangement to remove that devil-machine from Kabul—or my master is a dead man."

A devil-machine indeed! Would he never be rid of the confounded thing?

Thus Dick, in the privacy of his heart, while he briefly explained matters to the Wonderful Girl.

"It's the worst of luck. But I *must* go home at once and wire to Simla. It's all I can do. I'll come round again this evening. No fear!"

So they parted—for the moment—and there sped to the Military Secretary at Simla an urgent wire promising further unofficial explanation; begging, meantime, that the mind of the Amir might be promptly set at rest as regards the legacy left by a grateful British officer to Sirdar Hasan Khan.

To that end, the matter had to be laid before the Viceroy, who was not above enjoying the joke. Straightway, he dispatched a special firman to His Highness at Kabul, explaining the harmless and useful nature of an infernal machine the like of which was to be found in every cantonment throughout India.

In this fashion, at last, the ghost was laid; and Dick heard no more of the unauthorised incubus that had once threatened to tarnish the reputation of his regiment.

Sir Richard Chetwynd is a distinguished General now, with half the alphabet after his name; but it is doubtful whether any of his brilliant achievements in the field have ever given him quite the same satisfaction as that unnoticed exploit on the Shutargurdan Pass, whereby he not only saved the face of his Colonel, but supplied the Kabul Field Force with soda-water.

TO
MY FATHER

TWO RAJPUT SKETCHES FROM LIFE

I. LAKSHMI: DAUGHTER OF THE SUN-BORN

I

*As is water to the thirsty, so is the lover to the bride.
Who is there that will carry my news to my Beloved?*

KABIR.

IT was early evening. She was putting the last touches to her toilet,—the one serious business of the day: a deeper smudge of *kol* under her lashes; a brighter touch of red for the full lower lip. Then she sat pensive, mirror in hand, gravely debating whether to enhance the effect of her jade necklet with the new rope of pearls—her father's latest gift.

There was no resisting the pearls. They hung nearly to her waist and gleamed like a string of little moons on her brocaded bodice. A *sari* of palest green, with narrow gold border, fell loosely over her full skirt—indigo blue, like the sky at night. She had chosen her colours carefully for their meaning: green, for hope in the new life foreshadowed by arrangements now in progress for her marriage; indigo, the dye that will never wash out, for constancy in love—should she win to favour with her unknown husband.

In her restricted world of the Inside,[1] no girl was

[1] The *zenana*.

chidden for frank delight in trinkets and jewels, in the contents of the great carven chest that held her all. Since waking from her noon-day siesta, Lakshmi had spent an hour and more inspecting the contents of her own chest—fifty *saris*, twenty skirts, thirty bodices, muslins, silks, and many-coloured embroideries, all laid out and smoothed and refolded by her maid and girl-companion, Sarani. There had been much fun and laughter over her final choosings: and now she sat alone, considering the result, turning this way and that her heavy round mirror set with uncut gems.

It told her she was beautiful; and she loved it for telling her so; even as she loved her own image, with a vanity as naïvely unashamed as the egotism of a child. She, that was fifteen, a woman grown, how should she not take pleasure in the golden tint of her skin, the gloss of her oiled hair, the softly rounded cheeks and aquiline nose, lips redder than coral, softer than rose-petals, and the cunningly enhanced lustre of her dark eyes. It was the face of a true Rajputni—and she knew it; eyes and lips were quick with fire and passion and pride of race. On the day when negotiations and wedding rites were ended, he, the unknown one, would at last behold it; and then, if her eyes and lips failed not, he would surely take no other to wife; he would set her like a seal upon his heart.

From Arjuna—elder brother and playmate—she had contrived to coax details about those impending negotiations, even about the Prince himself; details that Little Mother and Big Mother would never divulge, even if they knew them. No dissolute, elderly husband for her! At her father's bidding, she would do almost anything (the un-

LAKSHMI

heroic reservation would creep in), but that—
never! Having himself encouraged her to drink
the bright, sweet waters of knowledge, he could
not expect her to be, in all things, like her sainted
mother. Tradition and the heritage of centuries
kept her still outwardly submissive to grand-
maternal authority; obedient to the letter of
Hindu domestic etiquette: but within, her venture-
some spirit was neither submissive nor obedient;
and in the main it was his own doing. For it is not
fathers, but mothers, and, above all, grandmothers
—supreme in sanctity and authority—who make
trouble in the matter of opening doors and
vanishing veils.

Her own father—who loved travel and had
fought for England in the Great War—had himself
been her earliest teacher. And now in the evenings
—the ceremony of his mealtime ended—he would
send for her to read with him, in the outer apart-
ments, where her mother rarely went and her
grandmother never. Together they would read
English stories of love and valour, passion and
greed: or legends and heroic deeds of their own
race—the fine flower of Indian chivalry, of kings
who were soldiers and soldiers who were kings. For,
in Rajputana, the two words are almost as one.

It was chiefly from the English tales and poems
that she had gleaned ideas about marriage which
would open the eyes of Big Mother. And from
them no doubt came her bold, unorthodox craving
to see, in a picture, the face of him to whom they
would presently hand her over, veiled and unknown.

Arjuna—most indulgent of brothers—had told
her he was young and of good repute; a prince of
moderate education, more given to sport than to

books : son of a greater chief than her father. And to Arjuna—who had met him in England—she had whispered, at last, her unmaidenly craving. Were there not photographs, for which comely young princes had a notorious weakness ? Could he not flatter his friend into giving him one, and secretly pass it on to her ?

Arjuna—scandalised but soft-hearted—had been pressed into admitting that the thing might be done. And she had straightway commanded that it should be done—or she would hold him unworthy the name of brother.

He was away now, on a visit to the State of her would-be bridegroom, taking part in a great week of *shikar*, organised in honour of the young Prince from England. At parting she had coaxed and pleaded, till he vowed ' by the sin of the sack of Chitor ' that he would not return without the coveted picture.

" And how if it does not meet with your approval ? " he had teased her, brother-like. " What can you do in a matter altogether outside your province ? "

And she—laughing at his simple masculinity—had replied : " I am neither a fool, nor a child, any more. Am I not fifteen—and a woman grown ? You can leave that to me."

The days of waiting had seemed like weeks : but this evening he would return.

All had been arranged between them. Screened by a friendly battlement on her roof-top corner, she was to wave a hand, signifying her presence : and he, if successful, would raise his, in a particular manner, to the ornament in his turban. Then she would know. And then he would come himself, to deliver his trophy.

LAKSHMI

The mischievous thought intruded : What would Little Mother say, or Big Mother—high priestess of *dastur*[1]—did they dream of these bold-faced doings ? The thought reduced her to a fit of girlish giggling ; tempted her—almost—to tell the tale (as if it were of another), and enjoy the fun of hearing them ' break the lightnings ' over her head, never suspecting the truth. But dread of discovery sobered her. Big Mother had the serpent's wisdom hid in her cunning old brain. Besides—by now Arjuna might be there.

Outside, up on her roof top, the battlements already made broad stripes of sun and shadow : and she, boldly advancing to the low wall, laid rosy, henna-tipped fingers on the warm stone that sent a queer thrill through her veins. No signs, yet, of the returning cavalcade.

Leaning farther forward, she looked down into the women's walled garden, cool and shadowed : stone paths and marble traceries and the great tank where four fountains made sprays of dancing waterdrops. The splash and tinkle of their falling came distinctly to her ears. Now and then, they danced higher, flashed in the sun like jewels of flame and green and gold ; fell—and became again mere water-drops, that pricked the still surface of the tank like a shower of pins.

Wide paths framed the tank ; and beyond, in the garden among the orange trees, all the roses of April were in bloom—crimson and creamy pink. Where the first blossoms had fallen, the white stone path was flecked with little crimson splashes like blood. And beyond the Palace walls, stood the greater walls of the city ; and beyond the city lay the desert—wave on wave of lifeless sand, and

[1] Custom.

out of the desert sprang the stark rose-red hills of
Rajputana. To her listening ears, the quietness
grew oppressive. Only that far tinkle of water and
the ceaseless kuru-koo-ing of doves.

All these familiar things her senses registered
automatically. Her thoughts were away with the
truant brother, who delayed his coming.

Sounds at last, from the far side overlooking
the courtyard; a confusion of hoofs and jingling
harness and laughter of men.

As a bird runs, she skimmed across the roof-top,
sari flying; flattened herself into the kink of a
buttress, near an opening in the masonry—and
peered cautiously through.

It was a stirring sight: horses, with gay saddle-
cloths and bridle reins, tossing heads and swishing
tails to brush away the flies; grooms running up,
riders dismounting. And there, foremost among
them, sat Arjuna, slim and erect, in the saddle with
its royal trappings of scarlet and gold; a Rajput
of the Rajputs; rider and warrior born, like all the
best men of his race; men of princely temper, of
blended chivalry and ruthlessness, vanity, and
courage.

He was laughing and talking, while, at the same
time, looking up carelessly at a particular corner
of the Palace wall. Through the slit in the
masonry, her fingers fluttered once. His went up
to his turban.

In the shadow, she stood and waited; hands
pressed to her heart that fluttered in her body like
a wild bird breaking its wings against its cage.
Would he never have done with formalities of
arrival, with tales of his own prowess?

Yes—at last!

He stood there before her, laughingly withholding her treasure, threatening to carry it straight to Big Mother.

Imperiously she flung out her small, clenched hands. "Give it me—*give* it, Arjuna-*bhai*.[1] It is mine."

"Nay, it is mine!" he teased her: but he gave it—a full-length portrait, in the uniform of the great Maharaja's army.

With shaking fingers and eyes cast down, she held it, while he stood awaiting her lively comments —that came not, because of the strange tumult in her heart and body.

She had not dreamed how it would be—this new sensation, so swift and disturbing—she, who had never so regarded any unrelated man of her own race. The princely carriage of him, the fire of pride in his eyes that looked straight, straight into her own, till the trembling passed from her fingers to her limbs . . . and still no words would come.

"Art thou not satisfied, little sister?" Arjuna's voice reached her through a confused ecstasy of sensation. "Talk of betrothal is already afoot. The omens are favourable. It were folly——"

At that her eyes shifted to his face with their familiar twinkle of mischief; and her lips moved of themselves.

"I am satisfied."

Her voice sounded so calm, that she could almost have cried out, in surprise, at her own hypocrisy.

And, with some jesting answer, he left her.

That night she could scarcely sleep for thinking of her picture. Every few minutes she must be slipping a hand under her pillow to make sure it

[1] Brother.

was there. When the moon rose and lighted the world as if it were day, she must fling off her light covering and creep out on to the roof-top, to look and look and look at those unknown eyes that boldly gazed into her own; stirring within her, afresh and afresh, that first confused ecstasy, past understanding.

She had read in English stories and poems of feelings that invaded the heart through love; but those who wrote either did not know, or did not tell all that there was to tell. How should they? Such secret feelings were not for everyday speech or for printed words. Had her gentle little mother, steeped in husband worship, ever felt this wild commotion in her breast?

Towards morning, she fell lightly asleep. On the instant of waking she remembered—and slid a hand under her pillow, foolishly fearful lest any should have stolen her treasure while she slept.

The photograph was still there.

II

If but once you should raise your loving eyes to my face, it would make my life sweet, beyond Death.—TAGORE.

FROM that night, onward, she became a new creature, self-dedicated, to one thought, one desire: keeping her treasure securely hid from all her feminine, chattering world.

No question of ought or ought not disturbed her passionate content; no qualms as to mild deceptions practised on those who would denounce and spurn her, did they guess that a daughter of their honourable house had brazenly looked even on the printed image of him she was to call husband. Surely none but a daughter of Rajputs would have so dared, even in these bold days. For of such were the women of her race ; foremost for courage and heroism among the many nations of India.

So April passed.

Then—one evening, Arjuna came to her with a grave face; and there, alone upon the housetop, he told her how difficulties had arisen in the marriage arrangements, just when all had promised so well for a speedy conclusion of the close bargaining that is part and parcel of marriages in the East. The State astrologers, consulted as to propitious dates, had declared that the omens were favourable ; that she, Lakshmi, would prove a model wife and bear many sons. Could the most exigent Prince ask more ?

" It is said," Arjuna told her, " that the Maharaja has doubts whether our house is sufficiently exalted for connection with one of such ancient lineage as his own."

And Lakshmi, hiding the pain at her heart, retorted in anger: " Are *we* not also Sesodia— sun-descended ? What lineage more ancient can they require ? "

Arjuna shook his head. " That is but talk, little sister ; a screen for the truth. Doubtless the holy men have secured a larger dowry from some wealthier State. Men talk of lineage, but they follow the chink of rupees as the cobra follows the snake charmer."

" And has my father no pride, no anger for such insult to our house ? "

" Canst ask ? His face is darkened so none dare approach him. But to what end ? Set the anger of a Rajah against the money bags of a *bunnia*— which will prevail ? Money is master in these low-caste days."

"Has the prince himself no word to say in the matter ? "

"It is reported that he marries to please his mother, being in no hurry to take a wife."

And Lakshmi, still hiding the pain at her heart, lifted her head a shade higher and answered not a word.

Later on, in the dark hours, she dropped bitter tears on the picture of him who had repudiated her —for all the rumours of her beauty and the favourable conspiracy of the stars. She had boasted to Arjuna that she was neither fool nor child, in such matters ; but against these far-off, unknown forces, her pride and anger dashed themselves in vain.

And there was worse news in store.

On a certain evening, while she sat reading with her father, Arjuna came in with a letter from a cousin—one who had known Prince Dyan Singh at the Mayo College, and held a confidential post in the Maharaja's household. He wrote that all had been hurriedly arranged for the Prince's immediate marriage to a child scarcely eight years old ; a proceeding her own father—apart from personal reasons—was sufficiently advanced to disapprove.

For Lakshmi that cruel news held only one grain of consolation—the Prince could not yet take her to wife. For several years the child bride would still remain in her father's house.

And while the men talked, anger flamed in her ; and the bitterness of disappointment, humiliation, was like oil poured upon the flame.

Suddenly she stood up—hands clenched to hide their trembling, soft eyes flashing.

"Of what use to talk—you who are men ? Shall there be such breaking of princely word, such insult to my father's house—and no retort, no demand that faith be kept with promises given ? "

Father and brother were silent a moment ; astonished doubtless and shamed a little, by that challenge to their manhood from a mere girl.

Arjuna was angry also. His eyes gave back fire for fire ; but her father spoke quietly, resting a hand upon her shoulder.

" It is easy for small people to make big talk, daughter of my heart. I, a Sesodia, swallow no insults to my House. I have long desired this union ; but these matters rest chiefly with the marriage-makers. And when there is accord between the holy men and the Inside nothing can come of flinging fiery words."

Dearly she loved and honoured her father ; but his quietness only angered her the more. In the madness of the moment, words broke from her— words unbecoming to girlish modesty and daughterly respect.

Of what avail to be men, Rajputs, and warriors ? Women-ridden, priest-ridden—were they princes only in name ? Rumour would spread abroad the news of her shameful rejection. She—daughter of Rajputs—was no doll, to be so lightly dishonoured. If she was but a woman behind the curtain, she had her pride and her wits. Let them wait a little—and they would see——

Then—breathless, afraid of her own daring, still more afraid because of her secret—she turned and sped down the long, dim corridors, back to the Inside, to the sanctuary of her roof-top and the darkness spangled with stars.

It was many evenings before her father sent for her to read with him again. But her words were no empty boast. By some means, by any means,

she would win him yet ; she would reign supreme,
in his heart, in his palace, second wife or no.
Were he the highest born Prince in all Rajputana,
he should not so spurn the daughter of Maharaja
Rajendra Singh. Let them wait only a little !
She would find a way.

For her, the waiting proved harder than for
them; but while those hateful wedding ceremonies
continued, even her impatience must contain
itself.

Meantime Big Mother became voluble, urging
her son to make fresh approaches elsewhere ; or
the girl would soon be too old for any right-minded
man to look at her. *She* did not uphold this
crazy new fashion of waiting for betrothal till
girls were old enough to fancy they had minds
of their own, and to make trouble ; disturbing,
through the vagaries of personal desire, the ordinance of heaven executed on earth by priests and
women.

Lakshmi, without question, had a mind of her
own : and she made trouble so effectually that her
father promised at last he would entreat his old
mother to have patience a little longer.

So, for a time, she ceased from troubling ; but
Lakshmi ceased not a moment from planning and
plotting ; wavered not a moment in her resolve to
win that laggard one by the inverted method of
the East—marry him first, and captivate him afterwards.

In the evenings, reading with her father, she would
beg leave to close the book, and would talk eloquently of the promise that—for the honour of
both houses—must be fulfilled ; pricking his Rajput
self-esteem to the quick with the delicate barb of

her woman's wit; still cloaking, with a show of pride and scorn, the hidden pain at her heart.

If Arjuna had his private suspicions, he said never a word. He was frankly her ally, do what she would. For she did not limit herself to upbraiding. Modern developments apart, the woman of Rajputana is more of an individual to be reckoned with than the majority of her kind. Wife and mother of warriors, she has the strain of heroism and adventure in her blood. To be strictly *purdanashin* is the hall-mark of aristocracy; but, in temper and talent, Lakshmi was no mere ' cage-bird.' Her father, by giving her education, had put the golden key into her hands. She could not only read, but write fluently, both in English and in her own tongue. Wits and talents, alike, she used without scruple to compass the desire of her infatuate heart. Talk of family pride might be on her lips; but within—pride itself, like all else, was burnt up in the fire that a pictured image had so swiftly and fiercely lighted in her breast.

She pleaded, she wrote, she intrigued, with the help of Arjuna, the faithful. All that a girl might do, she did—and more also. She insisted on re-opening negotiations and, in effect, from behind the curtain, she guided them herself. The greater the difficulties, the higher her gallant spirit rose to meet them. She pressed into her service the old chivalrous Rajput custom of sending the bracelet, whereby a maiden might claim the knightly service of any man whom she honoured with her token—be it of gold and jewels, or a few strands of silk. And the man, so chosen, might refuse no service asked of him. He became, virtually, her knight and she his lady; though, in this world, the two might never meet face to face.

With the lapse of war and its terrible emergencies, the custom has lapsed also ; but the sending of the bracelet would still be honoured by any Rajput gentleman worthy of the name.

So Lakshmi sent her token to that cousin at the greater Maharaja's court, thus enlisting him also in the fulfilling of her purpose.

And all the while, none but Arjuna knew of the hidden photograph that had lit the flame of passion and kept it burning ; that would not suffer her to rest her will and her wits ; that, surmounting every obstacle, prevailed at last.

From the great Maharaja came word that *if* pledges were deemed to have been given, they would be kept, for the honour of his house. After due consultation with his astrologers, the matter would be arranged.

That night, for the first time—since the birth of her bold resolve—Lakshmi's pillow was wet with tears that shook her body and would not be stilled. For the first time, her heart contracted with fear lest, after all, she had but snatched the husk of victory ; lest, having won the husband, she should fail of winning the man. And she knew enough of life behind the curtain to realise how bitter may be the portion of the unloved wife.

III

Life and death dance to the rhythm of this music.—KABIR.

ASTROLOGERS had decreed, at last, the auspicious hour. At last they two, bridegroom and bride, were seated together in the dusk of early evening, magnificently jewelled and arrayed. Side by side they sat, their right hands joined, a cloth of scarlet

and gold held screen-wise between their faces, till
the given moment of beholding.

Lakshmi—the graceful free-moving creature of
the roof-top and the Inside—was weary already
with the weight of gold-threaded brocades, of jewels
that hung about her neck and arms and drooped
from her delicate ears. Her head felt light and her
hands chilled from the conflict of emotions following
upon the long fastings and preparings decreed by
custom for this supreme sacrament of marriage; of
consecration and initiation; of ordered affection on
one side, and disciplined wifely devotion on the
other.

Before them were set symbolic images of their
respective ancestors; mute reminders that
marriage, for the true Hindu, is not vitally concerned
with the pursuit of personal happiness or the fusion
of passionate hearts. It is rather an ordained and
sanctified union between two transient incarnations
of the Great Spirit in a world of illusion—for the
sake of continuing the family and the race, for the
control of passions that hinder spiritual progress,
and the begetting of sons who will eventually
release the souls of their parents from the purgatory
of duties unfulfilled. Thus each in turn serves
each; and the chain of endlessly linked lives passes
unbroken through the ages.

So preached the holy ones, steeped in wisdom
of the Rishis; and so Lakshmi had been duly
taught to believe. But the written word and the
sacred decree were laid on beings of flesh and blood,
who could not, always, believe themselves unreal
creatures of illusion, dreams within a dream. Brahmans, in pursuit of holiness, might live as ghosts
clothed in dust of actuality. Not so—to Lakshmi's
knowledge—were the men of her desert race to be

cheated of belief in life's legitimate joys—joys of battle and friendship and shikar, of passion and woman's charms. No lean and lank-haired ascetics, they: and by their warrior caste, they had won priestly sanction for a certain freedom in spiritual affairs. As dwellers in a world of reality, however transient, they had framed their own chivalrous code of honour and courage, coloured by their own manly impulses, hopes, and desires.

For Lakshmi herself—true child of the soil—the husband whose hand enclosed hers, in a purely formal clasp, was god and lord of her life, but he was also man, capable of strong, jealous devotion to the wife who could rouse and hold him. And, in her eyes, the sacredness of marriage was not less, but more, because the scarlet thread of love and passion was so closely twined with the golden thread of wifely worship.

So, during the days of prayer and fasting, she had dreamed without false shame of delights that for her were not all illusion: dreams tinctured with one drop of secret bitterness—the knowledge that her young husband had come to claim her, indifferently, if not unwillingly, at his father's bidding; concerned only to fulfil pledges said to have been given, so that none might impugn the honour of his house.

These facts Arjuna had gathered from Suraj, cousin and bracelet brother: and she, for all her brother's reluctance, had wormed them out of him bit by bit. Now her heart throbbed painfully, recalling them, while the wailing of horns, the mutter of tom-toms and the nasal droning of priests chanting sacred texts sounded confusedly in her ears; and astrologers consulted a primitive water-clock for the auspicious moment of revealing.

And he, who knew not a line of her face, never dreamed (how should he ?) that every line of his own face was already dear and familiar to her eyes, had already lit in her veins the strange new fire of passionate love. Could it ever have been thus, she wondered, in all the annals of Hindu marriage ? Must she confess her unmaidenly daring ? Would he forgive her, when he knew ?

At last—the auspicious moment : the cloth drawn away, her *sari* pulled back a little, a round mirror put into her hands. And she must so hold it as to catch the reflection of her husband's face. Not even now might she look on him direct, as her woman's heart desired.

But the kindly mirror brought him nearer ; gave her his living image—the proud glance under thick black brows, the curve of his peach-pink turban, and the quiver of his jewelled plume ; the nose strong and manly, the trim moustache, and the princely olive tint of his skin—not too brown, like common men. His mouth looked sullen, a little. Doubtless he was weary of fastings and prayings and ceremonies without end. At his eyes she dared not look, lest they reveal too clearly his indifference to the new-made wife.

He also held a mirror ; and his glance into it was brief as her own. Had that glance waked a flicker of male curiosity—of desire to her actual self ? Now Lakshmi, Goddess of Fortune, look favourably on her name-child in this moment of moments !

At another sign from the holy ones, they had risen. Solemnly, hand in hand, they were pacing the seven steps round the sacrificial flame, thus consecrating their union, for this life—and beyond.

Then they halted ; and she, standing before him, head bowed, *sari* closely drawn, heard for the first time his deep voice pronouncing the sacred, immemorial injunction: " O Bride! Give your heart to my work. Make your mind agreeable to mine. May the God Brahaspati make you pleasing to me in all things."

Words and voice, alike, lifted her heart on a wave of mingled exaltation and dread, lest Brahaspati should fail to hear, or to fulfil, the prayer that meant infinitely more for her than for him who uttered it.

And still his deep voice went on, repeating the solemn oath that bound him, on his part, not to transgress his marriage vow either for wealth or for love. And still, through the far mutterings of tom-toms, the wail of the conches wandered, now high now low, like the crying of lost spirits that would not be comforted——

All was over: the interminable ceremonies within the Palace, interminable feastings in the courts without; largesse to priests and clamouring crowds; all the paraphernalia ordained by law and custom for the linking of two ephemeral beings in an unreal world.

Lakshmi—bride, but not yet wife—stood alone in an inner room furnished mainly with chandeliers and gilt mirrors, grass mats, and brightly coloured cushions. Wedding finery exchanged for a simple garment of silk fibre, she had been happily occupied in preparing her lord's first meal, the supreme duty and pleasure of a true wife, whether she be steeped in the disciplined sanctities of marriage or whether the dear illusion of love enters in.

Then, the gown sacred to that particular rite, and to prayer, had been discarded in favour of the shell-pink *sari* and the indigo skirt, in which she now stood awaiting the moment, when at last they two would meet and speak, as man and wife.

Should she straightway make full confession—demurely veiled—then fling back her *sari*, letting her face win pardon and more than pardon ?

The daring idea tempted her a moment: only a moment. She had woman's wit enough to know that confession, after conquest, might flatter his vanity; while confession, before conquest, might fatally wound his pride. She had not staked everything and strained every nerve, only to risk failure by a false step at the last.

Let him first see her face, hear her voice. Then —if he would not forgive all . . . ?

The door opened. He had entered.

Instinctively she drew her *sari* over her face and stood before him, head bowed in mute adoration, heart and pulses in commotion, as if a whole cageful of birds fluttered wildly within.

Then the deep-toned voice—deeper, manlier than Arjuna's—spoke his first husbandly command.

" O Wife, show me again thy face."

That one little word 'again' was in itself a foretaste of triumph.

"King of my life—live for ever," came her whispered answer.

Then, with lifted head and a graceful sweep of her arm, she drew back her *sari*. Bridal tremors and wifely modesties forgotten, she gazed deep, deep into his eyes, seeking one thing only— assurance of victory.

Gazing thus, entranced, she saw—and she knew: saw that the spell of her youth and beauty stirred in him the same emotion, swift as running flame, that his pictured image had aroused in her own breast; knew that from him she had nothing to fear any more.

Light-headed with fasting and endless ceremonies, faintness overpowered her. His transfigured face grew dim and wavered strangely. It was as if she were dying from excess of joy. Desperately she clung to the blurred and blissful sense of his presence; dimly she knew, as darkness enveloped her, that he had caught her in his arms to save her from falling; that he was holding her close against his heart——

In the Palace that evening all was disturbance and amazement and eager wagging of tongues. The bridegroom, it appeared, in one brief hour with his bride, had so swiftly caught fire from her beauty and her charms that he had broken all bonds of etiquette, of correct princely procedure, and had straightway carried her off to his own tents. He that had come, unwilling and indifferent, to fulfil a pledge of honour, had been bewitched at sight, like any hero of romance in the days before the veil.

And while tongues wagged and dependents feasted and night flung over camp and palace and city, her veil of darkness sewn with stars, Lakshmi knelt at the feet of her new-made husband and told him all.

Tremulous at first, she gained courage with the telling; courage that reaped reward beyond her wildest dreams.

He had no word of blame for her unmaidenly boldness; only wonder and a great pride in the girl-woman who could so dare, so achieve.

Never in all the annals of Rajasthan, he told her, had any Prince of the blood been in like manner wooed and won. For the child-wife, taken at command of his mother, he had no thought any more.

She whom he delighted to honour would be queen of his palace and himself. He would set her like a seal upon his heart ; content that, in all things, she should be ruler, no less than loving servant of her Prince.

1923.

II. THE GODS OF THE EAST

I

We be the Gods of the East,
  Older than all;
Masters of mourning and feast,
  How should we fall?

KIPLING.

A BREATHLESS, shadeless day, a day of monotonous brilliance, was slowly nearing its close. The sun hung rayless, a disc of flame over a rock-studded horizon, whose uncompromising outline—broken at intervals by ragged clumps of date-palms—was carven, crisp and clear, along the lower edges of a turquoise sky.

Neither shredded cloudlet nor haze of evening lent a softening influence to the stretches of yellow-grey sand, the jagged volcanic rocks, and dusty scrub of Western Rajputana. North and south, east and west, the gaunt profitless desert rose and fell, in billowing waves, and the level light streamed unhindered over its tawny surface.

A few moments more, and the sun was gone, leaving a crimson-purple stain upon the blue. Again a few moments, and, in that same blue, quivered the first palpitating stars.

With a soft strong rush of wings, the grey crane and the wild duck flew to their reedy resting places. The night-jar and fox-headed bat flitted ghost-like through the twilight in search of food. Here and there a trailing cloud of dust marked the track of some local herdsman driving his cattle byre-ward for the night.

One after one, like dropped stars, a group of home-lights revealed a village, hitherto almost indistinguishable from its surroundings: a mere cluster of mud-walled, sun-baked huts, huddled together on a bare billow of sand, as if from an actual sense of the vast loneliness around; and towards it trailing clouds converged from every point of the compass—for herdsmen of the desert roam far afield in search of green food.

At the billow's base, seven bedraggled date-palms clustered about a well; and beside the well a diminutive Hindu shrine was hewn from a boulder of red laterite.

Here, under drooping palm fronds in the glimmer of starlight, could be dimly discerned the figure of a man—tall, spare, muscular, and still as the slumbering earth.

For two hours he had sat thus, wrapt in the profound meditation of a mind and soul unharassed by the restless energy of modern civilisation. Desert-born and desert-bred, the silence and lifelessness of his surroundings oppressed him not at all; so absorbed was he in the secret communing of his own soul with the great unknown Soul of Things, to one of whose countless manifestations the grotesque red shrine by the well was dedicated. For Ram Singh was a Brahman and Rajput of caste and lineage unimpeachable; and—his evening service ended—it was his habit to devote the first hours of darkness to meditation and prayer.

The stern modelling of his features suggested fighting blood in his veins; but the face, as a whole, was that of a thinker rather than a warrior—a thinker who still retained unshaken faith in the gods of his forefathers, in traditions and customs handed down, through countless generations, even to his own.

A loud and cheerful voice from the heart of an approaching dust-cloud recalled him to earth and the affairs of earth.

"Oh-ho, Rama-ji, thou abidest late by the holy well. Hast some special favour to ask of Mai Lakshmi that thou flatterest her with such long devotions?"

"Not so, Durga Das," replied the Brahman, gravely. "I am beset by many thoughts. Surely thou hast heard that Munda Ram, banker, having failed to procure his moneys from Narain Das, thy kinsman, hath sworn to obtain them by *dharna?* And I—I am the herald who set my dagger to his bond."

The wreathed smiles vanished from the listener's face, and he pursed his thick lips with an air of tragic solemnity that sat strangely on his comedy countenance.

"*Hai—hai!* Thou hast need, then, brother, for thought and prayer. Who knows but thy life may be the payment? Then will there be much trouble with the police-*lōg*, whose eyes search out every hole and corner. For myself, I hold by the laws of the British Raj; and, if I mistake not, Narain Das is of the same opinion."

"Ay, that he is—cowardly son of a jackal!" spoke the Brahman, a flicker of mirth in his deep eyes. "But it will soon be seen whether his faith in their power will be of any avail in his dealings with me and mine. If the money be not paid, and that instantly, my death will be upon his head. There are but these two ways: and he will be loath to choose the last, chicken-hearted as he is."

Durga Das turned the palms of his hands outward in expressive native fashion.

"Who knows? His cowries are dear to him as his own heart's blood; but yet—a Brahman's death"—he wagged his bullet head slowly—"I would not be in *his dhoti* this day for all his hoarded treasure. Of a truth, thine house will grieve to hear thy tidings. Wilt along?"

"Nay, friend, not yet. Why should my feet make haste to bear ill news?"

The question needed no answer; and, with a sympathetic grunt, Durga Das went on his way, attended by trailing clouds of dust.

Ram Singh, left alone again with the darkening desert and the silence and the stars, faced unflinchingly the situation forced upon him by caste, custom, tradition—the all-powerful trinity of the East. This *dharna* he had spoken of was an ancient Hindu practice—the most singular and extravagant ever conceived by man—for enforcing the payment of a debt: a practice long since made punishable under the British penal code. But it takes time and harsh experience to convince the desert-bred Hindu that the penal code is a living power that snaps irreverent fingers at customs and traditions other than its own: so, in certain regions, *dharna* survived long after it had nominally been suppressed.

By its iron decree, if any injured suitor vainly demanded payment, he installed himself upon his neighbour's doorstep. There he squatted day and night—patient and inexorable as the grim gods he served—abstaining from all food and religious ordinances. His victim, if still obdurate, was compelled to follow his example; and, should the mutual fast be prolonged till the suitor died of starvation, the debtor was held responsible for his death. It need hardly be said that these strange proceedings were apt to prove more effectual if the applicant were a Brahman of birth and blood: so there had grown up a peculiar caste of heralds—known as *charan*—who made themselves responsible for the fulfilment of public engagements, bonds, or family contracts. The sign manual of their office was a dagger, which, in event of failure, they were bound to plunge into their own hearts. Nor was even this enough to satisfy the Hindu's innate love of the horrible and the grim. Should a herald have reason to fear that the indelible disgrace of causing a Brahman's death might fail to overawe the defaulter, he was constrained to take, instead, a life more sacred than his own—to kill, in open daylight, on the offender's doorsill, either his wife or his mother.

To be a herald, then, was to live in close fellowship with the idea of a sudden and violent end ; and thus had Ram Singh, and a long line of ancestors before him, lived from their youth up. Yet, when the critical moment came, it found him very humanly dismayed. A vision of his young wife, and of two lusty men-children, made his strong heart contract with fear of that which might shortly be in store for him and them.

And while he sat thus, his mind divided between prayer and foreboding, the moonless night fell round him like a curtain hiding all things from view.

II

What have women to do with thinking? They love and they suffer.—KIPLING.

"*Hai, hai!* My lord tarrieth late. These goodly chupattis will be quite unfit for his eating."

The young Brahman's wife crouched low before a brick oven, lamenting her husband's unpunctuality. A slim creature, in pale-coloured draperies, she looked scarcely capable of mothering the two plump babes who fought and scrambled gleefully a few paces from her side.

"And if he tarry, he hath some good reason," spoke a voice from a corner of the dimly lighted room. "Of what use are the hands of a wife if they cannot achieve the making of a new meal for a husband?"

It was the voice of Mai Chandebi, mother of the absentee. Full and strong, it sorted well with the tall, deep-chested figure that rose and moved into the area of flickering light given out by three cotton wicks laid in earthenware saucers filled with oil.

"Lo, even now, he cometh. Make ready with haste, Golabi."

And Golabi obeyed. Obedience was the first and last law of her young life; and she fulfilled it with a glad heart.

On the entrance of her lord, all was in order; and the women, as was meet, withdrew while he broke his fast. Golabi, a bare brown son on either hip, ventured an upward glance at him as she went; but his eyes were on his mother; and it was to her he spoke in carefully lowered tones.

"I would have speech with thee, mother, afterwards—alone."

Golabi's quick ears caught the words; and her arms tightened round her men-children. In them, she well knew, lay all her power.

Whilst the mother and wife sat together in an inner room, Ram Singh ate his meal alone and in silence, according to custom, squatting on the bare, baked earth, clad only in his loin-cloth and mystic Brahminical cord. And even as he blessed his wife's domestic skill, the touch of steel was sharp against his heart.

When the meal was ended, and his mother rejoined him, he arose, and the two faced one another—erect and silent. Their eyes met on one plane—steady and searching, and alight with a great love.

The woman spoke first.

"Hath it come so soon, my son? I might have known. Never falls the sword upon the neck of the willing victim."

"Thou knowest, then?"

"How should I *not* know? I have seen the sword's shadow in other eyes than thine, Rama-ji. To whom goest thou for the money?"

"To Narain Das, landholder."

"It will go hard with thee, son of my heart," she said, with a swift tightening of her finely carved lips.

"Ay; but it shall go hard with him also. I hate him and all of his mongrel breed. We shall see now whether his faith in the white man's law shall avail him against the decree of the gods."

"Thou hast not yet seen him?"

"I come from his very door."

"And of what like seemed his countenance?"

Her tone was steady, but the life had gone out of it.

"Even as I had foreseen. He laughed me to scorn, and bade me carry word to Munda Ram that he had best make application for his dues through the law courts of the English."

"And thou ? "

The words were a mere whisper.

" I answered him, that the white man's law was naught to me, but the honour of my caste was all; that on the morrow, soon after dawn, I should return and take up my post at his door. I said, moreover, that if my blood upon his head did not avail to shake his scorn, I would anoint his threshold with the blood of her—mother of my sons."

A twitch of pain crossed the stern face, and he turned it from the scrutiny of his mother's eyes. It was not an easy thing the gods demanded of him ; but the Great Ones take no count of such passing illusions, in a world of illusions, as the love of a man for his wife.

For a long moment neither was capable of speech. The inevitable lay like a stone upon their hearts.

At length, with purpose in every line of her powerful face, the old woman laid her hand on the man's arm.

" My son, thinkest thou that this thing shall be permitted while breath is in my body and blood in my veins ? Is it for naught that I am thy mother, and the widow of thy father ? . . . If there be any talk of death in this matter, it shall be *mine only*, . . . hearest thou, my son ? "

The fire of youth—dominant and masterful, flashed from her eyes: for in Rajputana even the women are soldiers at heart. But the man's strength of purpose matched hers. Was it not of her own bestowing ?

" Nay, mother," he answered sternly. " That is shameful talk. Thy life——"

" Is it more to thee than *hers*, Rama-ji ?

The agonised man caught her wrinkled hands in both his own.

"Mother, I entreat thee, speak not of this thing. Is not thy life sacred above all others? It cannot —it *shall* not be!"

Her excitement had subsided. She was erect again; eyes and mouth unflinching.

"And I say that it shall be, my son. Since when hast thou learnt to set thy will against mine? Let there be no more speech on the matter To-morrow I go with thee to the house of this man. She is young, Rama-ji. She hath borne thee men-children and shall bear thee yet more. But I—I am old, and a widow, and my life is a very little thing to give for thine honour, son of my heart."

Ram Singh could only clench his hands and groan, while she comforted him, tenderly, as though he had been a suffering child; but no further mention of the morrow's hideous necessity passed between them.

That night, lying beside his young wife, he felt her slender body shaken with stifled weeping. Very gently, he inquired the cause: and she answered him, brokenly, with another question:

"Hast naught to tell me also, O my husband? I am no weakling . . . I that bare thee two sons in one day. Wherefore hast thou locked thine heart against me?"

The man laid a hand upon her head, stilling its restless motion.

"Hush thee, light of my life. To-morrow thou shalt know all. The night is for rest; and I would have thee sleep, my pearl—sleep."

THE GODS OF THE EAST

III

Still Brahm dreams . . . and till he wakes the gods die not.
                                                    KIPLING.

THE first flush of dawn found the doomed household astir and going about their customary duties, which must be carried out whether hearts were at breaking point or no.

Mother and wife worked in silence, each at her appointed task—Golabi with moist lashes, for all her heroic maternal achievement; Chandebi with stern lips and dry, bright eyes

The two plump babes fought and rollicked as usual, laughing up into the faces of the silent women, whose fingers were mechanically manipulating rice-balls, flower-balls, and sweetmeats, to be offered during the *sraddha*[1] ceremonies, for the nourishment of Chandebi's ghost, when it should have discarded its mortal body, and for the formation of a new body in the regions of the blest. A grim occupation; but to your orthodox Hindu, custom renders all things possible and most things endurable.

The ceremony was long and dreary and solemn to the verge of stupefaction, involving much sprinkling of water, droning of prayers, and propitiating of priests. Ram Singh himself performed the principal rites, clad in spotless loincloth and white Brahminical thread; while his younger brothers were privileged to sprinkle flower-balls with water, and offer sweetmeats to insatiable priests. Custom decreed, moreover, that the interminable affair should be carried through

[1] A ceremony of propitiatory prayers and offerings to the spirits of departed ancestors, performed yearly and before any solemn undertaking.

fasting, to the mournful accompaniment of wailing chants. And it was so; while the ghost-to-be awaited its close with a stoicism born of lifelong submission to the decrees of caste and the gods.

The sun rose high in the blinding blue, when three tall, white-clad figures drew up before the threshold of Narain Das, defaulter.

The worthy landholder was a man of full habit, and of a cheerful, time-serving humour, inexorable only where his cherished horde of silver was concerned.

In answer to the formal summons, he came forth, beaming a benevolent welcome, clad in the short jacket and *dhoti* of his class. In a gap between the two garments a roll of brown flesh showed like a girdle round his ample form.

"Ohé, Rama-ji, thou art ever welcome," he began, in accents a shade too suave for sincerity: but at sight of Chandebi's draped figure and the bared blade in her son's hand, his flow of words forsook him, and uneasiness crept into his furtive eyes.

Not all his cringing reverence for the Sahib, or his dread of breaking the Great Queen's laws, could make him other than a Hindu of caste, which is to say that, in his eyes, the Great Queen herself was an inconsiderable personage compared with the man who stood before him, unflinching purpose in every line of his stern, spare face.

The landholder's small stock of valour was not proof against the flash of a naked sword in the sunlight. The prospect of seeing an old and reverend woman struck down in cold blood might well have shaken a braver man than he: and behind the horror of the whole thing lurked the hair-raising conviction that her blood, so spilt, would be upon his own head till the day of his death—and through untold lives beyond. A clammy dew broke out upon his forehead. The suavity of his smiles increased tenfold.

"Verily, I had forgot; 'tis to settle that little matter of the loan that thou art come—and in a fortunate hour, my friend. I was about to send word that at the month's end I may at length be able to pay my honoured creditor, Munda Ram. Then will all be well between us; as between brother and brother."

His fat brown hands moved nervously one over the other, as he lifted cunning, conciliatory eyes to the Rajput's face.

Ram Singh merely turned to his mother; and she, without quiver of hand or lip, kneeled down before him, her grey head bared in the sunlight.

"Thine honoured creditor asks a plain answer to a plain question. Wilt thou make payment at once—or no?"

The Rajput's tone was business-like and decisive; but the movement of his right arm sent a snake-like shiver down the defaulter's sleek back.

"Yea, I will make payment—by all means," he cried with a quavering assumption of cheerfulness; and the kneeling woman lifted her head. "But to procure so many rupees at one moment's notice is not within the power of this slave."

Chandebi bowed her head as before.

"At the in-gathering of harvest much money will accrue to me. Then, by the gods of my fathers, I will repay every cowrie I have borrowed from the great and worthy Munda Ram. He knows I am a poor man . . . a very poor man . . ."

His restless hands were clenched to hide the tremor that shook them. He dared not look again into the Brahman's face; but a blinding flash told him the sword had been swung high above the motionless grey head.

"Have done with thy goat's bleating, son of a jackal. Keep that for the law-cowits Make answer . . . yea, or nay."

Ram Singh's voice rang out like a trumpet; and the gaping crowd, that had gathered to look on at this unwonted *tamasha*, held its breath—knowing the end was near.

With lips visibly trembling, Narain Das spoke: "Stay thine hand, O Rama-ji: and by all that is holy I will pay a portion at least before the crops are in—a month . . . a little month . . ." his quavering assurances were unceremoniously cut short by a cry of horror that rang shudderingly upon the still air.

The curved sword had swept down with mighty force; and Chandebi's grey head lay in a pool of blood at the landholder's feet, to the lasting damage of his patent-leather shoes.

With a howl of terror he turned and fled into the house, closely followed by the Brahman's two brothers, who had still to enforce the customary mingling of his blood with that of the victim.

The awe-stricken crowd broke up into groups—and gradually drifted away. When the first gasp of horror had spent itself, the sleepy village buzzed with talk of the morning's tragedy; and within a very few hours a second deputation was drawn up before the house front of Narain Das.

It consisted of a company of yellow-turbaned native police, backed by an English civilian, pale and perspiring, demanding, in terms more peremptory than polite, the person of Ram Singh, Brahman and Rajput.

The man gave himself up with his habitual air of dignity. He acknowledged his act without a word of explanation or defence—and Golabi and her two lusty sons saw his face no more.

The law—being lamentably without sense upon so nice a point of family honour—and being concerned only for protection of life and limb, condemned Chandebi's high-minded son to transportation for life. He accepted its decree, as he had accepted most of life's ugly inevitables, stoically and in silence.

Not so Narain Das. His wailing was loud and long, and sleep forsook his eyes. A vision of that grey head, steeped in its own blood, was with him night and day; till this spurner of Brahm's decrees, in an agony of terror and remorse, voluntarily starved himself until he died.

TO
MY SON, CYRIL

SIEGE PERILOUS

SIEGE PERILOUS

*" A Shame," said I, " she should add just him
To her nine-and-ninety other spoils,
The hundredth—for a whim."*

BROWNING.

I

THE verandah of Mamūl Dak bungalow was saturated with May sunshine: the glory of it tempered by a breeze from the snows that gleamed, far and pure, along the northward horizon. Southward, the tortured plains of the Punjab were veiled in silver haze. Near at hand, between the bungalows and the snow-line, loomed the wooded hills of Dalhousie.

Mamūl rest-house is—or was—the last stage on the upward journey; a relic of unprogressive days, when one climbed from the plains to the heights by leisurely and delectable degrees.

In the empty verandah a tall Englishman was pacing to and fro; his head a little bent, his hands closed on a riding crop behind his back. At intervals he scanned the familiar glory of hill and valley with unseeing eyes. Once he abruptly stood still, took a letter from his breast pocket, and read it, frowning, for the third time.

The letter was signed ' Yours ever, Kenneth Malcolm '; and in the course of nearly two sheets a certain woman's name appeared with disturbing frequency: a trifling detail, in the case of a junior subaltern up on leave. But in the eyes of this particular Englishman, Kenneth Malcolm was not as other subalterns : and that trifle—no less—accounted for his presence at Mamūl.

Colonel Philip Hardynge, R.E.—a man of few intimates—was reputed a woman hater. Hatred is an ugly word—and misogynist an uglier ; but let it be conceded that he sedulously avoided and vaguely distrusted women in general ; that he acutely distrusted and disapproved of the woman, in particular, who was clearly fooling Kenneth to the top of his bent. True, he knew her only by hearsay. But hearsay, in India, is apt to be circumstantial, if not scrupulously exact. The Punjab—all of it that mattered—was free of her story—or, rather the club-and-tea-table story of her notoriously incompatible marriage ; her case against her husband, his case against her ; the unedifying divorce suit with Captain Woolford of the Gunners, for co-respondent ; the whisper, circulated in confidence by the strictly moral and charitable, that Woolford had offered marriage and had been refused. If the whisper ever reached him, he had neglected to refute it. Not overmuch time had been given him. For, instead of living to defend the woman he presumably loved, the careless fellow had let his pony slip over the khud, one rainy night, riding home from a dance—and both had been found dead in the morning.

So people had been left to think what they pleased, which commonly implies thinking the worst. The probabilities favoured it—given Marion Rex, known among the Simla wits as Marion Regina. Her good looks and her spirited fashion of ' facing the music ' had won her a measure of championship among the men, more especially those who knew Rex and the precise kind of bounder he was. They merely wondered, in their masculine sagacity, how the deuce she ever came to marry him. Women—with a few notable exceptions—had 'turned her down' on principle. For, in the day of Marion Rex's brief shining, divorce was divorce, not the mere *sauce piquante* of social life. In the opinion of those who were presumably qualified to sit in judgment, it was incumbent on her to retire gracefully and hide her too conspicuous light under a bushel at Home. Instead, she had confounded her critics by remaining in the Punjab, dancing and riding with one infatuated young man or another, generally keeping her head in the air and looking younger than ever.

Such, more or less, was Colonel Hardynge's mental conception of the woman whose name had been appearing too frequently in Kenneth's recent letters. Entirely unconcerned, he had accepted the general verdict without giving the original a second thought, beyond the fact that it confirmed his own opinion of the type. Now the old story cropped up again, in all its distastefulness; and he was no longer unconcerned. Confound the woman! Good or bad, she must be at least ten years older than Kenneth, who seemed in danger of losing his head and coming a cropper, unless he were speedily and discreetly removed from the toils.

To that end, Hardynge—no frequenter of Hill stations—was heading for Dalhousie, when he should have been making for the lone regions beyond Chamba with his gun and a couple of *shikarris*— the best he knew. To that end he was squandering one priceless week of his leave, a proceeding admittedly out of keeping with his rôle of confirmed bachelor and cynic. For private reasons of his own, the matter concerned him more deeply than he would have cared to confess. He would get no thanks for butting in. The mere fact that he had been Kenneth's guardian would make the boy only the more restive under his elderly sagacities. Yet there it was. Thanks or no, stumbling-blocks or no, he could *not* stand aside, indifferent to the fate of the boy who might have been his own son ; might have been—and was not. There lay the secret sting. . . .

As to this infernal, unknown woman, with the eyes and the figure and the more than doubtful reputation, whether she were crazy enough to dream of marriage, or was merely 'out for a fresh scalp,' she might prove a stumbling block of the first magnitude—Kenneth being what he was. Hardynge cursed himself for not having realised it sooner. But how could any sane man suppose——?

Sanity, it seemed, was at a discount ; and psychological niceties were not in Hardynge's line. In plain terms, Kenneth must be told a few home truths about his divinity. He must be diplomatically detached from Hill-station futilities and transplanted to the bracing atmosphere of snowfields and Shikar.

Hardynge still felt a trifle hazy as to how all this was to be achieved by a man of action, unskilled in the vagaries of women and the human heart. Yet he did not seem to see himself being bested by any Marion Rex of them all. . . .

At this point he lost patience ; shouted for his *sais ;* vaulted into the saddle and surrendered himself to the pleasure of the fourteen-mile ride in the company of his favourite mare.

II

*Why do I prate
Of women, that are things against my Fate?*
THOMAS RANDOLPH.

UP and up and up: the prospect nobler, the air keener with every mile of ascent, till the Post Office and the stolid little English Church hove in view, and a hand-gallop along the Mall brought them to their destination, Bullen's Hotel.

In the grateful shade of a young deodar, Hardynge dismounted and stood a moment caressing his mare, scanning the wooden verandah —smothered in roses and honeysuckle—that ran the whole length of the châlet-like building. The hotel was mainly a bachelor resort: two of them sprawled in long chairs near the entrance, scanning Home papers. But women wormed themselves in everywhere now. A man could never feel sure.

Throughout the verandah, at all events, not the flutter of a petticoat; but at the far end, Hardynge noted a suspicious-looking arrangement of chairs, rugs, and a Sutherland table, a spotless tea-cloth and a vase of roses—the orthodox cartwheel rosette of pink buds and maidenhair fern, in alternative rings, dear to every right-minded *māli* throughout the land.

From one of the many doors that opened on to the verandah came Kenneth himself, in R.E. blazer and flannels; very square as to the shoulders, very well-groomed and polished as to the thatch of reddish brown hair. Under a surface impression of youth and pliability, the groundwork of manhood showed clearer than ever to Hardynge's critically appraising eye. There was a touch of exaltation about him, too, that told its own tale, and angered Hardynge afresh. The devil's own luck, if he had stumbled on a tea-party.

Belinda was consigned to her groom. Hardynge lit a cigar and strolled forward, watching— between amusement and vexation—how Kenneth pulled the primly-set chairs and rugs this way and that, with careless nervous haste, lest any discover him in the act ; how he tweaked at the maidenhair, to loosen the nosegay, and the roses retaliated by toppling out and standing on their heads, with all their wet stalks in the air.

At that critical moment, enter Nasur Ali— Kenneth's man—bearing a tea-tray that confirmed the worst.

"*Wah—wah*, Sahib ! " he exclaimed, looking vainly round for the delinquent. No wind : not a dog in sight.

Hardynge's quick ear caught his low-toned, "Colonel Sahib *argya*."[1] And Kenneth, whose back was turned, swung sharply round.

"Hullo, Colonel ! " he called out, his friendly welcome tinged with evident surprise : and while the two men greeted, Nasur Ali, depositing his tray, proceeded to wedge in his floral cartwheel more firmly than ever.

"You got my wire ? " Hardynge asked superfluously, to cover the boy's momentary embarrassment.

"Oh, rather." Kenneth was himself again. "I booked your room, all *teek*.[2] Didn't think you'd be up quite so early——"

[1] Has come.   [2] Correct.

A disarming glance at his rugs and chairs moved Hardynge to a quizzical smile.

"Don't mind me, old boy. Ladies to tea?"

"Well—we've a sett on, at the courts. But of course——"

"Yes of course!" Hardynge's smile deepened. "As it's a foursome, I won't spoil sport. An iced peg instanter would be more to my taste."

Kenneth, very brisk and practical, gave the order, priding himself, no doubt, on having neatly dissembled his relief.

They sat down; and Hardynge bridged an awkward silence by proffering his cigar case.

The boy helped himself; beheaded his cigar, and asked casually, "You up for long, Colonel? I thought you barred Hill stations."

"So I do—except on urgent private affairs! I'm moving on to Pangi to-morrow or next day." He leaned an elbow on the table between them, brusquely jerking out his phrases. "I want you to come along with me. That's the idea. Bring a pal, if you like. I'll guarantee you good sport. Streets better than pat-ball and dancing attendance on petticoats, eh?"

At last he looked straight at Kenneth—and realised, in a measure, the effect of his bombshell.

"I'm awfully sorry, Colonel," the boy apologised, with an engaging mixture of deference and discomfort. "I mean—it's awfully good of you. It would be ripping—if—well you see—I can't leave Dalhousie, just at present. Didn't you get my last letter?"

"I did. To make no bones about it—that's why I'm here." He paused, nerving himself for the frontal attack. "In plain terms, Kenneth, you're either making a fool of yourself or letting this Mrs. Rex make a fool of you." He waved aside the boy's incipient protest. "Oh yes, I know it's a libel. It always is! Of course my guardianship goes for nothing now. But as you've given me your confidence——"

Again he paused. Kenneth remained ominously silent, looking straight before him. Something in his aspect, some reminder of earlier days, moved Hardynge to press his point, with a more friendly urgency. "Take my advice and come out of it, old boy, while you can call your soul your own."

Kenneth's smile seemed to set the older man politely at arm's length.

"As to that, Colonel, I'm afraid . . . it's a bit too late."

"Good God! You've only known the woman a month. You can take it from me, it's *not* too late—if you'll give yourself a sporting chance to recover your sanity."

"And you can take it from me, sir, I've never felt saner." The quiet of his tone lent force to the simple statement. "Of course I'm sorry to lose a shoot—with you. But you don't seem to understand——"

"I understand this much," Hardynge broke out, galled by an impending sense of failure, "that you—a boy of three and twenty, a promising soldier, with negligible means of your own—seem seriously to contemplate marrying a woman more than ten years older——"

"I don't believe it. She doesn't look thirty."

"Very clever of her! The fact remains, you can't pretend to know anything of her character—her past life——"

"As it happens, she has told me—some of it;

and there are other women pining to tell me more. Four years ago! About time they let it drop. That chap Rex must have been a proper brute."

"I never heard so. He was a bounder, all right. But presumably—she loved him." Kenneth flinched, and Hardynge added with merciless deliberation, "There are two sides to every case, remember; two versions of every tale. I *have* heard Rex had a good deal to put up with. The lady——"

"For God's sake, Colonel——!"

The boy rose and walked away in an access of anger and perturbation.

Hardynge, checked for the moment, took a long pull at his cigar. As bad as that, was it? His arguments had been addressed to Kenneth, the boy. Here was Kenneth, the man.

Turning in his stride, he came back and faced his Chief, with an aspect as near defiance as his military training would permit.

"Tell me, Colonel—have you ever met Mrs. Rex?"

"Never, my son. Safer so, perhaps!"

"And you condemn her on hearsay." He ignored the mild thrust. "You sit there and throw mud at her——"

"Which is a libel. But let that pass!"

"Well, you would—if I'd listen. But I won't listen. Isn't it about time you made her acquaintance? They'll be here any minute now, she and Miss Madison—a topping girl she's chaperoning. Stay and see her. Judge for yourself."

Hardynge flung away his cigar and looked thoughtfully at the boy, whose reasonableness was taking the wind out of his sails. His determined dash to the rescue must not be allowed to fizzle out in virtual capitulation ; but refusal would put him in the wrong. No harm, after all, to have a look at the disturber of traffic.

" Very well, old boy. As you won't accept my invite, I accept yours," he agreed with his satirical half-smile. " But I warn you, even if the lady has all the gifts and graces, I still bar the whole affair. —Hullo ! Battle and murder ? "

From the region of the hotel entrance came a sudden infuriated outburst of snarlings and growlings and chokings that could only proceed from two dogs fairly at each other's throats.

Kenneth sprang up. He owned a belligerent Airedale, the terror of the hotel.

" That's Jock—enjoying himself——! "

As he spoke, a woman came quickly down the path and up the steps into the verandah—a woman in a summer frock and hat too girlishly simple for her undisguisable maturity. Discreetly illumined, she might have had a chance ; but the pitiless afternoon sun betrayed her.

" The fair, fluffy kind," Hardynge summed her up at a glance. " The perennial innocent." Not at all the type he had pictured her—which was precisely what he should have expected, with his vaunted knowledge of life.

" Oh, Mr. Malcolm! Your Terror is devouring my Chow, behaving as if he owned the place ! " she said breathlessly, laying an intimate hand on Kenneth's arm, and taking swift stock of himself from the tail of her eye. " Come—*quick*. No one dare lay a finger on Jock but you."

" One minute, Colonel," Kenneth excused himself.

" As many as you please. Hurry up ! "

Without looking an inch beyond Kenneth, he

could feel the woman's eyes on him : but she only said, " Yes, *do* make haste, or it'll be murder ! "

And they hurried away together.

Hardynge, left alone, watched them go with a sort of sick disgust at his heart that Kenneth, of all people, should have been ensnared on the threshold of manhood, by a mere ' she-thing ' of that quality. If he couldn't see the cut of her with his own eyes, who else could make him ? With an impatient sigh, he sat down again and reverted to the unfailing solace of a cigar.

They had hardly been gone five minutes, when a gaily cushioned rickshaw rattled up, drawn by four men in blue and orange uniform. Another woman ! Confound the lot of them.

She called out an order to her men, who had put on a final spurt, and could not, at command, check the impetus of the vehicle. In their valiant effort they jerked it backward, grazed the opposite bank, and tilted one of the wheels.

Instantly Hardynge was down the steps, swearing at the men, clutching the rickshaw with one hand, the woman's arm with the other, just in time to prevent an overturn.

" Oh thank you—thank you ! "

Half laughing, she stumbled out ; and almost before she had found her feet, he unhanded her so abruptly that she laughed outright ; and he found himself looking full into a pair of limpid, blue-green eyes.

" It's all right. I'm not a stinging nettle ! Very kind of you to be so prompt. The wretches got racing and fairly ran away with me."

" You should fine them. They get out of hand nowadays," he gravely advised her, ignoring her raillery, as she, in turn, ignored his seriousness.

She just stood there smiling at him, frankly amused.

"May I ask—to whom I have the honour——? I know most of the Bullenites."

"I'm Colonel Hardynge, young Malcolm's Chief." He felt himself stiffening. "I've just arrived."

"O—oh, Colonel Hardynge!" (That also seemed to amuse her: he failed to see why.) "Was Mr. Malcolm—expecting you?"

"No."

"A sudden impulse?"

"Yes. A sudden impulse." (Anything more she would like to know?)

"He must be delighted. You see, we've all heard of you. Don't be alarmed! Your character's quite safe in his hands.—I caught sight of him, wrestling with Jock, as I flashed past. Ah—here they are."

She waved a welcome to Kenneth, who was returning quicker than he went.

As he reached them, a second rickshaw rattled up, and a girl's voice called out, "Tally ho, Marion! Thought I'd have to pick up the pieces!"

That name, coupled with the look in Kenneth's eyes, showed Hardynge, in a flash, his egregious error; told him that, here and now, he was confronting the enemy. This woman was another pair of sleeves.

The new-comer had sprung out of her rickshaw, a tall strip of a girl, with a fashion-plate air—all length and no breadth; a bell-shaped hat pulled ruthlessly down over her eyes, and two coils of fair hair hiding her ears; only her mouth and chin and the tip of her nose in evidence:—clearly the 'topping girl' who took Mrs. Rex at her own valuation.

Kenneth mumbled an introduction, with his eyes elsewhere.

"I say—have you introduced yourselves . . . you two ? " he asked, trying vainly to appear at ease.

"*He* has—I haven't! But he's probably guessed!"

This time Hardynge evaded her laughing eyes. She seemed easily amused.

" Colonel—let me . . . this is Mrs. Rex."

Kenneth jerked it out somehow, and Hardynge acknowledge the information with a formal bow.

" Charmed—I—er——"

" Oh, we've skipped all that ! " she took him up with her amazing assurance. " You've heard of me too, no doubt ? *I'm* not alarmed ! " She turned to Kenneth. " Sorry we're rather late. Shall we adjourn for tea ? "

They adjourned there and then. For both men it was a relief (though Hardynge hated tea-tables), simply to concern themselves with handing cups and plates and being trivially useful to a pair of very pleasant women—Mrs. Rex doing the honours, at Kenneth's request.

In these arduous duties they were presently assisted by Miss Madison's partner, Major Vyner— a smooth-faced epicure, who made a cult of popularity, and rather too insistently affected to grow younger as he grew older.

Hardynge knew the man little, and liked him less. He was clearly making up to Miss Madison—or her dollars ; and their mutual fooling eased things a trifle, from Hardynge's point of view. From their talk he learnt that the ' perennial innocent ' was one Mrs. Berkeley-Kerr (and woe betide any other kind of innocent who pronounced it Burkley-Kurr) ; that she was the solitary grass widow in a hotel full of bachelors, who were duly grateful—with reservations—for her sisterly, or maternal, attentions, as the case might be.

For a brief space, Mrs. Rex was mercifully preoccupied with the tea-pot and a polished tin kettle that murmured on a camp spirit stove at her elbow.

" When I come here," she explained conversationally to Hardynge, " Mr. Malcolm very kindly panders to my weakness for making tea myself."

But if her words were for him, her upward, intimate glance was for Kenneth, who stood at her elbow, prematurely proffering a plate of toasted buns.

While she manipulated the tea-things, Hardynge had leisure to take stock of the enemy at less embarrassingly close quarters, and honesty enough to admit a point or two in her favour. Besides those remarkable eyes, she had the grace of an alluring figure—not on up-to-date lines—squirrel brown hair, and—yes—Kenneth was not far out—she looked little over thirty, even in full sunlight. Grudgingly enough, he suspected that she was clever ; something of a personality. He would wager that manner of hers was a cloak—for what ?

" Milk ? Sugar ? " Her voice dispelled his musings. A slim jug in one hand, a spoonful of sugar in the other, she turned to him, with a challenging smile, as if she had read his thought. " No sugar for *you*, or my instinct deceives me ! "

" I take all I can get," he gravely informed her, not without a spice of relish at—even so trivially—putting her in the wrong.

She retaliated by doling three large spoonfuls into his cup.

" Do you really need sweetening to *that* extent ? "

"Wouldn't you suspect it, from the look of me?"

"Oh, well—since you make a point of it——" She surveyed him with amused deliberation, till he could have shaken her. "From the look of you, I should hail you as a fellow-cynic, stripped of illusions, incapable of seeing even a peach with the bloom on——!"

Kenneth's involuntary protest was dismissed with a perfectly manicured hand. "Don't worry, my dear boy. He's rather gratified than otherwise. If we give him a grain of encouragement, he'll own up!"

Her arched brows were for Hardynge, who acknowledged her shrewd hit with an ironical bow.

"I never presume to contradict a lady. And I confess I haven't seen a peach with the bloom on since I was last in Kashmir—if that amounts to owning up?"

"Honest man! I knew I was right. I felt it in my bones. Nothing blighting or blistering. Just the harmless necessary cynicism of the disappointed romantic. That's my diagnosis, for what it's worth."

"Now *isn't* she cute?" It was the lively young woman they called 'Bobbie,' breaking away from Vyner's assiduities. "Colonel Hardynge, do tell! *Are* you a disappointed romantic?"

"Mrs. Rex knows more about that than I do," Hardynge retorted drily.

"I shouldn't be surprised! You can take it from me, she'll size you up to an inch before you've swallowed your second cup of tea."

"Bobbie, you're unspeakable!" The light reproof had a touch of sharpness.

"I'm not. It's the truth that's unspeakable. That's why it's so seldom spoken."

"Major Vyner, *do* give her half a dozen éclairs to keep her quiet!"

Vyner, with fatuous solemnity, obeyed to the letter; and Bobbie, as solemnly, transferred each one, as it came, from her plate to his own.

Mrs. Rex, with a smile for their absurdities, held out her hand. "More tea, Colonel Hardynge?"

"I daren't—after Miss Madison's warning."

"You won't wriggle out of it that way!" Bobbie assured him, with her mouth full.

"You seem to be a very cocksure young lady."

"I know my Marion," she retorted darkly. "You must be up the night before, to get even with *her*. If she's marked you down, you haven't an earthly."

"Is that so?" Hardynge politely inquired of Mrs. Rex. "Forewarned's forearmed. Is it— war to the knife?"

For the second time in their brief acquaintance, he looked her full in the eyes, and he saw the blood stir perceptibly under her clear pallor.

"Is it ever anything else—between a man and a woman?" she flashed back at him, with the touch of flippancy that set his teeth on edge.

He regarded her a moment with narrowed gaze. "Talk of cynicism and lost illusions . . . !"

She tightened her lips. "Oh, mine were never very hardy, poor things. And they fell among thorns."

It was seriously spoken. She looked away from him, across the strip of garden, to a glimpse of blue hills seen through pine-stems reddening in the afternoon light; and her abrupt change of mood smote them all silent. From the compound came the wailing of a child, the garrulous, comfortable clucking of unseen hens.

Without venturing a glance at Kenneth, Hardynge could feel how furiously the boy must be girding at his failure in tact. Or was it she, who had skilfully put him in the wrong?

It seemed an age before Kenneth opened his cigarette case, with a click that startled him like a pistol shot, and handed it to Mrs. Rex.

"We ought to be getting a move on soon," he urged, "or we shall lose that court. It's latish now. Of course, if you don't mind——"

For reward, he had her kindest smile. "You know I mind—or you wouldn't bother about it. Now then, you people, ' palaver done set ' ! "

She picked up her lighter manner as she might have picked up a dropped glove. Her glance travelled past Hardynge to the other two: and Vyner, rising obediently, saluted with his racquet.

"Marchin' orders, Miss Madison. Death or glory—what? It's goin' to be a break through!"

Bobbie tranquilly demolished her last éclair.

" 'Fraid I've eaten one too many of these. But I'm game."

As they moved down the verandah, out-fooling each other, Kenneth rose briskly and turned to Mrs. Rex.

"I'm ready when you are."

"Right. Only my shoes and racquet. I left them in the rickshaw. If you'd be very kind——"

Kenneth's instinctive glance at Hardynge lit a twinkle in her eye. "*He's* all safe. I won't gobble him up!"

And the boy, confounded by her deliberate inversion of his thought, went reluctantly to do her bidding. Hardynge had risen; and the two, left alone, fronted one another with lightly veiled antagonism.

It was the woman who spoke first.

"Now we're acquainted, I hope we shall see more of you. Come and dine to-morrow, you two. My cook's rather a treasure, and I'm a skilled hand with the chafing dish. Ask—Mr. Malcolm."

Her aplomb accentuated his lack of it.

"Thanks very much," he said with formal politeness, "but I'm probably off again to-morrow."

"To-morrow?" Her surprise rang oddly like dismay. "You came up all this way, in the blazing heat, just for twenty-four hours?"

"No, I'm up for shikar. But I came fifty miles out of my way—to see Kenneth," he told her with a straight look. "Though I'm no longer his guardian——"

"You were afraid he was getting into mischief? I apologise. *I'm* quite safe, I assure you."

"I never doubted *that*, Mrs. Rex." His answer came sharply, like steel on steel, and the blood flamed in her cheek.

"You're detestable," she said very low, " and he's—adorable."

Kenneth—a very Hermes—reappeared with racquet and shoes; and she swept towards him, leaving Hardynge to make what he chose of her return thrust.

"Oh yes, we're quarrelling." She lightly patted his arm. "No bones broken, so far! But your meteoric Colonel Sahib says he's absconding to-morrow. My orders are, you persuade him to stay on a little, now he's got here."

Kenneth glanced from her to Hardynge, who was occupied with a cigarette.

"Not much use, I'm afraid. The Colonel bars Hill stations."

She rounded on Hardynge with eloquent brows.

"Do I actually see before me the Superior Person, who disapproves of Hill stations and all their works?"

Hardynge shrugged, without looking up from the match he was shielding.

"If you choose to put it so——"

"I don't choose to leave it so!" A portentous pause. "Suppose for once, you put your principles (or prejudices) in your pocket, and stay on in Dalhousie for a fortnight? I'll undertake to cure you of the disapproving superior touch."

"Thanks for the offer. I've no particular wish to be cured."

"The Superior Person never has! Do be sporting. It's a wager. My silver cigarette box (a beauty) against six pairs of long gloves. I can't say fairer."

Once again their eyes encountered with the directness of a challenge. It was Hardynge's turn to pause. A sudden idea had occurred to him.

"Done. Since you're so pressing," he said, at last, in a level tone, "*if* I stay on."

"Of course you will! Dinner at eight to-morrow." She turned to Kenneth, and detached her shoes. "Thank you so much. I won't be a minute changing. I'll borrow the bedroom of the Burkley-Kurr!"

There was a long silence in the verandah. Hardynge had nothing to say.

"Well, Colonel!" Kenneth ventured, looking absently at a cluster of Banksia roses.

"So far, I neither retract my opinion—nor my advice," Hardynge answered in the same low tone.

"But—can't you see?"

"See? She doesn't hide her light under a bushel. She's magnetic enough for two. She has all the arts and parts—*and* she knows it. I fancy she's fond of you—up to a point. As to marrying—she's no such fool. She'd fly at higher game on sight."

"Really, Colonel—I *must* ask you——" The boy checked himself and added shyly, "You can't judge, to-day. She's in one of her moods. But sometimes . . . Of course it's sheer arrogance——"

"Don't be a damned fool." The quiet of Hardynge's tone gave an added weight to the commonplace injunction. "For God's sake, listen to reason—and come out of it!"

Kenneth shook his head.

"You won't?"

"I've told you, Colonel—it's not a case of 'won't.'"

"Very *well* then——"

Hardynge rapped out the words on so sharp a note of decision, that Kenneth started and faced about; but whatever he might have said remained unspoken.

Mrs. Rex had reappeared, and was coming towards them.

III

*Yea, though my flowers be lost, they say,
A heart can never come too late.*

GEORGE HERBERT.

'SUNBEAM COTTAGE'—a doll's house affair—was shared by Mrs. Rex and Miss Madison. Set upon Dalhousie's highest hill, it jauntily surmounted a narrow ledge—little more than a gravel path and a strip of gay garden. Behind it loomed the rugged mass of Bakrota. Before it, the greater ranges—purple and amethyst and blue—swelled outward and upward to the snow-line, mistily clear in the early evening light.

On the topmost step of her doll's house verandah Marion Rex sat alone, leaning forward, elbows on her knees, chin cradled in her hands. Minute after minute she sat there in a dreamy stillness—as of a mystic seeking to merge the individual in the Real: her eyes fixed absently on a rugged peak in the north, all sunset-flushed. A row of pale sapphires round her throat and a cluster of pale sweet peas at her breast moved just perceptibly with the even rhythm of her breathing. At long intervals an eyelash flickered.

And while the outward semblance of her sat there motionless, bathed in the glow of sunset, the mercurial, proud, and combative spirit within her was alight with the flush of dawn. . . .

In little less than two weeks the miracle had come to pass. She—the trifler, the sceptic, smirched by the embittering experience of a misguided marriage, found herself incredibly, unmistakably, at the mercy of an emotion that hitherto she had alternately dallied with, derided, and misused. While many gifts had been given her—beauty, intelligence, and power to sway the emotions of men—she had missed altogether this particular experience by which ordinary mortals set such extraordinary store.

Reared by a widowed father, who saw life partially and saw it warped, her young mind had inevitably taken colour from his. Had she ever deigned to make out a case for herself against the righteous, who smote her unfriendly, she might have argued plausibly enough that she had not been brought up on the ten commandments. If she had broken one here and there, in the course of an ill-regulated life, possibly they had broken others, less amenable to enforcement by law. If they knew the facts—and facts can be curiously misleading—she alone knew the full force of the extenuating circumstances.

Looking backward and downward—oh, many miles downward—into the valley of degradation (the unholy estate of matrimony, as she had known it) was like looking back upon a bad dream, in the sane and safe light of morning. She had suffered scarcely a twinge of conscience in breaking away from a marriage that had been of her father's contriving for his own ends. Only in the matter of John Woolford her mind had never been set at rest—nor ever would be. She had at least been honest with him. She had made no pretence of loving—as he loved; but, because he was not as the others of her circle, he had won her affection, her high regard. He had offered her a way of escape, making no stipulation for himself. The temptation had been overwhelming, the straits desperate, her barrier of scruples, where Gerald was concerned, none too robust. In fine, she had gone off with Woolford towards Narkanda, leaving her Simla world to draw the obvious inference, and her husband to make the obvious move. To his credit, he had been prompt about it. She had won through purgatory, to freedom: and then, in fairness to John, in fairness to herself—as she saw it—she had refused to marry him. For her, the word 'marriage' was anathema. It had not been in the bond: but inevitably, being human, he had hoped——

And that night, riding home—how had it been? She knew no more than the others: she would never know. She only knew that she owed her freedom to the best man who had ever crossed her path; that, in return, she had possibly sent him to his death. The loss and the hideous lurking doubt had left a permanent ache deep down. In the face of that possibility, what mattered the mud splashes of a little brief notoriety?

In four years she had more or less discounted them by the simple process of ignoring them. She was not a woman's woman; but she had made a few fast friends here and there—Bobbie Madison among them. A cold-weather acquaintance, two years ago, had ripened swiftly into a warmer feeling, for all the wide gap in age between them. Marion, hardened and embittered, had found a measure of solace in the girl's uncritical, unquestioning loyalty. For Bobbie was impulsive and affectionate, an engaging mixture of naïveté and worldly wisdom. The spoilt child of rich American parents, making the tour of India, she had succeeded in persuading them to leave her out of the larger programme and let her remain in the Punjab with her new-found friend. From India, the Madisons had passed on to Arabia; and Bobbie's fitful plans for rejoining her parents had a way of falling through. Marion had no quarrel with the arrangement. If Bobbie chose to stay on with her, she was welcome. They were very much at ease together, with the surface ease of an intimacy that never probes too deep. The girl's affection lightened the inner loneliness that Marion refused to acknowledge, and gave her fresh excuse for not leaving India. Bobbie being no paragon of intellect or the sterner virtues, never sat in judgment; never even troubled her head about Marion's chequered history; and she herself was as straight as a nice boy—the right sort, in fact.

As to the other sort, Marion knew perfectly well that her magnetism was too potent, her light disdain of their domesticities too galling for her to expect mercy at their hands. And as she asked none—so she gave little, or none.

In any case, she frankly preferred men's society, and in India there was no lack of it. Cloaking the natural woman's need with the faintly contemptuous detachment of the embittered, she was willing to dance with them, flirt with them, ride with them—to do anything in reason except love them and marry them. Because two men, between them, had wrecked her early life, she would have none of them, except in the way of amusement. If occasionally they burnt their fingers, that was their look out: and if here and there she did them injustice, was she entirely to blame?

For the most part, from girlhood upward, base

metal had been offered her and she had given base metal in exchange. Passion she knew—and understood. Sentiment she knew—and despised. The rainbow bridge that connects and transcends both, she had neither known nor permitted herself to believe in—till now ; and the coming of love to an embittered woman of six and thirty is an affair of greater moment than the thrill of a young girl's instinctive response to the larger demands of life.

To Marion Rex it had come with a bewildering abruptness, a vehemence that amounted to pain, and struck at the roots of pride—so immediate had been her inner response to Hardynge's friendly overtures, so swiftly she had disarmed his frank antagonism. The man was patently no philanderer, no carpet knight. His implied relish for her society was, in itself, the subtlest form of flattery. Scarcely a day had passed without a meeting between the four of them on one pretext or another. Casually, unobtrusively, Kenneth had been elbowed aside, as it were, by the older man. She had tried not to see how the process hurt him. She had reproached herself for the secret joy, the secret hope—— It amounted to no more : for there remained the galling admission that, as yet, she had no inkling how far her own sensations were shared.

Piqued by his antagonism—genuinely disturbed by Kenneth's quiet insistence—she had flung down her gauge impulsively, in the form of a bet—and here was the astounding result ! Neither he nor she had referred to it again. The day after tomorrow her given fortnight would be up, but he had shown no sign of impending departure. Did that mean she had won—not merely her bet, but the man himself. And such a man! It felt like bringing down big game after potting tame partridges. How the simile would enrage him!

And in that case, what of poor Kenneth? She could feel for him now in fuller measure; but, being still the essential Marion, she encouraged the conviction that he was too young to suffer permanently on her account. In his saner moods, he must realise that the thing was impossible; seeing that she had—or believed she had—tacitly impressed it on him to the best of her ability. Only to her inmost heart would she admit that at moments there had been need to impress it on herself also. For all her surface cynicism, and the bitterness of disillusion, there were, admittedly, needs in her diverse nature that only marriage could fulfil—marriage with a genuine lover, and a Sahib to boot.

Hence the insidious temptation. . . .

Thank Heaven, awakening had come in time; awakening—and Philip Hardynge——

Unmistakably, in the last few days, there had been portents that—to a woman of wide experience —could have but one significance. He would manœuvre, with delightful awkwardness, to isolate her from the other two; and the moment they were alone, he would be tongue-tied, patently ill at ease, as though he had something urgent to impart, yet, for some mysterious masculine reason, could not frame it in words. Twice this had happened with the same vexatious result. She was determined it should not so happen again.

To-morrow a moonlight picnic and alfresco dance, given by a group of bachelors, would provide an ideal opportunity for giving him his chance. After some preliminary grumbling on his part—

and, on hers, just a suspicion of diplomatic pressure —he had been induced to accept: and if he failed to bring it off this time—he was not the man she took him for.

To-morrow—to-morrow! The lilt of it throbbed in her pulses. Beyond it she dared not look.

IV

Judge not the play, before the play is done.
FRANCIS QUARLES.

THE dance-picnic, with diversions on the banjo, was not a promiscuous affair. The bachelor hosts were *The* Bachelors of the station. They had a reputation in the matter of entertaining, and to-night they surpassed their own record.

The thing was perfect in detail: the menu, the music, the natural glade framed in groups of noble old trees, their boughs hung with Chinese lanterns that glowed in the moonlit dusk like strange tropical fruits in some enchanted garden. At one end, a leaping bonfire crackled and laughed in flame, filling the open space with impish shadows. On a long trestle table, with cushions for seats, there were picnic delicacies worthy of a ball supper. Beyond—in deeper darkness, where lanterns flickered—khitmutgars kept jealous guard over 'drinks' that ranged from innocuous 'nemolade' to baskets of iced champagne. And over all, the unclouded moon of May wove her gossamer web of eerie light and shade.

"Simply perfect, Major Vyner!" Marion Rex apostrophised her host of the moment, comprising, in one sweep of her arm, the whole magical scene. "Not too many fairy lamps, nor too many human beings—and just the right amount of moonlight turned on!"

"Now, Mrs. Rex, you're raggin'," protested

Vyner, radiating justifiable pride, "I can't go pinchin' credit for the moonlight. My stunt's the menu and the wine. If you'll honour me for dinner, I'll put you up to a tip or two worth havin'."

She vouchsafed so to honour him; and two minutes later heard her small sally doing duty as original wit, for the benefit of a fresh arrival.

"Fatuous ass, Vyner," Hardynge muttered at her elbow; and she flashed him a smile that was half a caress, noting the contrast and glorying in it. But to-night she had a kindly feeling even for Major Vyner.

"A well of self-complacence undefiled! I wish he wasn't quite so patently after Bobbie's dollars. But he has his points—like the rest of us. If we're his neighbours at dinner, we may appreciate them!"

That 'we' tacitly invited Hardynge to sit on her left; the which he did with his quiet air of appropriation. Together they explored Major Vyner's good points, profited by his 'tips' and delighted his simple soul by arguing over their merits. Hardynge gave the palm to quenelles in aspic, Marion to a certain Madeira jelly—'Vyner's special,' he proudly informed her. And she noted, with amusement, that most of it casually found its way on to Vyner's plate.

His absorption in the menu—distinctly one of his points—left her free to devote most of her attention to Hardynge, who seemed in an unusually grave, abstracted mood—a good omen, if she knew anything of his kind.

"Are you suffering torments under the infliction of quenelles and moonlight and champagne?" she rallied him, when the torrent of hilarity was in full spate. " Or are you grudgingly enjoying yourself ? I feel responsible."

" I'm enjoying myself all right, thanks—so far," he answered ; and if his tone had a faintly ironic tinge, his quick sidelong look sent her spirits up with a run.

Throughout the meal she maintained an airy flow of talk in her most irrepressible vein. An elixir more potent than champagne had gone to her head. The man was at her side : the first, among many lovers, to whom she could say proudly, ' I am altogether yours.' The moon and the summer night and the unconscious, complacent Bachelors were her accomplices ; and the music stealing out of the massed shadows, just loud enough not to hamper conversation.

' Never the time and the place and the loved one all together ' ? Browning was wrong. To-night—for a mere Marion Rex—the miracle had come to pass.

Only one disturbing thought intruded at intervals —Kenneth. He was sitting directly opposite, with Bobbie for partner. She caught snatches of their talk across the narrow table ; but his attention was patently riveted on Hardynge and herself. There was no getting away from the fact of his pain, or of his changed attitude toward the man for whom he cherished a carefully repressed admiration, rarely accorded by youth to incipient middle age. Worse than all—from her point of view—he had evidently no intention of accepting the dismissal indirect. For the last few days his manner had been uncomfortably tense and purposeful. To-night he had pressed her for several dances. She had limited him to three : and his muttered comment, " I suppose the *Colonel's* going to sweep the board," had warned her that she would need all her wits to head him off an open avowal.

Never, in all her varied experience, had the necessity troubled her as it troubled her to-night, hampered as she was by the fellow-feeling that makes us wondrous kind. Yet her decision held. The double event—detestable! Better thwart him diplomatically than deal the blow direct. Leave that till to-morrow—if——?

She had soothed him a little—how could one help it?—by giving him the first dance; and the moment dinner ended, he was at her side.

"Your innings, old boy?" Hardynge remarked good-humouredly, and strolled off to join a group of men very congenially occupied with sport and scandal, cigars, and old brandy.

As Kenneth watched him go, his goodly young face darkened with anger and jealousy that he was at no pains to hide.

"Come along, Kenneth," Marion roused him gently, "Major Vyner tells me the drugget has been chalked within an inch of its life!"

"Oh, it's a top-hole show," he agreed without enthusiasm. "But I thought you rather disliked dancing on drugget. Are you very keen?"

"I was under the impression that *you* were very keen!" She lightly shelved the tentative implication. "I'm not young enough to be blasé. Besides we were invited to dance—what else? Come on."

"Oh, of course—— All the same——"

He set his lips on the futile protest; and because he took his hurt like a man, she hated herself the more.

Still—it was rather vexatious of·him to spoil her enchanted hour by thrusting on her so unwelcome a reminder of 'Marion Rex that was.' Less than ever dared she risk even the five minutes' pause alone with him. He was counting on it. She saw it in his eyes—felt it in the clasp of his hand. . . .

Directly the music ceased, she demanded iced coffee; pounced on Bobbie and clung to her throughout the interval: a flagrant manœuvre, almost as exasperating to Vyner as to Kenneth himself. But what cared she, just then, for anyone or anything outside her own imperious need?

For the schottische—a concession to their Highland host-in-chief—Vyner claimed her hand. And as he pranced before her, ponderously yet delicately, with due respect for his dinner, she caught herself wondering, "Has any woman ever felt for this well-groomed, complacent travesty of manhood even a tithe of what I am feeling to-night?"

So strongly smitten was she, that the Great Obsession coloured her every thought. The 'god dishonoured' was abundantly avenged.

The waltz was Hardynge's, and he danced well: but it was more than dancing she desired of him. When she realised his intention, an idiotic shyness fettered her tongue: and, remembering Kenneth, she thought, "Serve me right."

Unreservedly she yielded herself to the rapture of the music and movement and the brief, light contact. . . .

When it ended she followed him, meekly as any débutante, to a secluded rustic seat and table supplied by bachelor hosts who knew what was what. She wanted to push on farther, to get right away from the whole frivolous affair; but all power of direction, all her practised skill in manipulating people and things seemed gone from her.

When they reached the seat, she sat down at one end, and he very much at the other. He handed her his cigarette case. They lit up and proceeded to talk platitudes in a jerky colourless fashion, till she fairly lost patience. If he had only brought her here to play cross-questions and crooked answers he should have no further assistance from her.

He simply went on smoking, accepting her rare silence with his unshakable equanimity. Then, for the first time, he asked her a direct question about herself.

"Are you—do you—think of stopping out here indefinitely?" His tone sounded quite concerned, as if he had her on his mind.

She sighed. "I never think ahead—indefinitely. The long view is simply paralysing, if one happens to be cursed with imagination. I've schooled myself to think in sections; and leave the rest— to 'whatever gods there be.' As to stopping on, for the next six months—yes; for the next year —perhaps. A good deal depends on Bobbie—and on the pace of the present landslide."

"'M. That's the point. Two women knocking round India alone—one dislikes the idea, these days. There are too many, out here and at home, doing their damnedest to make the country impossible for white men and women."

"Yes—is it deliberate? I've sometimes wondered. Trying to shake our nerve? They won't succeed! In spite of a certain jumpiness, I'm not exactly keen to turn my back on India, for good. With all its horror and cruelties, under the tinselled splendour, it's a curiously beguiling country—the real India. You understand?"

"Rather."

"People who don't are apt to think it's merely a pose. In my case, they probably call it bravado."

"Why worry? Let 'em think what they please."

"Oh, I've given them plenty of rope in that line! But there *are* moments when one's—well, one's vanity——"

She had rushed her fence, and she must clear it somehow. He made no move to help her out. He sat there looking away from her, plainly ill at ease. And she, intent on his half-averted face, was roused by a sudden whiff of burning. With a start, she dropped her cigarette, just in time to save a brand-new pair of evening gloves.

He turned on her abruptly.

"What is it?"

Her fright had brought her to her senses.

"Another instant, and my vanity would have cost me twenty rupees! I was only trying to say that—in some cases one *does* care whether one is being judged fairly, or dismissed à la Berkeley-Kerr. It's all very well—— *She's* not been—dragged in the mud——"

It was hard to go on; but to give it up were an open confession of defeat.

"Anyhow—please believe it took something stronger than mere bravado to keep me out here, when I could feel the charitable crowd expecting me to retire gracefully. The more I *felt* them expecting it, the more I felt wild horses wouldn't drag me out of the country."

She glanced at him sidelong. He neither spoke nor stirred; yet she could have sworn he was not unmoved. A faint bitterness invaded her tone.

"*You* were probably among them—if not one of them?"

"No," he denied flatly; and added with a touch of awkwardness, "I was at Home on leave, at the time. Afterwards, of course, one heard— the usual gup. But all that's dead and done with. Why rake it up?"

Again she glanced at him, wondering.

"'*Il y a des morts qui ne sont jamais assez morts,*'" she quoted in a low tone. "My experience is that dead things very often breed lively and malignant ghosts. Also—as I said—there *are* moments . . ." She checked herself, galled by his lack of response, racked by sudden uncertainty, determined to force a crisis of some sort there and then. "I'm afraid this doesn't sound much like an essay on the virtues of Hill stations! Have you realised, I wonder, that the two weeks I gave myself will be up to-morrow?"

"I'm realising it acutely at this moment."

"Does that mean? . . . Have I actually— achieved anything?"

"You've achieved a record fortnight's work," he said in a contained voice.

"A diplomatist's answer! It tells—precisely nothing. After all—there's a bet on! How about those long gloves? Have I won them? Or are you going off—unconverted, with my beloved silver box?"

"That's all it amounts to, eh?" He drew in a long whiff of smoke, and let it out slowly. "Well—when to-morrow comes, I'll let you know."

"This is dramatic! Exactly on the last stroke of twelve?"

"No. I'm not being merely perverse." He turned to her, at last, suddenly purposeful in look and tone. "The fact is . . . There's something I want to say—and I'm a bad hand at it——"

"——*Cats* some women are! And of course we were dead cuts ever after."

It was the unmistakable voice of Mrs. Berkeley-Kerr, followed by the unmistakable form of her, more than ever youthfully attired, with Kenneth for her temporary victim.

Hardynge straightened himself with a jerk. As for Marion, if thoughts could kill, the Berkeley-Kerr would have dropped dead at her feet.

The good lady's ingenuous, "O-oh! Hope we don't intrude!" fell upon silence; and the provocative opening bars of a fox-trot told Marion that her coveted, barren five minutes were over, unless——

He said nothing—he had a positive genius for saying nothing! And as they rose mechanically, it was Kenneth who claimed her.

"Our dance—isn't it?"

His carefully suppressed eagerness was at once distracting and engaging. It was his dance; but in an access of irritation with everyone and, everything, she basely feigned forgetfulness.

"Is it? But I thought——"

"Well, you *said*—this is missing two." His glance of veiled hostility at Hardynge was not carefully repressed. "Of course—if you've changed your mind——"

"You'd be nobly generous—and waive your claim?"

The instant it was out, the cruelty of it smote her almost as sharply as it had smitten him. His frank face took on its closed-up look. To her amazement, it was Hardynge who spoke.

"If it's a case of waiving claims—may *I* have the pleasure?"

"Hold hard, Colonel. That's not cricket,"

Kenneth broke out with smothered wrath. " It's *my* dance. I'm not waiving any claims. But, of course—if Mrs. Rex——? "

" Don't be an ass, old boy," Hardynge checked him with an abrupt laugh. " Or by Jove, I'll take you at your word."

Kenneth's baffled look from one to the other moved Marion to lay her fingers on his sleeve.

" My dear Ken, can't you rise to a joke ? If it's your dance, it's yours. But I bar my two best partners snarling over me like two dogs over a bone."

" As a matter of fact," Hardynge remarked crisply, " it occurs to me I'm dancing this with Miss Madison. If I don't look alive, she'll be hoping *I've* waived my claim ! "

Mrs. Berkeley-Kerr—all eyes and ears for an intriguing situation—tittered gleefully. Detestable woman ! She would pass that on to Bobbie, who was being difficult enough over Colonel Hardynge as it was. She would retail the whole trifling interlude, with embellishments, at the tennis courts and the Club. Kenneth had made a fool of himself. He must be more definitely discouraged. Between his insistence and her own new-born uncertainty, her winged mood had very completely dropped to earth.

The moment they were alone, she turned to him briskly.

" It was stupid of me—I'm sorry. But we won't waste any more of it. Come along."

Nothing of the sort. They were all out of hand to-night—Bobbie included. Already she was in open rebellion over Colonel Hardynge. At dinner she had been positively aggressive. As for Kenneth, he stood there looking unutterable things at her: very square and resolute and vexatiously good-looking in the moonlight.

"It's not the dancing I'm keen on. *You* know that. Mrs. Rex," he pleaded with shy fervour, "why *should* we? It's such a topping night. Do come for a stroll, instead?"

"Kenneth, you're a fraud," she hedged shamelessly, " I'm dying to dance. It's my pet tune——" Her foot tapped briskly, and she rattled on to drown incipient sympathy. "If I weakly consented to stroll, I should be jigging all the time and drive you crazy. And it isn't sporting. At these little shows one must play the game." Deliberately she made a forward move. But his tragic aspect moved her to a kindlier tone: "Later on, perhaps. Honestly—I'm not in the mood."

"You never are—these days. And we've only got *one* more. You might spare me another—— Oh, can't you *see*," he broke out with smothered passion, "you're driving me crazy? I never get a chance. It's always the *Colonel* with you—now."

Pushed into a corner, she took refuge again in lightness.

"Really, the perversity of men! I thought you particularly wanted me to be friends with him."

"Oh—*friends*! . . ." He hurled the word at her with incredulous scorn.

"Precisely. And I've done it—in record time; though he isn't exactly a responsive subject. All the same, under his rocky surface——"

It was useless. She could not keep it up. They were both too deeply and diversely involved. Her forced lightness broke down under an uprush of genuine pity.

"My dear old boy, *do* be reasonable. I know

it's difficult; but glooming and glowering won't improve matters one little bit. I'm as willing to be good friends with you as—as ever I was. But I can't say—what you want me to say. That's the unpalatable truth. So, for heaven's sake, come and dance."

Again she made a move; and this time he followed her with a mute docility that hurt her more than any passionate protest or appeal. The thing he craved to say, and manfully refrained from saying, spoke louder than words.

Almost at once they encountered Colonel Hardynge with Bobbie, looking younger and slimmer than ever in her straight-cut frock, a leaf fillet round her short fair hair.

"Absconding already?" Marion greeted them, marvelling what that might bode. "And here have I been lecturing Kenneth on the sin of shirking!"

"Well, the cap doesn't fit this child," Bobbie retorted with a wicked grimace at her partner. "I deserve a V.C. for trying to stick it out. Your Colonel Sahib waltzes like peaches and cream; but he can't fox-trot for toffee."

"Well, I warned you," Hardynge gravely reminded her.

"And for *once* you spoke the truth. Now it's to be a talking match." (The information was for Marion.)

"Anything to please you, I'm agreeable."

"Since when?" she queried innocently.

"Bobbie, be *quiet*!" Marion flashed in spite of herself. "Colonel Hardynge, do you let her go on like that all the time?"

"It seems to keep her happy. And I'm a pachydermatous animal."

"You wait!" Bobbie eyed him with awful significance. "See if I don't get a pin-prick through!"

Marion's involuntary glance at Hardynge was intercepted by Kenneth, which spoiled the effect.

"Dare I leave you to her tender mercies?" she asked him, only half in joke: but Bobbie, very much in command of the ship, airily waved her away.

"He's my partner. No poaching! Time you were fading along, you two; or we'll have Major Vyner regrettin' to observe that you're discouragin' the young from playin' the game—eh what?"

Hardynge chuckled, and Marion—for all her anxiety, laughed outright.

"Bobbie! If he heard you——"

"Bless you, he wouldn't turn a hair. It 'ud sound so natural. Kenneth, be a man, not a mouse, and take her off to dance."

"Well, *I'm* not stopping the way," Kenneth retorted with a touch of heat. Marion, on thorns, dared not risk so much as a glance at the girl. There was no reckoning with Bobbie on the war-path. She would say, or do, any hair-raising thing that entered her irresponsible head.

"Will you come?" Kenneth asked in his normal voice; and Marion, pacing silent and abstracted at his elbow, could only pray that, if it came to open hostilities, Colonel Hardynge might prove more than her match.

V

She is constant as a star,
And yet the maddest maiden

MEREDITH.

IF Marion suffered qualms, Bobbie Madison was
immune—and rightly so, in her own esteem ; her
conscience being clear. She was a young lady of
decided opinions ; and in the present case, her
conviction deepened daily that this intrusive,
entirely superfluous Colonel was playing a low-down
game. That he was falling in love with Marion
—honest injun—she simply did not believe. It
would be unspeakable if Marion ' came a cropper '
on his account ; and already Bobbie had a sneaking
suspicion that the damage was done. Some
people would say she deserved it. Not so Bobbie.
Of course it *had* been bad of her letting poor Ken
dangle around in a fool's paradise ; but she had
her excuses, multiplied by the fact that Bobbie
was genuinely fond of her.

For Colonel Hardynge, whatever his ' dark
designs ' might be, Bobbie would admit no shadow
of excuse. He had switched off Kenneth. He
had fooled Marion. He needn't fancy he was
going to fool *her*. Before the next dance struck
up, she would get a few pin-pricks through—even
if he *was* a pachyderm, and gloried in it.

Head erect, coolly purposeful, she piloted him
to the identical seat he had so lately left.

" This'll do nicely," she remarked, briefly

surveying a scene as ill-suited as Oberon's Wood to the sparrings and jarrings of mortals.

Above their rustic seat loomed a noble English chestnut, its long leaves weirdly illumined by a solitary Chinese lantern that glowed like a hollow melon lit from within. If Bobbie had little of sentiment in her make-up, she had an eye for natural beauty; for all she admired the Chinese-lantern effect quite as much as the eerie magic of the moon.

But at the moment, glades and lanterns and moons were trivial etceteras; herself and the Enemy were all. She turned and faced him as it were measuring swords.

" Sweetly romantic, isn't it ? "

" Oh, sweetly."

His tone belied him, and she arched innocent brows.

" Aren't we the pine-apple of politeness ? Never contradict a lady—and all that ? "

" Oh, if you're keen on being contradicted, it's one of my few accomplishments. But I can't rhapsodise. I'm not a romantic subject. Shall we sit ? "

For answer, she subsided gracefully, smiling up at him, and spreading out her narrow skirt to its full extent.

He retaliated by gravely abstracting a chair from a very confidential arrangement under a neighbouring tree, and setting it down on the far side of the little table.

" That's all right. You needn't be alarmed."

" Alarmed ? I'd be enchanted ! " She flung him a wicked look. " P'raps we're *hardly* secluded enough. Also—I've one or two things to say."

" Such as ? . . ."

He sat down with an air of amused resignation; and she, drawing the table nearer, planted her elbows on it, resting her chin in her hands.

"Such as—your last remark but one; you're *not* a romantic subject. And you're bored stiff with Hill stations. . . . Very *well* then—what's all the music about? Why don't you freeze on to your mountain goats and things, instead of crashing into other people's romances that are no concern of yours?"

It was a clean thrust; and it stiffened him. He was neither amused nor resigned any more.

"Sorry if I'm in your way. I stayed on for the simple reason that Mrs. Rex asked me to."

"O-oh? News to me. But I assure you that amounts to nothing, from Marion. And I'll bet you any odds you please, it just happened to suit your book."

"I'm not taking on any more bets, thanks."

(One pin-prick! Bobbie registered it with glee.)

"Well, if you'll look me straight in the eyes and swear it didn't——"

"I'll do nothing of the kind," he retorted sharply.

"Easy on!" She scrutinised him with embarrassing candour. "You've as good as admitted there *is* something behind it all: something that's making you feel mean—or you wouldn't be so huffy over it. And whatever it may be, it's a wicked shame the way you've upset those two."

That took some stiffening out of him: but he said nothing; and again she considered him pensively. She was beginning to wonder. . . .

"Of course, if I thought you'd got it in the neck—like poor old Ken——"

"That's neither here nor there."

"My mistake," she murmured with disarming meekness. "But there's no mistake about it— you've made Marion jumpy. You've made Kenneth pretty well hate you. (More than a pin-prick, that last.) And we were all getting along like a house on fire before you blew in."

"Look here, young lady——" (He was furious. He would snap her head off in a minute!) "If I know anything of Mrs. Rex, *she* wouldn't thank you for interfering."

"Which of us knows her best, I wonder?" Bobbie drew herself up, very dignified. "And *you* can't talk about interfering. You've done damage enough in that line. What I'm after is—when do you propose to clear out and leave us to pick up the pieces?"

"When it suits me. Not a minute sooner."

"Oh, if that's your line, it'll be daggers drawn." (She was thoroughly enjoying herself now.) "Marion's had her fill, one way and another. But she's going to hear what I think——"

"Good God! I've had enough of this."

He rose with a jerk that knocked the chair over, and stood scowling down at her. He looked rather nice when he was angry. "Miss Madison —*will* you leave Mrs. Rex alone?"

Bobbie, nothing abashed, stood up confronting him.

"Will *you* leave her alone?—that's the point."

"No. If she's going to hear you, she's going to hear me, too. In any case, I intended . . . speaking to her, to-night."

"You—intended——?" Bobbie gasped, feeling rather like a pricked air-ball. "For the Lord's sake, why didn't you say that sooner?"

"It was no concern of yours."

Something in his manner puzzled her.

"That's a matter of opinion. You mean ? . . ."

"I mean—what I say."

"So do I," she retorted, still puzzled, but defiant. "And I'm not going to be scared off with innuendoes either. So that's that."

He shut his mouth like a trap.

"Now we know where we are. As I've nothing to add to your concise summing up, you'd better come along and refresh. It's a fool's game, Miss Bobbie, trying to run other people's affairs."

His tone was positively paternal; and that 'Miss Bobbie' made her feel like an impertinent child slapped and put in the corner. After all, he was probably old enough to be her father; and she *had* cheeked him pretty freely. She admitted the fact with relish. What else could you do with a strong, silent pachyderm, anyhow ? And she had jolly well rattled him, for all his condescending airs.

The dance was just over; and at the buffet they ran into Marion, with Kenneth. Of course she had dragged him there to eat and drink, when he probably couldn't swallow a morsel. You could see it from the look of him. As for Marion, she seemed jumpier than ever, under all her lively talk. And there was the Viniferous Vyner—who had already crashed over a proposal—drowning his sorrows in drink, under cover of 'refreshing' the great Mrs. Berkeley-Kerr—the only one of them all as serene as she looked. And even she—perhaps——? You never could tell. In any case, they were all bound to keep it up somehow—jerking and grimacing like marionettes, because it was the rule of the game. What a life !

"*I* saw you fox-trotting, Colonel Hardynge ! Quite coming on ! "

That was Mrs. Berkeley-Kerr, who never seemed able to see that he couldn't abide her.

"Ask Miss Madison," he answered curtly.

"I prefer to form my own opinion!" She was positively arch. "Young things are always impatient. You must try again."

"Not for a kingdom, my dear lady."

It came out a shade too quick; and Mrs. Berkeley-Kerr—not all of a fool—had him on the nail.

"Don't lose your nerve, Colonel! *I've* no designs on you. I'm death on these devastating caviare sandwiches. Wasn't it Milton or someone, who wrote, 'Food is the last infirmity of noble minds?' *So* true. Let's be infirm together—even if we can't be noble!"

She pushed the plate towards him. He politely proffered it to Bobbie.

"Ladies first! Miss Madison has done 'some' talking. She's earned 'em."

Words and tone tempted Bobbie to tip the plate out of his hand. Only a grain of self-respect and a weakness for caviare sandwiches saved the situation; but, in her passing fluster, she missed the cream of some chaffing remark from Marion about mangling Milton that seemed to have ruffled the Berkeley-Kerr.

Major Vyner pounced on it of course—he was getting a shade hilarious.

"Don't know much about manglin'—or Milton —but the fella scored a bull's-eye with that 'last infirmity' touch! Tell you what, Colonel"—he confidentially nudged Hardynge's elbow—"my khit's got a bottle of old brandy in lurk that would make a defunct bishop sit up and take notice. If Miss Madison'll excuse you——"

"I'm sure Miss Madison will be charmed!"

The light shaft was so pointed that Bobbie had eyes for nothing but her sandwich. Even through her lowered lids, she could *feel* Marion looking her way, thinking unspeakable things; swiftly she laid her simple plan to get her own innings before the banjo interlude.

"I wouldn't be responsible for keeping any man away from a glass of old brandy," she answered demurely, addressing her remark to Major Vyner, not to the Enemy. "Anyway, I'm booked for a stroll with Mrs. Rex before you start tuning up for the sing-song."

That was a neat one for the Colonel Sahib: and if it did startle Marion, she submitted like a lamb, when Bobbie boldly slipped a hand through her arm, trying not to be aware of poor Ken's blank dismay.

"You come along, too, m'lad." Major Vyner waggled an inviting finger. "You're lookin' rather white about the gills; and you're down for a rousin' item presently."

The two men moved off; and Kenneth, basely deserted, had no choice but to follow them.

Bobbie, having gained her point, took no further interest in the merits of old brandy.

"You crazy child—what *are* you up to?" Marion demanded, when they were comparatively alone among the shadowy, lamp-lit trees.

"Oh, just getting you away for a breather. You ought to be grateful."

"So I am," Marion unexpectedly agreed. "It's a positive relief to be quit of them all."

"Even Colonel Hardynge?"

"Even Colonel Hardynge."

Bobbie made incredulous eyes at her.

"Done-gone-finish? Is the world coming to an end?"

Marion sighed.

"Oh dear no. Nothing so drastic. Only perhaps—one incarnation of one not very admirable woman."

"Switch it off! You and your incarnations! Is that a kind of sidelong admission that you're treating Ken disgracefully? Not so long ago nothing was good enough for him. And now—— It makes me mad. He's pure wool, that boy."

"Oh, obviously and patently. He's a darling. That's been the trouble all along."

"And he's had to pay a pretty tall price for his darlingness. It's the devil that gets the ha'pence and the darling gets the kicks. You ought to be ashamed of yourself."

"I *am*. That doesn't help much."

She halted near a couple of secluded chairs, and sat down on one of them with a sigh of weary impatience, looking straight before her. . . .

Bobbie followed suit. She could hold her tongue at need, or she would not have remained Marion's friend for two years. If she wanted to get in her word about Colonel Hardynge, she also wanted to hear anything Marion might be moved to say about him.

So she lit a cigarette; and Marion, absently watching her, went on: "For all you're a babe, my Bobbie, you've some grains of worldly wisdom. Just consider a moment. A boy of Kenneth's quality—and my lamentably battered self: my age, my many 'regrettable incidents' . . . even if I were fool enough . . . oh, he's utterly impossible——"

SIEGE PERILOUS

"Not more than he was a month ago," Bobbie insinuated cruelly.

"N—no, I suppose not."

"Well, then—why did you let him?"

"*Let* him? My dear girl, you've got two eyes in your head. Did he wait to be let? If a boy *will* put his fingers in the fire——" She shut her teeth on that, and added in quite another tone, "But I didn't come here to talk about Kenneth."

"No more did I—though he's miles and away the better man. It's Colonel Hardynge——"

"Yes, it's Colonel Hardynge," Marion briskly cut in. "What do you *mean* by it? You've been badgering him. He looked quite worried."

"Did he? Did it really show?" Bobbie triumphed shamelessly. "Then I *must* have got some pin-pricks through!"

But Marion was in no mood for raillery.

"Tell me what you said—I insist."

Bobbie, devoted but diplomatic, leaned coaxingly nearer.

"I was only trying to fight your battles, old darling—not with conspicuous success."

"Very dear of you." The constraint in Marion's tone scarcely matched her words. "But rather superfluous. There really isn't any battle to fight."

"Deluded woman! I've the evidence of my senses."

"The most unreliable evidence on earth."

Bobbie drew herself up dramatically.

"Well—if I'm *cast* out of your confidence——"

"*When* there is anything to confide——" Marion vouchsafed her a sudden straight look, "you'll probably be the first to hear it."

"Which it's no more than I deserve. And there's

a sporting chance," Bobbie nodded mysteriously, " that it may be happening along to-night. He said——"

" Who said ? "

" Why, Colonel Hardynge, of course."

" What's *he* got to do with it ? "

" That's your cue, not mine. But I tell you flat, Marion—I don't trust your Colonel Sahib— not one inch."

" Poor dear man. What an awful calamity ! And you hardly know him."

" Do *you* know him ? " It was Bobbie's turn to be in earnest ; and Marion promptly mounted her pedestal.

" I should say Kenneth's feeling for him— apart from my own judgment—is quite sufficient guarantee."

" That's hedging," Bobbie sternly reproved her. " You ask Ken straight what he thinks—now. It'll be a startler. Anyhow I've treated his High-and-Mightiness to a valuable piece of my mind. Hope it won't give him bad indigestion."

That jerked Marion off her pedestal.

" Bobbie, you little fool ! *What* did you say ? "

" Oh, we're all fools, when we happen to disagree with the other fools. I said—what I thought of him. P'raps I ought to have spoken sooner. But that *you* should be in earnest——"

" Who said I was in earnest ? "

" You mean to tell me you'll refuse him—if that's what he's after ? "

" I don't mean to tell you anything. I've said so once. For heaven's sake, child, can't you leave me alone ? "

" Why, certainly—from this time forth for evermore ! " With exaggerated dignity she stood up

SIEGE PERILOUS

to take her leave. "*I'm* not a pachyderm; and I'm sure I hope you'll be happy. You've shunted Kenneth. You've shunted me. But no doubt your precious Colonel Hardynge will make it up to you a hundredfold."

On the word, she swung round and walked briskly away.

"Bobbie, you darling little fool—come *back*," Marion called after her low and urgently; but Bobbie, having tasted defeat once that evening, clung to her shred of victory.

Marion was a graceless, ungrateful wretch, talking like that after the noble way she—Bobbie —had fairly put her head between the lion's jaws and had it snapped off for her pains. And of course she hadn't enjoyed tackling Colonel Hardynge— oh no, not a mite! Let Marion try it on herself, if she was so dead keen on him. Bobbie hated being disagreeable, especially to Marion; but her feelings were hurt.

So she merely glanced over her shoulder and remarked: "Time's up. They're settling round the bonfire for the sing-song. You'd better come along too, and manœuvre for a position."

VI

Truth's a weighty matter;
And, truth at issue, we can't flatter.
ROBERT BROWNING.

MARION followed at her leisure—too profoundly disturbed by all that Bobbie had said and left unsaid to take even the mildest interest in manœuvring for a position. An interlude of banjo thrumming and songs with rousing choruses stretched interminably between her and the one real event of the evening—two consecutive dances which she had bestowed on Colonel Hardynge, with full intent to dance neither.

She secured an inconspicuous seat near the outer edge of the circle. The syncopated rhythm of a lively coon song strayed, as it were, through her brain, while her gaze travelled here and there, seeking—but not finding—the tall, familiar, figure; and as disheartened at her failure as any raw girl in her teens.

Song and banjo, banjo and song, alternately assailed her inattentive ears. The interlude was half over before she became aware of his presence. From the farther side of the bonfire, he was strolling towards her, with an admirably casual air. At his approach, she looked up: and he, without a word, established himself beside her, reclining on one elbow, his long legs stretched out upon the grassy slope.

"Not half a bad show, after all," he remarked

in a careful undertone, as the chorus subsided.
" This sort of thing suits my barbarous taste
better than the rest of it."

" Well, I won't insist on dancing when *our* turn
comes again ! "

" That's all right," he said, and let his eyes linger
a moment in hers.

Then he fell silent altogether—and she preferred
it so. The thrill of his nearness made talk difficult ;
and silence left her free to watch, undetected, the
play of firelight on the admirable masculinity of
his face. Good looking he was not, even to her
enamoured eyes ; but the whole man—face, figure,
and hands—bore the satisfactory stamp of distinction and strength. The strain of hardness and
bitterness in him merely caused her to yearn over
him the more. He had so plainly lacked all the
softening elements of life. . . .

The band struck up a one-step. The group
round the bonfire dissolved into couples. Her
moment had come.

Colonel Hardynge rose deliberately ; seemed to
hesitate a moment ; then proffered a helping hand
and drew her to her feet.

" Ours—I think," he said, with grave formality.

" Yes—ours," she echoed ; and because of the
tremor within, forced herself to add lightly, " And
you are not to be victimised this time ! "

" Quite sure—it's not the other way about ? "

" Quite sure."

He did not reply to that ; and they moved
leisurely away from the open space, toward the
wooded fringe of the glade, where the moon
wrought ghostly arabesques, and stray groups of
trees made bars and pools of shadow.

A prolonged silence fell on them. And still they walked on and on. For the first time in her life Marion Rex felt hopelessly at a loss. She had done her part. What demon of masculine perversity withheld him from doing his?

An involuntary sigh escaped her. He started and looked round.

"I'm sorry," he said abruptly, as if he had been jerked out of a dream. "I've got something to say—to ask." An ominous pause. "We can't go on this way. It's about time we understood one another."

"Don't we—understand one another?" she asked very low.

"Up to a point—yes. Fellow-cynics—eh?—as you were quick to recognise. At least, that was my impression . . . not knowing you."

"And now—you *do* know me? . . ."

"I can only throw myself on your generosity," he answered, looking away from her.

Involuntarily she drew a sharp breath, half pain, half impatience at his hesitancy; and again, as before, he turned to her, suddenly purposeful.

"Mrs. Rex—I am an inexpert bungler at this sort of thing. But having broken the ice, I must take my chance. As I said—I've something difficult to ask. It's about Kenneth, as you've probably been feeling in your bones."

"About—*Kenneth*?"

It was as if he had flung a glass of cold water in her face. The shiver of it ran all through her. Only when it had passed did his unwittingly ironic hit at her intuition strike home. For a few bewildering moments, she was so dazed and hurt, so thankful for the uncertain light, that she only heard the deep vibrations of his voice without gathering the sense of the words, which it plainly cost him a painful effort to speak. . . .

When at last she emerged, chilled and rigid, from her confused blur of sensations, he was still talking of Kenneth. Had he no other concern on earth? Or was it . . . perhaps . . . A flicker of hope revived in her.

" You mean—can you be in any doubt ? " she murmured.

" Doubt ? No, *I* never doubted that you were simply passing the time. The trouble was—to convince him. A straight-run boy like that, infatuated with a woman—like you." The words seemed forced out of him, giving an additional bluntness to his manner. " As you know, our relation's rather an intimate one. I care for the boy, and I can't break the habit of feeling responsible. I tried to get him away by plain speaking. God knows I had no taste for—*this* sort of expedient——"

He paused awkwardly—puzzled, perhaps, by her lack of response.

" What sort of expedient ? " she asked in a toneless voice; and it seemed an age before his answer came.

" Well, if you insist on dotting all the i's. It was my simple duty, as I saw it, to disillusion Kenneth, get him out of his fool's paradise, one way or another. I said what I could, to no purpose. Naturally, in his state, he spurned my cynical assurance that it was simply a case of propinquity and no rival in the field. Then *you* turned up—and heaven knows why—flung me that bet. Like a fool, I took it. And, it struck me suddenly, one might try the effect . . . of an object-lesson——"

Again he broke off. His distress was evident. In a blinding flash, she saw it all: but pity was far from her. She would spare him nothing.

"In plain English," she said, "your assumed admiration for me has been merely a clever piece of acting . . . for Kenneth's benefit: a studied insult to a woman who has done *you* no harm——"

"Before God, I never meant it so!" he broke out passionately. His control seemed to be slipping from him as hers gained ground. "Have some mercy on a blundering man, who has made an unholy mess of things. I've admitted Kenneth *was* my first concern. But confound it all—as to acting . . . or studied insult . . ."

Her sigh had a touch of impatience. "Really, I can't pretend to understand you. But I quite understand *I'm* only a side issue."

She turned as if to leave him. He put out a detaining hand.

"Mrs. Rex—one moment—Kenneth——"

"Yes—Kenneth?" she queried with a frigid lift of her brows. She was in no mood to help him out.

He answered without looking at her. "I needn't tell you I've failed to convince him. I've simply alienated him. He thinks I'm playing a common, low-down game."

"Is he—so very far out?"

"I leave it to you." (Tone and manner told her the thrust had gone home, and she was glad: she who had quarrelled with Bobbie on his account.) "Anyhow, nothing now will make him believe he never had a chance, except a clear statement from you. That's the request I've been boggling over. . . ."

"I'm not surprised." She confronted him with

rising wrath. " You have the effrontery to suggest I should vilify myself for *your* benefit, that Kenneth may be cured of his chivalrous—infatuation ? Do you know, I think he would be rather angry if he heard you ! "

" Oh, no doubt." He tacitly accepted the implied rebuke. " I've done for myself all round. The common fate of the meddler. . . ."

The note of pain in his voice struck through her shell of hardness, and set her vaguely wondering . . . ? But she would dally with no more illusions.

" Colonel Hardynge "—her tone had a studied quietness—" did you seriously suppose I would belittle myself to that extent, in his eyes—for the asking ? "

" I—well—I could see no other way. You seemed to care for the boy—up to a point. I thought there might be a sporting chance if I didn't badly bungle things."

She drew an audible breath.

" Thank you. That's the one real compliment you have paid me. I *do*—care for the boy. I have treated him disgracefully. So have you. He has taken it like a man. I would do almost anything to atone. He was trying—to speak this evening, but I stopped him. I can't bear hurting him any more. I've half a mind—to go straight back, tell him what I think of him . . . and say . . . I'm willing . . . to marry him——"

" Good God—*no !* "

The man broke in with smothered vehemence ; and again she was startled. But by this time her emotions were well in hand.

" Would it be such a dire disaster—for him ? " she asked gently.

"No—not that." He braced his shoulders, and spoke stiffly in jerks. "I beg your pardon. It was a trifle unexpected. Of course, if you've been fooling me—if you do really care, there's no more to be said. You have the advantage of me all round. I don't profess to understand women."

"You have made that abundantly clear," she confirmed him with the ghost of a smile. "Kenneth can give you points every way. I'll go to him at once. It will be easier."

"Mrs. Rex——" he began; but she had endured enough.

"Spare me . . . your thanks. I don't deserve them."

For the first time a tinge of bitterness crept into her voice; and, turning away, she walked briskly back to the peopled region round the bonfire, thankful that he made no effort to keep level with her. Stray couples were strolling towards them. No more could be said; and, once within the safety zone, she slackened speed.

The search for Kenneth proved unavailing. He was nowhere to be found. Bobbie had noticed him moving away from the bonfire when the music struck up. No one had seen him since; and again the sharply sundered pair stood isolated—nonplussed. A mocking sense of anti-climax jarred Marion's nerves, already overstrung.

"Perhaps," she suggested hopefully, "the poor boy has just gone home."

He nodded.

"Well, I'd like to go, too, if you'll excuse me . . . the other dances?"

"They are excused—in any case. I don't think —we have anything more to say to one another. I will see Kenneth, or write to him, to-morrow.

And as I've lost my bet, I will send you my silver box as a memento—of this amazing interlude."

She looked full at him now, but he set his lips, and answered nothing. Was the human envelope so dense that he could stand within a yard of her, uncomprehending, unaware . . . Without word or gesture of leave-taking, she turned away, and left him standing there in the moonlight, mute and motionless, like a man under a spell. . . .

The gentle slope seemed unusually steep. All the lightness and ecstasy of youth renewed had gone out of her. Even in the turmoil of her immediate misery, she found herself wondering, with a queer, dull detachment, why so much pain and bitterness should be her portion—tacitly refusing to perceive that, in large measure, the cause and the sufferer were one.

Before she reached the bonfire, she heard him shout for his *sais* ; heard Major Vyner hail him in his most convivial vein : " Cheerio, Colonel ! Two lonely bachelors, eh ? Come an' have a drink. Just a little one. Tell you what—my khit's got a bottle of old brandy up his sleeve . . ."

She hurried out of earshot, sick to death of the whole trivial affair that had seemed to her a thing of beauty and miracle less than two hours ago.

VII

*What I seem to myself, do you ask of me?
No hero, I confess.*

BROWNING.

HARDYNGE, left alone, summarily released himself from Vyner, secured Belinda, and set off at a brisk canter along the narrow, unrailed track—a proceeding for which he would have rated a younger man. The fury of bitterness and self-castigation that consumed him demanded the relief of rapid movement: and if, by chance, a root, a stone or a deceptive patch of moonlight happened to make an end of him—who would be any the worse for it?

Kenneth would survive; and she—— ? A twinge of regret, perhaps, for the merciless precision with which she had let fly the shafts of her scorn. Perhaps—she would even marry Kenneth. His ear was haunted still by her "I *do* care for the boy "—the ring of genuine feeling in her voice. And what a voice it was! What effortless charms and spells she wove to ensnare the unwary, even were they fools enough to believe themselves immune.

Seen through her eyes, his bungling attempt at bringing Kenneth to reason took on quite a new aspect—by no means flattering to his self-esteem. To Kenneth it must seem as if—under cover of paternal zeal—he had deliberately stepped in and stolen the treasure he affected to despise. He saw himself, every way, condemned to self-repression; the more so that his own feeling was plainly

not shared by her. She had merely found him—as
he anticipated—more congenial company than a
love-sick boy of three and twenty; while he,
confidently steeled against woman and her wiles,
had not dreamed of danger for himself.

Was ever man more ironically 'hoist with his
own petard'?

Nothing now remained but to get square with
Kenneth—a tough job on the face of it; then lay
his dák for Chumba and the passes beyond, there
to stalk markhor and ooryal and bend his will to
conquer a futile obsession. In future, he would
stick to work and shikar. If Kenneth showed any
further propensity for tying himself into knots,
he must be left to the educative experience of
unravelling them to the best of his ability.

Arrived at the hotel, he hurried along the
verandah to the boy's door. No light gleamed
through the 'chick.' He lifted it and surveyed an
empty room. No sign anywhere of Kenneth's
return. What the devil did it mean? A twinge
of acute anxiety mocked at his resolve of a few
moments earlier. Had the boy gone off in a fit of
depression, or bottled-up anger. He had been
notably silent and unapproachable the last few
days. Suppose he had ridden recklessly, and gone
over the khud?

Questions and speculations were useless; equally
useless to ride back in search of him. For more
than half an hour Hardynge paced the empty
verandah cursing the malicious perversity of
things in general. Finally, he cursed himself for
a nerve-ridden fool. He and Kenneth were in the
same plight after all. No doubt the boy had gone
for a ride to work it off. Bed was more to the
point than pacing a damned verandah. But

unluckily bed did not imply sleep; and he lay a long while, with closed eyes, straining his ears for the sound of hoofs that never came . . .

In the end, he slept heavily and woke, later than usual, with a drugged brain and a dead weight on body and spirit. Then he remembered . . .

Springing up, he slipped on a dressing-gown, and opened the connecting door into Kenneth's room, that was next his own. Emptiness still: but emptiness revealing action and direction. The place was cleared of Kenneth's belongings. A strapped trunk and gaping bag betokened instant departure.

While he stood looking blankly at those eloquent inanimates, Nasur Ali appeared in the doorway.

"Where's Malcolm Sahib? Has he breakfasted?"

Nasur Ali salaamed. "Very early, Hazúr. Ohé, he is without sense this morning! Some devil must have entered in."

"When did he return?"

"Long past midnight, Hazúr. He awoke this slave; and, not regarding inconvenience, gave orders to pack—*jut-put*.[1] Twenty years I have known the madness of soldier Sahibs. But Malcolm Sahib has never given trouble like this. It may be, if your honour spoke, he would hear——"

"Well, I go to breakfast now," Hardynge interrupted brusquely. "Tell the Sahib I must see him before he leaves. The matter is urgent. Where is he gone?"

"God knows. He went out for some purpose."

"When he returns, say the Colonel Sahib bids him wait."

[1] Immediately.

It did not take Hardynge many minutes to dispose of his tepid, belated breakfast. While he mechanically chewed and swallowed unappetising morsels, his brain was absorbed in an imaginary conversation with Kenneth—that would probably never come off.

Returning to the bedroom, he found the boy alone, hunting feverishly for something in the bag that stood on a table near his bed.

" Hullo, Kenneth—what the devil's the meaning of this ? " he asked, without preamble.

Kenneth started and stood up. " Oh—good morning, Colonel," he said stiffly. " Pretty obvious, isn't it ? I recognise—the game's up. That's all. I suppose I ought—to congratulate you."

" Me ? " Hardynge echoed blankly. Speech was going to be more difficult than he had foreseen.

Kenneth nodded, and went on fumbling in his bag. Misery seemed to be thawing, a little, the ice of his antagonism, his young dignity : but resentment burned him. And suddenly he faced about.

" Damn it all, Colonel—*was* it fair play to come dashing up here—and then—to cut in, on your own . . . ? "

" It may interest you to know I have done nothing of the kind," Hardynge interposed in a level tone.

Kenneth stared blankly. " I—I suppose I'm dense, but I don't understand. All I know is that last night she wouldn't give me a chance. But when *your* turn came—I saw her—I heard her. And I knew it was time to clear out. I didn't want any blooming fuss, only to get away, and be let alone. Not awfully much to ask—is it ?—when you've got everything. In fact—I'm taking your original prescription."

"Very dutiful; but a trifle belated. Pity you didn't wait a bit last night, before bolting—on insufficient evidence. The plain fact is—I've got nothing."

His tone roused Kenneth for the first time from absorption in his own misery. For the first time, he dispassionately considered the man, who had so long been his friend, in the finest sense, for all the years between. He had scarcely the aspect of an accepted lover. Kenneth had never seen his face look so old and strained.

"D'you mean—did she—refuse you?" he asked, blankly incredulous.

"No. I never asked her. I never meant to ask her. So now you know."

"You never *meant* to——!" Sympathy evaporated. A gleam of anger dawned in his eyes.

"Precisely." Hardynge took him up. "Is it any use trying to convince you that—first and last—I have been actuated by one motive . . . the same that originally brought me here?"

Kenneth gasped, and sat down rather abruptly on the nearest chair. Hardynge flung his cigar into the grate, leaned an elbow on the mantel-piece, and regarded him with grave, inscrutable eyes.

"I don't want to bore you, Kenneth. But to make things clear, we must go back a little. You may remember, I did what I could. I asked you to come away with me. You refused. When— Mrs. Rex pressed me to stay, I gave you a last chance. You may recall my remark about flying at higher game? Sounds conceited, on the face of it. But as you wouldn't listen to reason—an ocular demonstration seemed worth trying. In one sense I succeeded. In my main object, I have egregiously failed."

He paused, absently fingering a japanned candlestick; his eyes still searching Kenneth's face. A clearer understanding, it seemed, had not abated his wrath.

"*Colonel!* You mean to imply that, for my benefit—because you thought me a romantic young fool—you set out, in cold blood, to make Mrs. Rex . . . seem worthless in my eyes. Didn't you give a thought—to *her* ? "

The merciless indictment roused Hardynge's temper.

"Kenneth—you forget yourself," he said on a sharp note of command.

" I'm sorry, sir—you must make allowances——"

" I'm making every allowance. And as to Mrs. Rex "—his grave eyes showed a glint of his ironic humour—" I confess I didn't think my reputation was so shady that friendship with me would be likely to damage hers. But I don't understand women ; and I made a mess of things last night."

Kenneth was not to be so flagrantly side-tracked.

" Colonel, you know what I mean—the risk. Supposing—she got to care for you ? "

" Damn it, I'm *not* as conceited as all that. And I happen to know—it's out of the question."

" It isn't. I tell you—she *does*."

Hardynge jerked, as if the words had been missiles flung at him: but the wounds she had inflicted were still raw, and he the least credulous of men.

" If that's so, she has a damned original way of showing it. As a matter of fact—it's all up between us. I'm turned down—lock, stock, and barrel, if that's any consolation to you."

In spite of himself, the undernote of pain sounded through the surface bitterness; and

Kenneth knew that here also his intuition had not been deceived.

"Oh—I see," he said in a changed voice.

Hardynge flung him a quick glance.

"If you're so damn' clever, what *do* you see?"

"Something—that makes a lot of difference all round."

"Look here, Kenneth, I've said what I had to say. That's enough. You drop it—and stick to your own affairs."

"But this is tremendously my affair," Kenneth insisted, in flat defiance. "You said you wanted to make things clear, and you've landed me in a hopeless fog. For God's sake, Colonel, tell me—*what* went wrong last night?"

"Everything went wrong," Hardynge no longer troubled to hide his pain. "I bungled badly. And, having missed fire, I saw nothing for it, but to own up frankly—and be off."

Kenneth stared, in dazed dismay.

"You—you told *her*?"

"I told her—the truth, which I suppose is the last thing any man in his senses should tell any woman——"

"Not the whole truth, Colonel. If she'd known——"

"Listen, Kenneth. Don't interrupt."

Thus adjured, Kenneth listened, while the older man bluntly and lamely told, in part, the tale of his egregious confession and request.

"You see," he concluded, frowning at the candlestick, "my notion was that if you wouldn't believe *me*, at least you'd believe plain speaking—from her——"

"Good God!" Kenneth fairly exploded; and in the stress of agitation he got up and walked away to the verandah door, still blind to everything but the woman's pain—the woman's point of view.

"Of course it was a hateful job." Hardynge addressed his reply to Kenneth's broad shoulders. "But I'd fairly let myself in; so I had to pull it through somehow. And she took it—squarely. It was I who got the knock. I gather . . . the odds are in your favour. If you hadn't been in such a deuce of a hurry "—he hesitated awkwardly —" however, if you've the sense to stand your ground, you'll hear from her, or see her to-day."

At that Kenneth swung round, his blue eyes alight.

"If I *do* see her, Colonel, I'll have something to tell her—on my own account."

"Then you shall *not* see her—unless you give me your word to leave me out of your cryptic disclosures."

"Sorry. That's impossible." He came nearer, and spoke urgently. "Colonel—you don't realise. She has suffered so much—I can't bear that she should suffer any more."

"Not likely, Ken, on *my* account," Hardynge reassured him, moved by the boy's chivalrous concern. "You've got the wrong end of the stick."

"I've not. I won't leave Dalhousie till I've proved it."

The complete volte-face of their positions moved Hardynge to a bitter half-smile; and again Kenneth's attention was sharply arrested.

"Colonel—why on earth did you do all this . . . just because of me?"

"Perhaps not altogether . . . because of you," Hardynge said in a changed tone.

He was silent a moment, feeling with thumb and finger in his waistcoat pocket. Then, with a kind of resolute reluctance: " I never thought I should have to tell you. But now, it may help you a bit—to understand."

He pulled out his watch-strap in speaking, and with it a round flat locket, which Kenneth had speculated about in younger days. Opening it with a click, he held it out for inspection.

" D'you recognise that ? "

It was a tinted photograph of a girl in the early twenties ; a singularly appealing face. The low broad brow, the reddish fair hair and serious grey-blue eyes were Kenneth's own.

" Mother ? " Kenneth said on an indrawn breath. " The best I've seen. It's beautiful."

" She was beautiful . . . every way."

" And you—— ? "

Hardynge nodded.

" Did—things go wrong ? "

" Very much so. Partly my own fault."

He paused, looking intently at his dream-woman —out-rivalled at last, yet secure in the supremacy of death and distance.

" I was a young duffer—not out of Woolwich. A bit ahead of my age. She was three years older ; and—there was a little money, as you know. In the circumstances, I hadn't the face to propose marriage. And while I havered, things happened. There were muddles and misunderstandings. A woman responsible, of course. Your father's mother. It's a longish tale, and a saddish one. Some day I'll tell you more. She—Margaret— was taken off on a continental trip. I was booked for India. I never saw her again. I had only— the memory, and the maddening sense of having been manœuvred. Heavens, how I hated Mrs. Malcolm ! I've hated the society type ever since."

He drew a deep breath. The rest was more difficult.

"Six months later—just when I'd screwed myself up to write your mother a desperate letter—I saw the announcement of her marriage. And I vowed I'd never go through *that* again, for any woman in creation. Naturally it convinced me she had never cared a rap. I was wrong. But how that marriage happened, I don't know to this day. Naturally I suspected his mother. I never wrote. Later on, I heard . . . it was not a conspicuous success."

"N—no. It wasn't. I used to feel as if something was wrong—underneath; but I was too young to understand. And—your guardianship? Was it her wish?"

"Yes. Her answer to my unworthy doubts, that had made me steel myself against passion and emotion. When your father died—I was tempted. But youth and ardour were gone. I dreaded failure. And very soon—the end came. Then I heard I was appointed your guardian. And among her papers they found a letter sealed; to be given me after she was gone. You must realise, Kenneth, what it meant to me, that message from the dead; and how it was that I——"

"Of course. It alters everything." Kenneth leaned forward, and held out his hand. "Thank you, Colonel—for telling me," he said simply.

Hardynge returned his clasp without a word, and Kenneth growing bolder, added, "Life's a queer job, isn't it? My father standing in your light. And now——"

"Oh, damn queer——"

The gruff voice of Nasur Ali at the door announced a chit from Rex Mem-sahib—and the present sprang sharply to life again.

A parcel for Hardynge—by hand of her *sais*: and for Kenneth a message. "The Mem-sahib waits below. If Malcolm Sahib has leisure, will he ride with her. The coolies also wait, Hazúr. All is in readiness."

It was Hardynge who answered, "Send the coolies to Jehannum. There is no departure to-day. Bid the *sais* take word that the Sahib is coming."

Nasur Ali retreated, muttering of *baksheesh*, and scratching his head over the indubitable craziness of Sahibs.

The two men, left alone, confronted one another —resolute, opposed, but antagonistic no longer.

"Not *this* Sahib," Kenneth said quietly. "I didn't give you my word. And it's up to you."

"Is it? I'm quite unconvinced, you know."

"Well, go along down, sir, and—let *her* convince you."

There was that in the boy's low tone which made Hardynge look up from his parcel.

"You put me to shame," he said; and began gingerly undoing the string.

Kenneth, unable to answer, stood watching him, a strange clash of jealousy and passion and exaltation in his heart.

On the top of the silver box lay Marion's card; Hardynge turned it over mechanically, and discovered a few pencilled lines on the back.

"I spoke harshly last night. Forgive me—if you can. I don't find forgiveness easy, myself. But when I see Kenneth, I will do my best to make amends.—M. R."

He had barely glanced through them, when Kenneth found his voice again.

"*Do* go, Colonel. She's waiting."

SIEGE PERILOUS 141

"For you." Hardynge reminded him.

"Oh, I'm out of it." His eyes were on the familiar cigarette box. "What's that?" he asked.

"She sent it. The bet—you remember; the mustard seed from which all this sprang up." He handed Kenneth the card. "You see what she thinks of me. I'm unforgiven."

"Naturally. But when she knows—— After all, sir, you brought it on yourself. It's your move now."

"That won't work, old boy." All the bitterness was gone from his tone. "She's asked *you* to go for a ride. . . . It's 'yes' or 'no.' If you intend to come along with me, the least you can do is to see her, and explain yourself."

"Very well, Colonel." Neatly cornered, he had suddenly seen his chance. "As you wish it, I *will* see her—and explain."

His tone enlightened Hardynge.

"Stick to your own affairs, mind. I—oh, good Lord——"

He stepped backward, his face went suddenly blank; and Kenneth, swinging round, saw Marion Rex, in her riding gear, framed in the open doorway.

The moment his back was turned, Hardynge slipped quietly into his own room.

The boy had eyes and ears, just then, for only one being on earth. Embarrassed, utterly unprepared, he took a step forward.

"I—I'm awfully sorry," he stammered; but she silenced him with a gesture.

"It's for me to apologise. I'm afraid I interrupted. But something your man said gave me an impression you might be going to decamp again—in earnest. So I made bold to come straight up."

But she remained on the threshold.

"Colonel Hardynge was touchingly anxious last night that we should quite understand one another. You were very foolish to run away. But if you'll come for a ride——"

Her smile, her unusual hesitancy, made his self-imposed ordeal harder than ever, with the Colonel standing behind him and all.

"The truth is—I'm going——" he began in desperation, glancing nervously round—and realised they were alone. "Hul-*lo*! The Colonel's bolted."

"Naturally. What more has he got to do with it?" she asked in a changed voice.

"Everything." Kenneth was himself again. "Please come in. There's a good deal to explain. You made a big mistake last night. So did he. We've got to clear it up, between us. Half a minute, Mrs. Rex."

Turning from her, he pulled open the door of Hardynge's room, thrust his head in and said briskly:

"You're wanted, Colonel. Mrs. Rex is here." ("That'll do it," he thought. And it did.)

Hardynge might curse the boy's too complete command of affairs, but he could not flatly disregard that summons; he could only disguise his agony of embarrassment under a frozen exterior.

"Good morning." He bowed stiffly in the direction of the woman who had dismissed him out of her life. "I must apologise for intruding. This is—Kenneth's show."

"Perhaps you're right, sir," Kenneth agreed, looking tentatively from one to the other, and wondering—what next?

It was Mrs. Rex who came to his aid.

"Really this is quite intriguing! Has he also

got an explanation up his sleeve ? " She addressed
herself pointedly to Kenneth. Her deliberate
lightness had an undernote of strain. " Which of
us is to have first innings ? May I suggest—ladies
first ? And to start with—do let's sit down."

Kenneth—bewildered, but obedient—mechanically proffered a chair, closed the verandah door,
in response to her glance that way, and made a
feint of sitting on the edge of the centre table.
Hardynge remained on the hearth-rug, ruefully
considering the odd juxtaposition of Mrs. Rex
and his half-opened parcel.

There fell an excruciating silence. It was one
thing to claim the first word—another thing to
speak it in an atmosphere electrical with repressed
emotion. The men were tongue-tied, utterly ;
their thoughts securely hid, waiting her pleasure.

" I'm not exactly enjoying this," she flung out
at last, still pointedly addressing Kenneth. " And
I don't imagine you two are either. So let's get it
over. It's all your fault, you know. If you
hadn't basely absconded, I could have made my
amends becomingly, by moonlight."

" What amends ? "

Kenneth looked blank ; and Hardynge braced
himself for a bad quarter of an hour that was not
in the bond.

" Well, you see, in Colonel Hardynge's opinion,
I've been guilty of giving you a false impression of
my worthless self. Seeing you were in earnest, I
failed to administer the right brand of discouragement—to advertise the fact that I never had—that
I never could . . ."

" Mrs. Rex—*please* ! " Kenneth leaned towards
her, pain and pleading in his tone.

Hardynge shut his teeth upon a stifled protest.

"My dear boy, I can't keep it up. Forgive me —if you can. That's all it amounts to." She had dropped her mask. Her face was all tenderness now. "I may be a hardened sinner, but I've the grace to know a man when I see one. And I got so much too fond of you, I hadn't the moral courage to hurt you—even for your own good. Yet now I'm goaded, by a galvanised conscience, into hurting you worse than ever."

"You're *not*. You're justifying me, over and over." The young fervour of it hurt Hardynge more than all that had gone before.

"But you do understand—— ?" she pressed him.

"Oh yes . . . I understand . . . now. But the point is——" He gripped the edge of the table, "I want *you* to understand that I—that is—the Colonel——"

"Dry up, Kenneth," Hardynge commanded in a voice of steel; but Kenneth was impervious to commands.

"Well—you're for it, Colonel. Unless you tell Mrs. Rex the truth——"

"I don't know what you're talking about," Hardynge muttered, unable to look at either of them after that flagrant lie.

It was Marion who spoke, in a changed tone:

"I think Colonel Hardynge and I said all we have to say to one another last night."

"*He* didn't. He left out—the main thing."

The utter unexpectedness of it startled Hardynge into vehement speech:

"Kenneth, for God's sake—Mrs. Rex has had enough to put up with. I *won't* have her pestered——"

"Hazúr, the coolie people are making trouble," Nasur Ali's voice intruded through the gingerly opened door—not before Hardynge had caught her small gasp of surprise. "If it is not the Sahib's pleasure to start this morning, they make demand for *baksheesh*."

"Oh, damn!" Kenneth swore under his breath. "Yes—yes—I'm going all right," he called out briskly. "Let them wait."

As the door closed, Marion turned on him tenderly reproachful. "Kenneth—it's too foolish. Both of you?"

"No."

"*Yes*."

The two opposing statements, sharp as pistol shots and almost simultaneous, moved Marion to a faint smile.

"Well—which *am* I to believe?"

Kenneth had risen and moved close to Hardynge. With his back to Mrs. Rex, he said low and rapidly, "I'm game to stick it, Colonel—*if*——"

Hardynge saw the words, rather than heard them. His straight look acknowledged that final proof of the boy's quality: and Kenneth, not glancing in Marion's direction, went quickly out, leaving them alone.

For several seconds they stood without speech or movement, half resentful, wholly at a loss; still sundered by the memory of last night's parting, for all Kenneth's summary proceedings.

In Hardynge, hope was extinct. By no lightest sign—so far as he could see—had Mrs. Rex confirmed Kenneth's crazy statement. Let in, every way, maddened by an insensate longing simply to step forward and take possession of her, what the devil was a civilised, self-respecting man to do . . . ?

And to Marion, standing a few feet away from him, absently studying the pattern of certain cracks in the whitewashed wall, he seemed rigidly unapproachable—miles removed. Yet was hope not utterly extinct. Her woman's intuition told her that Kenneth would not wantonly have subjected her to this. Kenneth must know. To her quick nature, the tension of their embarrassed silence was unendurable. It may have lasted a minute; to her it seemed an age, before she turned her face to him, and encountered his eyes.

"I confess—I'm altogether at sea," she said, in a carefully contained voice. "I thought—I understood—— Perhaps *you* can tell me what it all means?"

Clearly it was his move; but her manner did little to reassure him. His eye lighted on the silver box. He picked it out of its wrappings, and gravely held it out to her.

"It means—for one thing—that you have not lost your bet. Many thanks for sending it."

He almost thrust it at her; and her fingers closed on it mechanically.

"But why? Last night——" she stammered, self-possession slipping from her, with the uprush of hope revived.

"Oh, *then*—I was in a horrid fix. I had to go through with things, for reasons I have given to Kenneth—purely personal. I needn't bore you with them. If I've been a clumsy meddler, I've got my deserts . . . burnt my own fingers——"

He turned brusquely away from her in a futile attempt to hide his pain and embarrassment, picked up the paper wrapper and folded it with mechanical precision, wishing to heaven she would go; dreading to hear her move away.

Instead, he heard her come nearer, and stand almost at his elbow.

"Burnt *your*—fingers?" she echoed, her low voice shaken with the impact of the truth.

"Yes. You may as well know it, as Kenneth insists. Of course I don't blame you upholding him—and turning me down."

"Are you . . . so very sure . . . I'm turning you down, after all?"

Startled, incredulous, he rounded on her with the abrupt impatience of a strong man tangled in a web of feminine subtleties.

"What do you *mean* by that?"

Startled in her turn, the colour flooded her face. She stood there, all eloquent: no misreading, now, the message in her eyes.

"*Marion!*" he cried—and remained gazing at her, slowly taking it in. "Kenneth—was right?"

"Yes. Kenneth was right."

The words were barely audible, but irresistibly her hands went out to him.

He caught and held them fast. Beyond that, he made no move; but his eyes never left hers. It was as if, having found them at last, he could not let them go.

"God knows, I don't deserve the miracle—of your forgiveness," he said at last.

"It's more than *that* I'm giving you," she gently reminded him. "You must have known—once the truth was out, you could not but be forgiven?"

"Kenneth knew. I hadn't the effrontery . . . I exhausted my small stock of that last night."

"But this isn't last night—Philip."

At that word from her, his long inner tension snapped with an almost physical pang.

Deliberately, without a word, he drew her into his arms . . .

When at length, reluctantly, they moved apart, his hands were shaking. Tears stood in her eyes.

"Let's get away from here," she said quickly, unsteadily. "Shall we ride?"

"Yes, by all means." His look thanked her for understanding. "I must leave a line for Kenneth."

"Oh, he's splendid, that boy!"

Hardynge gravely inclined his head. The thought of telling Kenneth almost unnerved him.

No sign of the boy anywhere, either in the verandah or in the hotel compound. Neither of them named him; but he was uppermost in their thoughts as they set out at a foot's pace, along Terah Mall.

They met other riders. They met scurrying *jhampannies* in fantastic uniforms. They exchanged greetings with mere human beings, who hailed them cheerfully unaware. Everything, everyone was quite amazingly as usual. Yet they two, man and woman—who had presumably outgrown the divine follies of youth—seemed to be riding in a new-made world.

"Where are we going?" she asked presently, turning so radiant a face to him that he felt he had not known her till that hour.

"The Grove, of course—where I did all the damage," he answered with a long look: and they urged their horses to canter, yielded themselves to the rhythmic motion, the keen sweetness of the morning air. For the moment, even Kenneth was forgotten—Kenneth, to whom they owed everything.

From the bend of an upper path, he watched them go; and once again he suffered that discordant clash of jealousy, passion, and exaltation: but ultimately it was exaltation that prevailed.

1920.

TO
MY SISTER, VIOLET

SUNIA: DAUGHTER OF THE HILLS

SUNIA: DAUGHTER OF THE HILLS

I

Oh very woman—god at once and child.—SWINBURNE.

THE pearly shimmer of dawn was over the mountains; the far-off snows gleamed ghostly pale and pure against the dove-like tones of the sky. Away across the valley loomed Kalatope ridge, serrated and majestic, its outline printed sharply upon the brightness beyond.

A Himalayan dawn is brief as it is beautiful. Sudden and swift as magic, the full splendour of morning flashed along the sky. Rapier-like shafts of light pierced the purple lengths of shadow which lay along the deeper ravines and engulfed the slumbering valley. They threaded their golden way through the sombre pine-boughs of Kalatope forest, and stretched out their radiant length along the verandah of a low wooden bungalow that stood alone in the heart of this silent, smiling mountain world.

In that verandah a solitary Englishman sat peeling a banana and drinking tea, in full view of the valley and the brightening east. From time to time his eyes rested on the magnificent scene before him with the quiet satisfaction of one who looks on the familiar face of a friend; for, under the high-sounding title of Deputy Conservator of Government Forests, Phil Brodie reigned sole

monarch of this his paradise—a peaceful and
satisfactory form of kingship.

Having eaten his last banana, he rose and
sauntered over to the wooden railing, hat in hand.
He was a long, lean man of sportsmanlike build,
though the face—sallow, deeply scored and self-
contained, with a hint of cynicism about the
mouth—suggested cultured thought and feeling.

While he stood so, his keen eyes brightened
curiously—not without reason.

From the black mass of pine and deodar to
his right the figure of a young girl emerged, and
drew near with swift, elastic step. Dress, face,
and carriage proclaimed her a child of the Himalayas—a child-woman, typical product of the East.

When a Hill girl is beautiful, you will scarce find
her match in the five continents; and Sunia was
beautiful past question. For eighteen months,
morning after morning, Brodie had watched her
approach him thus, bearing on her head his daily
tribute of fruit and flowers; yet did her beauty
still surprise him afresh and demand a reiterated
recognition of its quality. There were horrid
moments, when he realised that in five years'
time she would be coarse and common-place; in
ten a wrinkled hag. But at present she was incom-
parable—and she did not know it! There lay
the miracle.

The face was a pure oval, with flower-like curves
of cheek and chin, and eyes of that rare pale brown
only found among true Hill folk, and that too
frequently. A flower-like silver ornament in one
of her nostrils seemed coquettishly designed to
accentuate its delicate curves. The soft fullness
of her lips suggested passionate possibilities, and
the scarlet of betel-nut upon them made an en-

chanting incident of colour among the dusky tints of her face and her homespun dress, a few shades darker than her skin.

The graceless, close-fitting 'pyjamas' were partially concealed by a rough brown tunic girdled with coils of twisted goat's hair and fastened loosely across her breast with a silver pin. Round her throat she wore a necklet of goat's hair strung with lumps of raw turquoise, onyx and amber, and a grotesquely patterned plaque of hammered silver. Her small ears drooped with silver trinkets; bangles and anklets of glass and silver clinked musically as she walked.

A flat basket, piled conically with garden produce, crowned her close-fitting cap of yellow cotton, from which her hair fell in one long braid, almost to her knees. Brodie knew—and Sunia probably cared not who knew—that two-thirds of this same braid, its wearer's dearest bit of vanity, had been borrowed from the back of a mountain goat.

With a gracious sweep of her arms, she uncrowned herself, laid her *dáli* at Brodie's feet, and lowered her forehead thrice to the ground.

"Live for ever, Lord of my Life!" she murmured. The conventional greeting was uttered with passionate fervour.

Brodie stooped and lightly touched the quaint assortment of almonds, walnuts, and early vegetables, symmetrically encircled with alternate clumps of blood-red rhododendron blossoms and the first wild white roses of the year. One of these last he chose, and placed in his buttonhole.

"Roses, Sunia!" he said, speaking the soft Hill dialect as musically as the girl herself. "Thou hast been far afoot to glean so fine a sheaf of blossoms?"

She stood before him now slim and upright as the young pines all about her, and a flush showed dimly through her olive skin.

"What matter how far, so my lord be pleased?" she made answer with veiled eyes. "Away there, in the valley, they were scattered like stars of silver; and I said in my heart, their shining will make beautiful the Hazur's house and give pleasure to my lord. If the Sahib permits, I will bear them now to Dhunnu, that they faint not for lack of water?"

Brodie inclined his head. Then, with eyes averted, and a smile half quizzical, half tender, he noted how she surreptitiously plucked two roses from the same bunch as his own and set them, Hill-fashion, above her ear. That done, she abased herself once more, took up her burden, and departed with much delicate jingling of anklet and armlet.

Brodie watched her reflectively till she passed out of sight. "She's a queer child," he mused. "Shows her gratitude in the prettiest fashion."

He raised the lapel of his coat and glanced down at the wild white blossom, whose fragrance filled his nostrils.

"She must have tramped miles to get so many," was the thought in his mind. "And slaving for me all these months—refusing payment. Pure gratitude—I wonder? Saves analysis, anyhow. Bah! I'm a conceited ass. It's the nature of the race."

Nevertheless, a vision of Sunia choosing the two blossoms nearest his own, her nervous haste, her tell-tale blush, forced itself again and again on

Brodie's mind that morning. And he said to himself, " This won't do." Conventional morality apart, he favoured ' fair play ' in all his works and ways. It irked him to think that by some inadvertent kindliness on his part, he might have sown in Sunia's passionate Oriental heart a seedling that could bear only bitter fruit.

Briefly, this curious relationship between Primitive Passion and Cultured Complexity had arisen in this wise:

Eighteen months earlier, while ' shikarring ' bear in the Chamba hills, Brodie had stumbled upon a pitiful scene that remained vividly printed on his memory; still more vividly, perhaps, on hers. A small, tawny figure at the roadside, crouched under a beetling rock; and, not twenty paces off, the huge upright form of a bear, shuffling, swaying towards his prize, with a low snarling sound, hideous to hear. Unseen by the girl he had deliberately covered the brute's heart and fired. . . .

With a grunt, the shaggy monster rolled over— and was still. And while his men ran forward, Brodie had found himself held up by two brown arms, that clung about his boots, and a voice from the earth that blessed him with the fulsome fervour of the East. Stooping, he had raised the girl to her feet; and, in so doing, had looked on Sunia's face for the first time—a sensation no man would be likely to forget.

From that day she had attached herself to his establishment; steadily refusing to give any information as to the whereabouts of her village; working as only a Hill woman can work; spurning the suggestion of payment in any form.

In time it transpired that her mother had been

out with her cutting wood that day ; but, in abject terror at sight of the bear, had stumbled backwards off the narrow path and been hurled to death in the boulder-strewn gorge below. Further personal history Sunia had none that she chose to tell. With a captivating mixture of dignity and obstinacy she merely reiterated her intention of remaining with the ' Heaven-born,' the ' Preserver of her life,' and serving him so long as her fingers could bind a faggot or wield an axe. And he had not been man could he have turned her away.

Dhunnu, *máli*, a one-eyed, ape-like old gentleman of irreproachable lineage, had been induced, on payment of monthly *baksheesh*, to receive the new-comer under his own roof, as one of his household. A small patch of garden had been handed over to her care, and its tillage had become for her almost a religious rite; its every flower and vegetable laid in her *dáli*—a self-imposed tribute —at her master's feet.

As for Brodie, he had regarded these dumb expressions of devotion, at first, with a tolerant amusement, later, with a lurking tenderness, tempered by an innate reluctance to take his own or anyone else's emotions too seriously. But when an Englishman encounters Oriental passion, in its pristine simplicity and strength, he is compelled to take it seriously, first or last.

Brodie was beginning to realise this; and the discovery made him feel a little anxious and uncomfortable.

There were others, also, who were growing daily more anxious on Sunia's account. For the one-eyed *máli*, and Mai Râdha, his grizzled wife, had knowledge of which Brodie dreamed not.

They knew of a treasured box containing withered flowers, to which one or two were added daily. The box had once held a hundred Havannahs, and had lived on Brodie's office-table. They knew of long night-watches spent in stringing scented wreaths of marigolds, and white, waxen 'champa' blossoms; of secret flittings, in the first glimmer of morning, to the hamlet that clung to the hillside two hundred feet below. They knew that Sunia's wreaths—yea, even fruit and flowers from her cherished garden—were destined for the 'Mundar,' or shrine of Kála Dévi, the dread goddess of whom every pious Hindu stands in holy awe. And the knowledge troubled Mai Râdha's practical soul.

"Truly it is fool's talk, and shameful," she protested to her milder spouse. "A maid, young and good to look upon! There are men of our own *ját*, who would give rupees in plenty for so fair a chattel—a true Rajpoot, with a face like the morning. I had looked that from this girl's dower we should purchase rest in our old age. Nearly two years have I been to her as a mother, and the ingrate rewards me thus! Were't not a fool, thou wouldest speak to the Sahib of this madness."

But Dhunnu, a chicken-hearted little man, turned his hands outward in expressive native fashion.

"*Ná, ná*, valiant one, I thrust my head betwixt a lion's teeth. Speak thou, if thou art minded to."

And Mai Râdha did speak, fluently, drastically; not to Brodie, but to the delinquent herself—with totally unexpected results.

Sunia—her eyes dilated, her small hands clenched till the knuckles stood out sharp and white—

gave her back eloquence for eloquence, good measure, pressed down.

"What sayest thou of shame that a maid should live unwed ? It is thou, grey-head, that utterest shameful talk. I will not hear it. I am none of thine ! "

"*Ai tobah !*[1] These be brave words, insolent, from one who hath eaten my salt these many months," the elder woman retorted in shrill wrath.

"Not one grain of thine have I eaten, oh Mai Râdha. Hast forgotten whence come the rupees ? And should *I* take to myself a man ? I, who own one lord of my life, and my body, and my heart ! I, who would be dust, as is my mother, but for the strength of his arm ! Talk not to me of men-folk. Betrothed was I, long since, to a son of mine own people ; but now am I my lord's slave till I die—till I die ! "

Her lips quivered on the last words, and two tear-drops hung on her lashes.

But Mai Râdha having eyes, saw not. She was a woman, and old. This girl stood between her and the money her fingers itched to grasp. So she spoke harshly, as before.

"Oh fool, and blind ! This thy lord hath never a thought of *thee.* Thus it is with these English : stone-hearts all. As the wind blows, and the water flows, kind calls to kind. He will take to wife some bold white 'Miss,' with hair like sunshine and eyes like the noonday sky. What will be thy portion then, O thriftless one ? "

Slowly the blood ebbed from the girl's cheeks : but her lips were steady now ; her eyes dry and bright.

"There is always—Death," she made answer

[1] Shame.

quietly. " Mai Kali must needs accept my life, if no other offering availeth."

On Brodie's office table, in a wineglass of water, the wild white rose of the morning bloomed fresh and fragrant still. He could scarcely tell what had prompted his impulse to preserve it ; nor did he trouble himself to analyse the reason for so unusual a freak of sentiment.

But Sunia, not knowing of the rose, went heavily for many days, a haunting fear at her heart, a ceaseless prayer upon her lips. Also she redoubled her offerings at the ' Mundar ' of Kála Devi, who, being a woman, must surely understand, and hear.

II

Love, that keeps all the choir of lives in chime ;
Love, that is blood within the veins of time !
SWINBURNE.

BUT Mai Kali was deaf, or hard of heart in those days ; or, maybe, she was busy with the affairs of wealthier folk. For, as June drew to a close, and the patient pines sighed for the great monsoon, there came to the hut on the hill-top the ' white Miss ' of Mai Râdha's prophecy, ' with hair like sunshine and eyes like the noonday sky.' And Sunia's heart dried up like an autumn leaf ; for she knew her hour had come.

In prosaic Western terms, the fateful event amounted to no more than the chance advent of Miss Edith Lindon, escorted by her brother and by a certain Polden of Brodie's acquaintance. They had been riding into Dalhousie one sultry afternoon, on their return from the yearly race-meeting at Kajiar. They were hot and thirsty ; for they had ridden eight miles, and the air, even at that height, was heavy with the coming rains.

It was Colonel Polden who suggested a raid on Brodie's hut, for refreshment ; and as they went, he had entertained Miss Lindon with rhapsodical praises, half jesting, half sincere, of Brodie's ' bewitching little Hill beauty.'

"Saved her from the embraces of an amorous bear, year before last," he wound up. "And she's served him for love ever since. A pretty little woodland romance—what ? "

"Charming ! You must persuade your friend to let us see the girl. Perhaps I might even be allowed to sketch her. I'm making a collection of Indian figure studies to take home ; and the Hill costume is ripping."

If Sunia could have heard ! She saw, however, which was more than enough in the way of anguish.

Crouching in the shade, behind a group of deodars, she saw Brodie lift the girl from her saddle ; saw her yellow hair flash in the sunlight ; saw the blue eyes, the magic pink and white of her cheeks. Then she glanced down at her own brown, shapely hands, and shuddered.

"Mai Râdha spoke true," she whispered. "I have been a fool, and blind—blind ! "

Tinkling laughter from the verandah made her wince and shiver ; yet she felt powerless to move away. She could only look and listen with feverish eagerness.

Tea was served in the verandah : a typical Khansamah's tea ; Rockingham tea-pot, with a damaged spout ; plush tea-cosy ; pale slabs of cake, and a plate of *meta biscoot*.[1] The ' bold white Miss ' presided with as much ease and freedom

[1] Mixed biscuits.

as though she were mistress of the house; as, indeed, she was already, in Sunia's excited fancy. The Sahib had sent money, doubtless, to his own land, and the grey-head, her father, had brought him this, his bride.

Gradually a grey cloud darkened the face of the sun. The parched pine-boughs stirred and whispered mysteriously. Sunia knew the sound and its meaning well. Two minutes later a snaky streak of lightning flashed; and a sound like the rattle of musketry rent the sky. Then, like liquid bullets, fell the first rain drops of the great monsoon.

Within five minutes the clouds were dissolving in a sheet of water, on the thirsty hills, and all the pines were creaking in the wind.

Sunia fled, drenched, to her smoke-grimed hovel; and endured, in silence, Mai Râdha's caustic comments on the new turn of affairs.

In Brodie's hut a council of war had resulted in a definite decision. "No going on to-night," he said to young Lindon, as they surveyed the drowned landscape. "If your sister doesn't mind using my room, she is more than welcome to it; and I think my little grass-cut girl could manage to act as ayah, once in a way. You two fellows can have the second room. I'll sleep on the lounge in here. Hope Miss Lindon won't be beastly uncomfortable."

"Rather not. Awfully good of you. She'll be as right as a trivet, thanks," Lindon assured him with brotherly unconcern. "She's not a faddy sort at all."

And it appeared that he spoke truth.

"Quite a lark!" the fair Edith declared with a naïve frankness which did not ill-become her. "And will your little Hill beauty *really* consent to do ayah for me?"

Her arch look at Brodie missed its mark.

"She will obey my orders," he returned with grave politeness.

His assurance proved a trifle premature. For once in her life, Sunia was spurred to rebellion. When the order reached her that she should make herself clean and carry hot water and a lamp to the Miss-sahib's room, she sent answer flatly: "Tell the Sahib that I cannot do this thing." Yet, even in speaking, she knew that love and long habit would compel her to eat her own brave words.

At the sound of Brodie's voice calling her from the back verandah, she sped across the rain-lashed compound, and flung herself, dripping, at his feet.

"Oh, my lord, forgive thy slave for unseemly words. Let the Sahib command what he will. It shall be done."

Then she rose and faced him; hands clenched, her body quivering with emotion desperately held in check.

Brodie was not a little mystified. Her words and manner so strangely stirred him, that he would willingly have annulled his order, but that he shrank from Miss Lindon's arch comments, and Colonel Polden's quizzical asides. As it was, he spoke soothingly.

"I make no command, Sunia. I ask only this small service because it would be shameful talk that a Miss-sahib should be alone in my house, having no woman to wait on her—and that thou knowest."

"It is enough, Sahib. I go."

And she went, fulfilled with righteous resolve, but very sore at heart.

Edith Lindon was not more light-minded than others of her sex and age; but she was young, and attractive; and—perhaps not without reason —very well satisfied with herself and the world at large. She was just now ardently engaged in 'doing' India; because it was the correct thing to 'do' India—to roll Bombay, Delhi, and a Native State or two, and fragments of the Himalayas, into one great dust-coated pill; to swallow it whole, and dispense it—with harmless necessary embellishments—at Western dinner-tables, for the benefit of the great uninitiated.

She regarded her present predicament chiefly in the light of an excellent prospective anecdote, needing only one item to complete it—a sketch of Sunia herself. But on that point her host had proved politely obdurate; and Edith must content herself with a mental photograph of the girl's appearance; a process which entailed a good deal of frank staring on Miss Lindon's part, when at last Sunia entered with hot water and towels. It did not occur to the Western girl that the 'wild little Hill creature' could possibly resent being inspected. So she inspected her carefully, not without evident admiration.

But—for all her barbaric dress, and her prejudices in the matter of cleanliness—Sunia was human. A dull flush burnt through her brown skin, making her look more charming than ever; and she preserved her Sphinx-like gravity of expression.

The goat's-hair necklace, with its rough stones and silver pendant, captured Miss Lindon's fancy.

She coveted it for her 'curio' table at home. Happy thought! Perhaps the girl would sell it.

With the easy assurance of a spoilt child, she stepped up to Sunia, and laid an irreverent finger on a mottled lump of turquoise.

"*Burra accha chēse. Hum mangta*,"[1] she remarked smilingly. Her Hindustani, though limited, was terse and to the point. "*Kitna dām? Panch rupee?*"[2]

Sunia recoiled as though she had been struck. "These be mine own jewels, Miss-sahib. I am not of the *Bunnia-lôg*, that I should bargain with white folk for rupees."

Miss Lindon was taken aback. But a moment's thought convinced her that her offer had not been large enough.

"*Dus rupeea déga. Bus—aur nahin.*"[3] And she held out an expectant hand.

Sunia, with a glance of speechless scorn, turned and fled through the blustering night.

This, then, was the bride-elect of her Sahib, her demi-god among men—this smiling, insolent, pink-faced miss! The strong rush and roar of the storm through the forest drowned the passionate sobs which racked her body half through the night.

III

THE sun rose on a green, babbling world next morning. Prismatic hues flashed from swaying boughs; birds, brooks, and cicadas rejoiced in chorus, and, from moist fissures of rock, the little brown *krait* (viper), with others of his kindred, slid stealthily, to vanish at once in the moist verdure

---

[1] Very good thing. I want it.
[2] What price? Five rupees?
[3] I will give ten rupees. That is all—no more.

of the flower-beds. Away over the plains, a billowy mass of cloud surged and dissolved and flowed together again till the higher hills seemed no longer rooted in earth.

Brodie and his guests were early astir. By eight o'clock the latter were in their saddles.

As her host lifted Edith Lindon to her Arab, she reminded him laughingly of some English violets he had promised her overnight.

"Please don't trouble about them now, though," she added sweetly: "I'll forgive you for forgetting!"

But Brodie was already in the verandah.

"Won't take me two minutes," he called back as he went.

He had made a hobby of his little garden; and there were certain flowers kept sacred even from Dhunnu's zealous fingers. So he knelt down bareheaded in the sunlight, and plunged his hands among the dripping violet leaves. The violet beds being at the back of the house, and the horses in front, he was alone—or apparently so. At all events, he was unconscious of eager eyes that devoured his face from within the sheltering shadow of the deodars.

Those eyes, in spite of their absorption and the tears that were in them, saw what his did not—a slimy, living streak of brown close to his left hand. In a flash Sunia was beside him, her own hand laid on his—not one second too soon.

Brodie sprang to his feet with a cry, and made a futile lunge at the vanishing snakeling, whose name is Death.

Then he turned to Sunia.

"How didst see the reptile? Good God—look! Did he bite thee, child?"

"Ay, Hazúr, he bit me—and—I die. But what matter, so the Sahib lives—to make marriage with the—the white Miss ? And I—I pay my debt."

She swayed where she stood, and a little quiver convulsed her frame. Quick as thought Brodie's arm went round her, and with a sharp little sob she leaned her light weight upon its strength.

"*Kohi hai!* Nizam Din ! " he shouted. "Take these flowers to the Miss-sahib, and tell the Sahibs to go forward. I cannot come. Bring me *at once* coffee of the blackest, and the flask of brandy from my dressing-case. Run ! "

Then, with voice and face all tenderness, he turned to the dying girl.

"Walk, child, walk—for the love of God ! The brandy may be here in time."

Feebly she resisted his effort to hurry her forward.

"Nay, Sahib, I have chosen, and—I die. When my lord taketh to him a Mem-sahib, and goeth hence, what shall come to this slave ? Death is easy. And I—I pay my debt."

All her worshipping soul was in her eyes, and Brodie read it like an open book.

"There stands no debt betwixt us, Sunia-ji. And why talk of Mem-sahibs ? I take no Miss-sahib to wife."

"But the white 'Miss,' who came—who spoke——"

Her voice broke, and she shuddered again.

Brodie tightened his hold. He saw the whole thing, suddenly, through her eyes. "But, Sunia, the white ' Miss ' is naught to me—naught. She is gone ; I shall never see her again. Here is the brandy. Drink. Thy Sahib commands thee—drink ! "

He forced the glass between her lips. She took one sip; then shook her head wearily.

"It is Kismet, Sahib. I take no brandy. Let . . . him go—I die."

Further argument was useless. The poison was working swiftly; for the krait knows no half measures.

With a stern, "*Kohi mut aou*,"[1] Brodie waved Nazim Din away, and drew the girl's lagging feet toward the verandah.

He laid her tenderly in his own long chair, and leaned close to her as he spoke; his face strangely illumined.

"Sunia, thou art dying, speak truth. What *right* hadst thou to do this thing?"

The glazing eyes lightened for an instant, and the lips parted in a radiant smile.

"The only right that belongs to women-folk, Hazúr—I love."

"And I? What thinkest thou?"

In the emotion of the moment he did not weigh his words.

"I think naught, Sahib. I love—it is enough."

Her voice was a whisper now. But her eyes clung desperately to his face. Impelled by an irresistible impulse, Brodie stooped and kissed her fervently on the lips and brow.

"Live for ever, Lord of my Life," came the familiar greeting. But he saw the words rather than heard them.

Then Mai Râdha came, and smote the hill-sides with vociferous grief; for she claimed her right to mourn as foster mother to the child.

Brodie retreated to his office, and sat there for

[1] "Let no one come."

two full hours, staring blankly at a half-written letter, and considering the strange thing that had come to pass.

He was a lonely man—sisterless, motherless—but, until this moment, he had scarcely been aware of the fact. Slowly it dawned on him that he was not, and would never be again, quite as he had been. A hitherto unacknowledged element had been added to his conception of life. He had seen with his own eyes the love that is strong as death; and to see that once in a lifetime is a wholesome thing for a man.

*TO
BIRD*

COMPLETE SURRENDER

COMPLETE SURRENDER

To hold by leaving, to take by letting go;
Leaving and again leaving . . .
This is the Law.

EDWARD CARPENTER.

I

"*Complete Surrender.* Baby boy, one year old. Healthy, gentle birth. Mother unable to support. Good references, No institution need apply. C.B. 37 Garland Street, Upper Tooting."

CLARISSA BROWNE, idly exploring the front page of the *Morning Post*, paused and re-read those few, curt phrases, brief and bald as a telegram, with a little shock of sympathy and protest. Her quick imagination visualised their underlying tragedy—a tragedy all too common in these first years after the war. But the common tragedies remain the supreme tragedies. Clarissa knew. The war had taken her only son.

Hundreds of people, comfortably breakfasting this morning, would glance at that pitiful advertisement without giving it a thought. Hundreds more would not even catch sight of it. The fact that she had seen it—that it hurt her so acutely—seemed almost to constitute a claim on her; though common sense told her it was no concern of hers that one more woman and one more child should fall by the way. The trouble was she could never see it so. Even at fifty-three, she had not arrived at taking such things for granted. Candid friends told her it was nothing but sentimentalism, that she let her sympathies run away with her, which, of course, she stoutly denied; adding, with true Irish logic, that even if they occasionally did, why should one think shame of doing a kindness to one's neighbour?

'Complete Surrender.' How the deeper significance of those two words struck home! To give —and to give up; woman's eternal crown of glory and of thorns—whether one chanced to be a distracted girl-mother in Upper Tooting, or a thirty-years' wife delicately crunching toast and honey at a perfectly appointed breakfast table in Chelsea.

Instinctively, while her thoughts roamed, her fastidious eye appraised five coppery-pink roses set in a dwarf goblet of old Venetian glass. Her Los Angeles bushes were excelling themselves this year. Beyond the breakfast table, the open French window framed a sun-bright parallelogram of flagged pathway, lawn, and rose-beds, dappled with restless shadows of a beloved and ancient lime-tree, where the bees hummed incessantly these blazing late June days. At the far end of the path a fountain flickered and splashed. Its centre figure—a Hermes poised for flight—seemed the guardian spirit of the place.

What excitement there had been when Derek discovered him in the back-yard of an old picture-dealer's shop; bargained for him, and carried him home in a taxi for her 'birthday surprise.' A red-letter year that had been for them both: the year they two had persuaded his father that, for him, there was only one conceivable career—Art. Godfrey had always favoured the Army; but Derek was of her mind, of her moulding. Between them, they had prevailed; and the unspoken dread of her heart had been exorcised—to her inexpressible relief.

But relief had been short-lived. She had reckoned without Europe at war. She had grudged her boy to the Army—and the Army had the last word after all. It was as if, in some secret corner of her being, she had foreknown.

At this point her husband—immersed in the lion's share of the *Morning Post*—emitted a grunt of dissatisfaction.

"Not enough backbone left in the country, even to fire this rank, rotten Government!"

He was a full-figured man, ruggedly built, outside and in. Still muttering combatively, he pushed his saucer towards her.

"Only half a cup, me dear."

It almost amounted to a ritual; every morning —these, how many years? Most days she complied mechanically. To-day, for some reason, the mere fact that she knew precisely what was coming —that nothing could stop it from coming—waked a crazy impulse in her to seize the cup and dash it on the ground. The sameness of that little accustomed interlude seemed suddenly to epitomise the inexorable sameness of the revolving nights and days, through which she moved, serene and smiling—shattered inside, while externally unscarred. It was almost as if a clock should go on ticking with the works broken. But, whatever befell, one could not turn away from life like a fretful child, push aside one's toys and refuse to play any more; whatever befell, her woman's heart of pity and kindness would live on, unextinguished, inextinguishable, except by death.

And always there was Godfrey, needing her now

more than ever; though at times the fact might not appear self-evident. The bitterness of his grief had eaten into him, as rust eats into iron. He could not speak of it, even to her. When the bad moments came, he withdrew into himself; and it was lonely work standing outside, even if one intimately understood how, in such moods, he was helpless to open the door of his heart.

Things had gone ill with him lately; and this morning, beyond the ritual of the coffee cup and that solitary grumble, he had scarcely said a word. He had not even noticed her surreptitious abstraction of the outer sheets from his sacred paper. Undeniably, she *had* spoilt him in early days. And yet—would she have him otherwise?

Instinctively she suppressed a sigh he would not have heard; and again her eye fell on the advertisement. It contracted her heart—the thought of that girl-mother and the yearling babe she proffered to an indifferent world; and those final words ' No institution need apply ' struck an instant chord of sympathy. Clarissa hated institutions, their ruthless efficiency, their stereotyped attitude to tragedies and follies, pitifully human. No doubt, they in their turn anathematised women like herself, at the mercy of their sympathies, over-ready to thrust inexpert fingers, on impulse, into alien lives.

She had made her own muddles here and there; and would doubtless make them again, thanks to an incorrigible streak in her.

Already at the back of her mind, a decision was forming to answer that advertisement in person; see what could be done—supposing the child proved to be legitimate. She had decided views about separating child and mother; but . . . if it had to be . . . ?

For some months the idea of adopting a boy had lain dormant in her. Now it was definitely astir. They had much to give, she and Godfrey, could they only bring themselves to take into their lives, into their affections, a child not their own; a child to keep them in touch with youth, to fill, however inadequately, the empty niche of the grandson who would never now be theirs.

She had not yet ventured to speak her thought. She had no idea how Godfrey would take it, if she did.

The barrier of the *Morning Post* rustled ominously. Something was vexing him again. She felt suddenly tempted to read him the advertisement, by way of a ' feeler '; but a glance at his profile sufficed. Breakfast was rarely a good moment for unauthorised intrusions. Her mild adventure would either be extinguished or provoke a lacerating wrangle. She would wait; she would take base advantage of the friendlier influences of the study, and his morning pipe.

It was a relief when he rose, with a rumbled threat of writing to the paper, that nowadays rarely went beyond a threat: and she dispatched her brief duties with her mind very much elsewhere.

Ten minutes in the green sanctuary of her garden, snipping off wilted roses, soothed her nerves and crystallised her decision to make a personal raid on 37 Garland Street, Upper Tooting. Finally she entered the study—up three steps and through the French window—a basket of fragrant petals on her arm, the stolen sheets so folded that the advertisement readily met the eye.

He sat deep in his arm-chair, smoking; the paper laid aside. He looked round at her entrance, shifted the pipe from his lips and smiled.

The cloud of ill-humour had vanished. It was the look, the smile of another man—the real man whom she had loved and served and ' spoilt '—as the foolish saying has it—for thirty years and more.

These things she saw; but she could not see how ten minutes with her flowers and the flutter of a new, living interest had wrought a subtle change in her own aspect; how the slant sunlight shed over her comely face and greying hair a passing illusion of youth. She only knew there would be no wrangling now.

Smiling, she held up her neatly folded sheets.

" You never missed them ! "

" I did. I was just thinking, for all I knew, anything might have happened to anybody. But as you seemed to have frozen on to them, I was waiting."

She stood rebuked. He had wanted them—and waited ! The possibility had simply not occurred to her.

" What a shame ! But I happened to notice a personal advertisement that rather seized me. And *I* was waiting—— ! "

Their eyes met in a twinkle of understanding. Behind the twinkle, she divined a shade of apprehension.

" What sort of a wild-goose chase are you after now ? "

" Only trying to help another woman—and her child. Read that."

He read it, either very leisurely, or twice over, and emitted an unpromising grunt.

" Hard luck. But it's a very common dilemma, my dear."

" Which makes it none the less tragic."

"No. But they soon get toughened—that sort. They know their way about." His glance shifted from the printed page to her face. A combative note invaded his voice. "You're not going to *answer* that?"

"Well—no." She met his implicit challenge with her most disarming smile. "I thought of going there myself, this afternoon, to see the girl, and find out more—if I can."

"And come back with a stray baby under your arm!" His temper was rising, but he had the sense to postpone direct opposition. "Take my advice, Clarissa, and keep out of it. All the minx wants is to be rid of an encumbrance."

"More probably all she wants is a fresh chance."

"She'll get *that* right enough."

"Will she? And—the child . . . ? Oh, it's easy being an optimist over other people's tragedies."

He winced at the implied rebuke—rare enough, from her, to take effect.

"I didn't mean it so, Clarissa, but you know I can't abide your messing round with that sort."

"Why conclude she's—that sort? Anyway, I'm going to find out."

"And she'll fool you all along the line."

"I must risk that. Of course I'll be on my guard. I hate vexing you, Godfrey." She came nearer and spoke more urgently. "Call it one of my unreasoning impulses. It came over me the moment I read the advertisement. If I didn't go now, they'd simply haunt me—the pair of them. My own initials—look!"

"You old sentimentalist!" he grumbled.

By that she knew hostilities were at an end; and stooping, lightly kissed the top of his head.

"I could name worse epithets that the average

man thinks no shame of! One needs an occasional holiday from being sane and prudent."

He chuckled.

"You can be as insane and imprudent as you please, so long as you don't ask me to join in the orgy. Upper Tooting in this blazing heat! It'll only prostrate you—to no purpose. Take a taxi, mind—*and* your smelling salts."

"And camphor balls in my pocket? And be sure and send my poor little mother (if she *is* that sort) to some inhumanly virtuous institution? In your heart, O Solomon, I know you think I'm a perfect fool."

"I'm waiting and seeing!" he informed her, with one eye on the bald daily record of man's three great adventures.

II

"Oh *do* give over, Agnes. It's sick to death of it all I am!"

"And it's sick as a cat you'd be, my fine lady, if your 'ad' fell flat as a pancake: your last spare shillings blewed, with nothing to show for it. A good sister I've been to you, for all your fine airs and feckless ways; and you're welcome to me best bedroom a bit longer, if you'll up and try for a job, and quit invaliding around as if you owned the earth. You look alive an' answer those two. Pile on the sentiment. That'll do it."

"Well, I won't, then. They're not the sort. I wouldn't be giving *them* me lovely boy, not if they went on their knees for 'm."

"Likely—ain't it?" sneered the elder girl. She was dark, with a ferret-like sharpness about her long nose and close-set eyes; a good-natured ferret—up to a point.

"Send 'm along by special messenger to Buckingham Palace, eh? A present for her Majesty. The best's about good enough for Captain the Honourable Napoleon Horatio de Boots!"

"Oh, Aggie—you *beast*! And me head's splitting. An' there isn't a breath. Push the window up a bit, do. Quietly—not to wake him."

The young mother's eyes—periwinkle blue they were, with ink-black lashes—reverted anxiously to the swinging cot beside her, and the child's head nestling on the pillow. His fair hair, damp with heat, was clustered in tight little rings; and the sweet familiar look of him sleeping there—not troubling a mite—made her heart jerk in the queerest way. She lay there, fainting almost, limp as the damp towel that hung on her brass bed-rail.

Invaliding around, was she? How would Aggie like it, then, to feel the way she did? Every bone in her body seemed to have gone soft with the heat and the worry, and something the kind doctor called 'general debility.' It wasn't exactly an illness; so Aggie (who must have things cut and dried) rounded on her for a fraud, and a 'sponge,' taking her ease in the best bedroom. Such a rare one it was, too! The mattress in lumps for want of picking, a knob gone from the foot rail, the pink carpet with monster roses all messed and faded; and you couldn't make the blinds hang straight anyhow.

Here she checked herself feebly. The ungrateful villain she was! But for Aggie and her manicuring job and her practical way with money, she—Colleen —wouldn't be having so much as a lumpy mattress to lie on at all, at all. But her brain was almost melted with the strong afternoon heat that poured in beneath the limp, half-lowered blinds, and her thoughts just drifted about in it anyhow.

Ungrateful or no, she was dead sick of lying there partly dressed, through feeling bad when she had tried; sick of the cheap 'oak' furniture, the drawers that wouldn't pull open, the cupboard that wouldn't stay shut, and the flies buzzing and crawling, fit to drive you mad, and the clatter-rattle of the everlasting old tram at the end of the road. Sicker than all she was, to-day, between hope and dread of some kind lady, you couldn't be refusing, who would want to take away the boy, the light of her eyes. She'd spent the money —she had: and she'd think shame of herself not to hope; but the terror was there, too, taking all the stiffening out of her worse than the heat——

The screech of the window under Agnes's impatient fingers, wrenched her back to the miseries more immediate. It also disturbed the boy. He stirred and whimpered in his sleep. Worried with his teeth, poor lamb! The flies buzzed round and round him, settled and crawled. The tiniest thing in fists—carved out of wax, it seemed—moved restlessly, brushing them away. Drat the things! They wouldn't even let him sleep.

Leaning sideways, she swayed the cot and waved them away. From the window came Aggie's voice. Quite excited she was.

"Heavens above! A taxi—and the lady at *our* door-bell, too! Bet she's after the Honourable Nap. Coming herself and all—looks like business."

Colleen felt her breath come short and the tug at her heart again. It made her want to scream. Instead, she dropped back on the pillow and shut her eyes; but there was no shutting out Aggie's voice. She came close to the bed, and went on speaking in her quick, hard way.

"Listen here, Colleen, an' quit your lackadaisical airs. I'm going down meself. I'm smart at sizing people up in a twink; and I believe we've struck a winner. With a trifle of tact, we'll make a good thing out of her. Leave it to me."

Colleen shook her head. She knew from experience, her step-sister's idea of a 'good thing.' Aggie was their mother's daughter by an English husband. No streak in her of the Irish pride that Colleen had from her own father.

"No, Aggie, I can't—I won't," she said, gently but unshakably. "The boy's mine. It's my affair."

Aggie thrust out her pointed chin.

"Oh, is it, then? There might be two opinions to that. Do it your own fool way, if you like. But *do* it; or I warn you straight, I'll wash my hands of you and the kid—if he *is* the sole surviving heir to the empty family stocking! Now I'm off. Pity things don't look a bit tidier—you and your lazy ways."

Aggie was gone. The door was shut. In two or three minutes it would open again—and then——

"Oh dear God, what *did* you make us for—us and our babies?" wailed the mother's distracted heart. But she would go through it somehow, she would; not because of Aggie, but because of the boy.

She had dragged herself off the bed and was hurriedly dabbing her face with toilet vinegar, dusting her small shapely nose with powder, thrusting hairpins into her rebellious bright brown hair. He had loved her hair; and she—in those days—had loved her own prettiness. Now she almost hated it. Impossible to dress in two minutes; moving quickly made her feel giddy. She could only slip on her crumpled blue dressing-jacket, and drop back on her crumpled pillows, pulling the light quilt across her knees.

The lamb lay there sleeping as sound, as sound. A mercy she had put that soothing stuff in the bottle. If he woke and cried, it would be the finish of her.

Not a sound of those two. What was Aggie saying down there? Taking a mean advantage? No. Hark! They were coming. Past the landing, they were now.

Oh, but she couldn't—she wouldn't . . . !

Sudden rage flamed in her; a frantic impulse to spring up and lock the door in their faces, and shout at them to go away, and leave her with her own baby. Her own, he *was*; and she a wicked, unnatural mother to be advertising him like shop-goods. She'd pull through somehow, sooner than turn him over to a stranger.

In a fever of excitement, she sat up and pushed the quilt aside.

It was useless. Weakness flowed through her, and the bitter knowledge that the mere physical effort was beyond her strength. With a small gasp, she dropped back on her pillows again, and mechanically straightened the quilt.

They were there outside the door. The lady was speaking in a soft, kind voice; its very kindness pricked her sensitive pride, overwrought as she was, and disheartened by the failure of her heroic impulse. No charity airs for her. A clear business arrangement for the boy.

They were in the room now; but still she kept her eyes shut, desperately warding them off.

When she opened them, the lady was standing by her bed; a real lady, you could tell at a glance. A silky grey cloak she had on, and a grey feather to her hat; and smiling eyes, kind, like her voice. Holding out her hand, she was at once—and *that* showed.

"You're ill, you poor child," she said in the friendliest way, a touch of shyness with it, too. "I saw your advertisement, and I felt I would rather come than write. But if you're not well—if it's inconvenient . . ."

Colleen jerked herself together and shook hands.

"Dear no, madam. It's honoured we are. Let you sit down. *This* one's safe!" She touched the chair nearest her with a wavering smile. "There's a leg astray on the other."

But the lady's hand was on the cot-rail, and she watching the boy.

"Nothing wrong with *him*. He looks lovely," she said; and you could tell she was a mother the way she moved the cot and spoke quietly, not to wake him. If only Aggie would clear out! But she just went over to the window, and she'd be listening with all her ears.

"Oh, yes, he's grand an' all." Colleen's tone was faintly combative, as she gave the needful assurance. "Only a bit fretty, in this heat. His teeth coming too quick. *I'm* not the sort to palm off a sick one. It's straight I am."

"My dear girl, naturally . . ."

The kind lady seemed a shade embarrassed, but she kept on looking at the boy; then she sat down and laid her ungloved hand on the quilt.

"I felt, when I read your advertisement, that you really cared, that you were—straight, as you say. And I want to help you, if I can to—to a fresh start—a fresh chance——"

"Chance!" Colleen stared, and the lady turned faintly pink. "It's not chances I'm after.

It's just—the boy. His father was an officer—
and a gentleman, which you couldn't be saying for
all of them, in this war. An' I want he should be
reared a gentleman too. Proper schools an' all.
And it's past me power, if I work till I drop. So
I've *got* to let him go. It seems a shame . . ."

Sudden tears blinded her; but she would not
break down.

" It *is*, my dear," the gentle voice echoed, and
a hand was laid on hers. " I'm very much against
it. In fact, I hoped—if you would be frank with
me—I might find work for you that would help
you to keep him—for a time."

"*Keep* him!" The thought of it came near
breaking her in two; but she held together somehow. " It's ever so kind you are. But if he must
go—it 'ud only come harder. All I'm wanting is
. . he should be reared a gentleman—like . . like . .
my husband——"

" Husband? You're married? "

The words came quick and low, as if they
tumbled out by accident; and for one wild, bad
moment, Colleen saw red. She wanted to hit
out at that soft-voiced, misbelieving woman; give
her a clean one between the eyes. But she put a
great restraint on herself—because of the boy;
hardly even raised her voice, angry as she was.

" Married? What else would I be? Palming
off on you a poor little come-by-chance baby?
Trust *your* kind to think the worst on sight!"

" No—no, forgive me—I didn't mean——"

Distress and embarrassment robbed Clarissa of
coherence. What, precisely, did she mean—she,
who had instinctively been making allowances for
a creature so attractive, so volcanic?

Colleen paid no heed. She was speaking again,

quickly, a little breathlessly. For all her spurt of temper, she wanted this lady to understand.

"There's me ring. Put on in church it was, like your own." She flung out her thin left hand, hitherto unrevealed. "Doing things in a hurry— an' all that came of it—wasn't *his* fault . . it was mine. I'm his widow—an' proud to be. An' I've set my heart on it the boy should grow up so as his father might feel proud of *him* . . . if it's true he sees and remembers us . . . where he's gone..."

She choked ignominiously, fighting back the tears that ached in her throat, while the kind lady was saying soft things, and pressing her hands. And there was Aggie by the window, twitching her shoulders, thinking them, for sure, a pair of sentimental fools; wondering when they'd be coming to business.

They came to it, after a fashion, when Colleen had swallowed her tears. If the visitor's manner was a shade nervous and fluttery, she had her plans quite clear. She wanted to carry them off —herself and the boy; feed her up; put strength into her—and then . . .

But Colleen, however reckless, had the slender, unbending streak in her of Irish perversity and pride. Would she be advertising, just to try and catch some good-hearted lady, and grab all she could from her? Agnes might think her a fool. That wasn't *her* way. The most she could finally be persuaded to accept was the loan of ten pounds that would give her a month's quiet and change of air at Seaford. She had friends there, who would take her in cheaply.

"An' it'll be as good as a tonic," she added bravely, "knowing the boy's well cared for. And after . . ."

"Yes—yes. We'll leave all that till you're

stronger. Then—if you really feel . . if you're willing to let me keep him . . . we can go into business details. . . ."

Colleen caught her breath.

" I'll bring me lines an' all."

" Of course, of course." The lady was rather nervously pulling at the catch of her bag. She took out five one-pound notes and laid them on the sheet. " I'll send the rest. I've only silver left."

The good heart she had! And what *could* you say? Colleen could only murmur about signing an I.O.U. The lady laughed softly.

" Oh, well—as a matter of form. . . ."

From her miracle bag she took a sheet of paper and a gold-rimmed fountain pen; scribbled the usual formula; and the girl, propped on one elbow, signed her name—" Colleen Mary Browne."

The lady, reading it, twitched her eyebrows.

" That's my name, too! " she said; and Colleen stared.

" Well, of all the queer turns——"

" It's a very common name, of course. But we're not ashamed of it, are we? And perhaps it's a good omen! "

" Sure it is—for *me*." Colleen's eyes softened. " I'm thinking . . . if you keep . . . my boy, he'll still be having his Dad's name."

" So he will. And what's his other name? "

" I call him Christopher."

The lady had risen, and was looking at the boy again—a sad sort of longing look.

" I'm thinking . . . you'll be a mother yourself? " Colleen ventured; and the lady nodded.

" The war took—my only son."

" *O-oh!* An' it took—my man. It was a cruel war."

In the silence, Aggie's feet could be heard shifting impatiently, and the rattle of that everlasting tram down Holliwell Road.

The lady moved closer to the cot.

"Shall I . . . wouldn't it be better to take him now, if you have his little things ready? I want you to wire to your friends, to get away at once from—from all this."

Colleen caught her breath. Terror seized her. She wanted to scream.

But she heard herself saying, in a strange, suppressed voice:

"Yes—take him . . . *take* him. There's a few things ready. We'll send the rest."

To put a hard face on it, to be practical like Aggie; that was her only chance.

Very gently the lady picked him up. He half woke and whimpered a little; and the loving way she cuddled and rocked him quiet was at once a torment and a comfort to Colleen's distracted heart.

Aggie—in her element at last—was thrusting all she could into the Japanese basket with the strap —half packed this morning to be ready in case . . .

Oh, it was wicked and cruel! If she'd guessed how it would feel, she would never have let Aggie push her into it—not yet.

Half dazed, she saw that the lady was holding little Chris out to her—for good-bye.

Hungrily she took him, and crushed him against her breast. The feel of him there was ecstasy and anguish running into one. Would he wake or no, she *must* kiss him and kiss him with such terrible intensity, she felt as if her heart would burst. He opened his lovely eyes and smiled; but the lids drooped again, so sleepy he was; and fumbling for the forbidden 'sucker,' she insinuated it between his lips.

Then—she loosed her hold and let him be taken from her, without a word, without a tear. Her eyes were burning. A buzzing sound filled her ears. The kind lady was saying something; not a word of it reached her brain.

In a deadly, unnatural calm, she sat there and watched them walking to the door; Mrs. Browne first, with Chris in her arms (just as if she had bought him for five pounds!), Agnes following with the strapped basket.

The door shut upon them. She was alone . . .

Clarissa carefully descending the narrow stairs, stumbled more than once. Her eyes were heavy with tears, for a pang she too intimately understood. It made her feel no less a thief. And what on earth would Godfrey say to it all?

She had been hopelessly unbusinesslike; and she knew it. Shy and sensitive, in the face of that attractive creature's hyper-sensitive temper and pride, she had rushed her fences, had asked for no references, made no drastic inquiries. He would tell her, truthfully enough, that the whole transaction had been feminine and sentimental to a degree. Extravagant, too; for she had kept her taxi waiting, fearful of not finding another in this brick-and-mortar wilderness of trams, lorries, and tradesmen's carts. Probably that was the only item Godfrey could be trusted to approve.

Settled in her seat, with the very plebeian basket for a foot-rest, she gave her card to the sensible, unlikeable half-sister, promised to write soon and bade her arrange matters without delay.

Then the purring began, and she leaned back,

lost to all but the renewal of a dear and familiar sensation—the warmth and weight of a child asleep against her heart.

And behind her, in the high, narrow house saturated with afternoon heat, the unlikeable Agnes sped upstairs to say her say, already too long bottled up.

She found Colleen sitting as they had left her, staring at nothing—and it startled her. Good Lord, if she went daft now ? You never could tell with Colleen.

"Buck up, old dear," she admonished her, with rough kindliness. "Mrs. B.'s the goods, all right. You've done a sound stroke—in spite of yerself, so to speak. But *I'd* have done streets better. The dear Lord knows which of you's the bigger fool—she, flinging her money round, swallowing your tale on trust ; or you, getting such a soft in tow, and not squeezing her for all she's worth. She'd have taken on the two of you—like a bird. *Colleen* . . . For the Lord's sake——!"

But Colleen—hearing nothing, answering nothing—dropped limply sideways in a dead faint.

III

It was cool in the shade of the old lime-tree. A light breeze among the higher boughs made restless shadow-patterns on the grass. The fountain sang its own little song—eternally the same, yet never wearisome. The rumble of London traffic, dulled by intervening houses, had a soothing sound, as of waves breaking on an unseen shore. The air was still sweet with the scent of roses, though it was the time of ramblers, and July nearing an end.

Clarissa sat in a garden chair, under the tree that was her summer drawing-room, knitting a minute pair of cream silk socks with blue diamonds round the top. Close by, a square of movable railings enclosed a space of grass, occupied at the moment by a blue ball and white woolly dog with his legs in the air, staring up into the lime-trees with a glassy golden eye. Chris was out for his airing in the gardens. Presently he would come in for his morning sleep. At the prospect, a gentle warmth invaded her heart.

Only four weeks—it seemed incredible! Already the whole household revolved about his sleepings and wakings, his goings out and comings in. She had feared the maids might cavil at the extra work involved, though indeed she did most of it herself; but Esther, a shy quiet-spoken girl, had discreetly murmured that, if you asked her, there was 'nothin'' in life to touch a baby.' And it is certain her mistress agreed with her. So, between them, they delighted to serve him, till the ideal nurse could be found.

Of course there had been trouble with Godfrey —at first. Clarissa had need of all her wifely diplomacy to carry off her flagrant fulfilment of his prophecy. Not a word of the hidden motive underlying what he called her 'lame-dog mania,' till she saw his interest stirred, his antagonism disarmed, by the child's happy nature and engaging ways. Then, tentatively, she had broached her secret wish—with ultimate success.

His slow nature abhorred hasty decisions, it had taken him a full week to look searchingly all round an idea that had never entered his sober head. A child might prove a disturbing element; but undeniably the house seemed livelier since his coming. There persisted a certain masculine distaste for fathering (or even grandfathering) a child not his own: but dimly—as far as a man may—he realised her ingrained woman's need of ministering to life, were it only to flowers in a garden. If he said little, he saw how these few weeks, her face had softened and grown younger. So, for himself, he had accepted the risk on the clear understanding that the girl must produce unimpeachable references, marriage lines, and so forth, and be fully prepared to surrender all claim on the child.

It was the last that chiefly troubled Clarissa. It was inevitable, of course, yet how utterly unhuman! Could she—could Colleen—when it came to the point?

It was but one of countless cases in which her too keen sympathies became a positive curse. Knowing her own weakness, she ought to have avoided personal contact, or kept it purely formal. As it was, the look in Colleen's eyes that morning haunted her memory. Yet the girl's few and brief letters gave no indication that she was missing the child, or wavering in her resolve to give him up for his own sake, which was distinctly a relief. Clarissa, in her kindness, had written at some length, and sent snapshots taken by herself. Finally, she had announced her husband's willingness to adopt the boy, if references proved satisfactory, and if Colleen were ready to accept the usual conditions. No answer, so far, to this, her first businesslike letter.

Meanwhile, from day to day, the looks and ways of this stranger child—the mere babyhood of him —irresistibly invaded her untreasured heart, brought her nearer to healing and happiness than she could have believed possible within two years of her loss. There were moments, at once quickening and disturbing, when the illusion of having recaptured her own child was eerie in its vividness; a sensation she wisely kept to herself, knowing it for sheer fantasy. But Godfrey's slow, half-unwilling subjugation to the creature's overtures for friendship was no fantasy. It was a sight to warm the heart.

Sounds of laughter from the house; and she looked up to see Godfrey himself standing just outside the study window, Chris perched on his shoulder, snatching at a coveted spray of clematis, which Godfrey playfully jerked out of reach.

Watching them thus—with a sudden pang for what had been, what might have been—she was aware of Esther bringing the midday post.

One envelope—in Colleen's hand. Leisurely she opened it and read:

"DEAR KIND LADY,

"I'm ashamed of myself, I *am*, and I must ask your pardon for what I'm going to say. It was gospel truth, all I told you, and I never thought to go back on it. But I just couldn't see ahead how it would feel being without him. Now I know I *can't* give him up, even to the kindest lady I ever struck. I'll get stronger, I'll work and *work*. He shall have his schooling somehow. I'll pay back the £10, and I'll never be able to thank you enough for your goodness.

"Don't be too angry with me, please. But I can't wait. I'm coming at once. I'll be turning up in the afternoon about tea-time. But *I had to write* all this—I couldn't for the world say it to your face——".

There was a good deal more—grateful, incoherent, transparently honest; but so unexpected, so cruelly unwelcome, that Clarissa found the lines wavering, and dashed an impatient hand across her eyes. Idiotically, but undeniably, she felt furious with the girl for a volte-face as natural as it was distracting. Like a fool, she had too completely let herself go. It unnerved her even to think of losing the boy, now . . .

There they were—still at their game. Chris had captured his spray. He had no further use for it. Godfrey must be a horse; and he became a horse at command. With snortings and absurd prancings, he was bearing down upon her; the boy, jolted this way and that, emitting small shrieks of glee. It hurt her horribly. And now she must hurt him—which was worse still. But why worry him prematurely?

Obedient to the instinct of a lifetime, she slipped the envelope into her knitting-bag; but her move was not quick enough. He had seen.

"What's the mysterious document, old lady?" he challenged her quizzically, and she gave it up. She was a poor dissembler at best. She could only smile and shake her head at the pair of them.

"It's—from Colleen. Rather worrying." She hesitated. "Oh, you'd better read it yourself."

Fishing out the horrid thing, she handed it to him, and received the boy in exchange; pressed him closer with a little convulsive movement, and kissed the top of his head. Then she looked up at her husband. He was angry. There would be ructions.

He could barely have skimmed the letter when he broke out:

"This won't *do*! Can't have her wobbling over it, worrying you to death. She offered the boy.

We've taken him. There's an end of it. He's a jolly little chap, and I won't go back on him."

She sighed, secretly overjoyed at his changed attitude; bitterly aware that they were powerless against a mother's inalienable rights.

"Don't you worry, old lady," he added more gently. "You leave it to me. Of course she feels bad, when it comes to the point, or she'd be an unnatural rotter. Just a touch of hysteria. We've got to tell her it won't work."

"Oh, it sounds very simple, put that way." She smiled at his masculine assurance. "But you haven't seen her. I have. She's crazed on the child. And he's hers, after all——"

"Hers—to starve and drag back into the gutter! That may be the law; but she'll hear something from me first. It's up to us to make her see the clear advantages of the arrangement for the boy—and for herself. Plain business: no 'sob-stuff.' Leave it to me. I'll see her for you when she comes."

"Oh, Godfrey, it's good of you; but I *must* see her first."

He regarded her dubiously. "You're too soft. If the girl started crying, you'd knuckle under."

Of course she denied that stoutly, knowing perfectly well it was true.

"But I *must*," she pleaded. "Let me have a chance."

"Oh, very well. It's a woman's job. If you're stumped, turn her over to me."

And they left it at that.

Tea was laid out in the long low studio that ran through the width of the house: a room so saturate with memories of Derck that Clarissa could hardly bear the thought of using it again, as an informal day nursery for herself and the child; but, no other room being available, she had succumbed to the dictates of common sense. And she had her reward. For here, in the studio they had planned together—his pictures stacked as he had left them, the unfinished one still on its easel—he seemed mysteriously yet intimately nearer to her than he had ever been since that terrible spring of 1915, when his training ended and the flood tide of war swept them apart.

Now she sat there, in his deep arm-chair of Oxford days, awaiting the advent of Colleen; telling her sore spirit that Godfrey was right, that the girl was acting selfishly by Chris, and she ought to be made to see it; trying to ignore an uncomfortable suspicion that, in the circumstances, she would do precisely the same herself.

Chris sat in his railed enclosure, crooning happy nothings to a realistic pony on wheels, serenely unaware. Since the coming of that letter, Clarissa could hardly trust herself to caress him or play with him. The folly of it smote here; but the fact remained.

The door opened. "A lady to see you, 'm."

The door closed'; and Colleen stood there—transformed, the flush of health in her cheeks, her gaze riveted on the child in his blue smock on the blue-and-white play-rug.

Clarissa rose and held out her hand. Colleen's fingers closed on it with a convulsive pressure.

"You . . . you got . . . my letter?"

"Yes—I got it."

Clarissa's tone was unmistakable: and for an embarrassing moment they stood tongue-tied. Apart, on paper, they had been drawn a little nearer. Now, at sight—each instinctively on guard against the other—they knew themselves utter strangers, with the chasm of class and the clash of suppressed emotions widening the gulf between.

"Were you—very angry?" Colleen ventured at last.

"I was naturally very disappointed—just when things seemed settled." Already Clarissa felt her sympathies getting out of hand; but remembering Godfrey, she pulled herself together.

Colleen drew in her lip like a chidden child.

"I was hoping you'd understand——" Her eyes shifted irresistibly to Chris again. "It's the good angel you've been to him. He *does* look lovely."

As she spoke, he lifted his head and regarded her with wide eyes—interested, as at any new phenomenon in a world of wonders.

"He's clean *forgot*," she murmured, like a stricken thing. Then in a changed tone. "Isn't he—Mummy's boy?"

At the familiar word, light dawned.

"Mum—mum," the creature cooed, and held up his arms.

She was on her knees beside him. She had snatched him out of his enclosure, and was clutching him, kissing him, in the same tense, fervent fashion as on the day of parting. Did that imply a lurking indecision? Clarissa, keeping a tight hand on her insurgent sympathies, shamelessly hoped that the child's aspect and surroundings, coupled with her own attitude, were already taking effect.

When Colleen tried to put him down, he clung to her, but she skilfully diverted his attention to the pony; and rising, confronted Clarissa, her blue eyes bright with tears.

"The selfish fool of a mother-woman, you're thinking me, to be snatching him away from all this, only to ease me own starving heart. But I *did* make a fight for it. I wish I may never go through such weeks again. He's all I've got . . . of his father——"

"Yes, yes—you poor child. It's natural. Don't upset yourself."

Clarissa gently installed her in a low chair near the tea-tray. "Of course if you feel fit to work—if you can *find* work . . ."

In spite of awakening sympathy, she emphasised the last; and quite unaggressively, in the intervals of dispensing tea, she set forth her own invincible arguments on the other side: all that the boy would gain, later on; all they had been planning to do for him; all he would inherit when they died.

From the sentimental standpoint, she was being simply cruel—and she knew it; but the bitterness of her own disappointment, and an undersense of Godfrey in the background, impelled her to make one decisive effort in the dim hope of reviving the spirit that had prompted Colleen's advertisement and her ensuing surrender.

And through it all the girl sat meekly attentive, not even trying to answer the unanswerable. As to whether the unanswerable was producing the remotest effect, her sweet, still face gave no sign. Was she pondering the words of wisdom, or were they passing clean over her head . . . ?

Distracted with doubt, Clarissa ceased at last. Nothing palls sooner than an uncontested argument; and Colleen looked up.

"It's wonderful—the way you can tell it all. And the truth it is . . . every word——"

"Well, in that case," Clarissa prompted her

hopefully. "It's simply a question—isn't it?—whether you care more for the boy's welfare or for your own happiness in having him with you."

"Whether I *care* . . ?" Colleen echoed in a shaken voice, her tear-blurred eyes widened in a strange fixed gaze, as though she saw a vision. "There—there's something queer about this room——"

The words were barely audible; and if Clarissa felt faintly startled, Colleen, for her part, was oblivious of anything outside her own tremor of amazement and exaltation.

For while she sat there listening—torn between her deep mother-craving and her heroic inspiration—she became aware, through gathering tears, of a face so strangely like her dead husband that, to her excited fancy, it seemed as if his spirit had come to reproach her for wicked selfishness, because no persuasions would move her to part with his gift.

Hardly aware of having spoken, she brushed away her tears, and sprang to her feet with a cry.

It was no fancy. He was there, on the mantelpiece; the fine head and shoulders of him in the familiar uniform——

"Why, it's *him*!" she broke out. "Did you know him. . . ."

"*Know* him?" Clarissa echoed blankly—seeing, yet refusing to see, the truth that flashed across her brain. "That's my dear dead son. I don't understand——"

And Colleen, absorbed in her own sensations, answered very low: "All I know is . . . it's my . . . dead husband."

"Your—husband!"

"Why not, then? *He* thought no shame of it." Head erect, her sensitive pride in arms, she challenged Derek's mother, who had no answer at command.

For a full minute, they stood so, silently facing each other, taking it all in. The incredible strangeness of it! The joy of it, in one sense, the pain of it in another—to the elder woman, who had believed herself, not without reason, supreme in the heart and in the confidence of her only son. The thing was past crediting.

Not without a sharp struggle could she bring herself to face and accept all that the girl's simple, staggering statement implied. She could only repeat lamely: " I don't understand. There *must* be some mistake. He would never . . . he could never . . ."

" But he did," Colleen assured her with unconscious cruelty. " And it's not *him* that would be wishing there was—a mistake, I promise you. Captain Derek Browne, he was, of the Monmouths. I've brought me lines and all. And to think it should be *you*! No wonder I liked you straight off. Is it hating me, you are? Could you be wishing—you that reared him—he'd not been straight with me . . . ? "

The words, spoken low and swiftly, scarcely reached his mother's brain. The voice of her own distracted heart was too loud in her ears. Her Derek had loved—had married, secretly, this unknown girl—not even one of themselves, for all her Celtic refinement and charm. And he had never told her—he, who had appeared to tell her everything. In the acute revulsion of the moment, she almost hated that other, who stood there saying such unbelievable things about her beloved dead. . . .

Suddenly it dawned on her that Colleen had changed her tone.

"Oh, if *that's* how you're taking it——" Her voice quivered between pain and anger—"If there's no love in your heart . . . even for his own boy, it's good-bye to you, Mrs. Browne. And I'll take my Chris straight; and you can be sending his things—them that *I* made him."

"Colleen—for heaven's sake——!"

Clarissa flung out her hands with a desperate gesture, as the girl swung away from her to pick up the child.

"Well, there's no other way to it—if it makes you feel so bad."

And Clarissa answered truthfully: "It makes me feel—dizzy. I can't take it in . . . why he never *told* me?"

"He wanted to tell you. He meant to. But you see . . ."

Her obvious hesitation stabbed the older woman afresh; stabbed her, this time, broad awake. Incredulity, resentment, possessive jealousy paled before her simple mother-craving to hear all—she who had fatuously believed she knew all. . . .

"No—honestly—I *don't* see," she confessed, not without an undernote of bitterness. "I thought I did. I would have sworn it was impossible . . . But it seems I didn't really know . . . my own son. Does any mother—ever? Oh, tell me, Colleen—tell me everything."

The girl's clear eyes softened at the frank appeal.

"Let me only comfort him a mite. The pattern he's been, playing by his lone."

With a crooning sound she caught up the boy and leaned her cheek against his bright hair, a picture to charm away all evil humours.

"It's the twin of himself he'll be presently,

barring me eyes and me hair. Can you see it—
now ? "

Yes, Clarissa could see it now. Some unerring
instinct in her must have guessed it all along. *His*
son ! The supreme gift she had desired of him,
while secretly dreading the inevitable wife. For
the first time, since the shock of revelation, a faint
tenderness invaded her heart; but words were
difficult.

" Why—didn't you call him Derek ? " was all
she managed to say.

Colleen shook her head.

" Ah no ! I'm a proper fool that way. Derek
was—himself. I couldn't bear it on me lips for
another, not even for *this* one." She gave the
creature a convulsive squeeze that seemed to say,
' He's mine again—mine ! ' " It's Christopher
Derek, he is. Somehow the name took me
fancy."

" It's a beautiful name."

Stooping, she kissed the child's upturned cheek,
hesitated the fraction of a second, then kissed his
mother—Derek's wife ! Not yet could those incredible words carry conviction to her protesting
heart.

" We must love each other, my dear," she
murmured, " because—he loved us both. Sit
down now, and tell me all you can. When . . .
and how . . . ? And why he never told *me*—of all
people."

Colleen, chilled by that perceptible pause, sat
down obediently in the low arm-chair.

Sitting there, with Derek's boy in her arms,
she told their brief, passionate story, shyly but
straightly, with vivid touches and her picturesque
turns of phrase : how she had ' done her bit ' in

a Y.M.C.A. hut at Boulogne; how he had found her there and set her ' heart in a blaze.'

"Like a lightning stroke on me, it was," she confessed simply, gaining courage from the face of him up there, not venturing a glance at his mother. "And me not knowing, when he went, if ever I'd set eyes on him again. Twice he came, after that. They kept him a spell at the base for fever and sleeplessness. And before he went back, that time, 'twas all out between us. Then it was he told me about . . . about his father and . . . you——"

An agony of hesitation here. How could she say all to this mother, whose jealous devotion and aristocratic fastidiousness had been the root of the trouble: and he, longing to tell her, like the straight one he was ?

"Well—what about me?" came the quiet, demanding voice. "If . . . if it was my own fault, I've the right to know—I would rather."

"Oh, but you couldn't call it that, only to be thinking the world of him . . . so nobody 'ud be good enough, let alone a chit of a thing like me; no lady an' all; though me father *was* well born, but feckless. So he slipped down a bit, and married beneath him. I'm a chip of him, I am, and proud to be—if he *did* give more trouble than mother."

Lightly, rapidly, she had skidded over the worst of it somehow. Impossible, it was, to be telling a mother, and she bereaved, how she'd made her own boy feel restive through holding on too hard. It was easier to tell how she, Colleen, had begged him to let her be, and forget her quick, sooner than make trouble at home; how the recall snatched him back to those cruel trenches—and she, sick with terror for fear he'd be seeing wisdom

and do her bidding: how his letter came, telling
he'd got ninety-six hours' leave and he was coming
—to her. Giving her up was beyond him. He
would make his mother understand. Then—oh
then, there was no holding her at all, at all: and
it was she that begged they should be married
right off, so she would be his wife for always, whatever came—three days and nights of a honeymoon
they'd have, anyway. And they had it. And it
was their all of married life.

" So you couldn't be grudging me just that," she
apologised meekly. " You that had him close on
thirty years."

But the other was fiercely grudging her every
hour of it, as Colleen knew without telling; for
she, being his mother, would have grudged it
herself.

A sigh was all her answer: and her own voice
failed. She found it hard to go on.

" Just crazed with happiness, we were, in that
morsel of time. And if he didn't think to write
. . . let you forgive him. He vowed he would—
after—and make everything square for me. But
before his time was up, came the recall, and
then——" Her voice shook uncontrollably. " Ah,
you *know* how it was! "

The silent figure beside her nodded mutely. Of
a truth, she knew how it was—the sudden and
violent enemy onslaught; the agony of waiting
for news, of vacillations between hope and dread;
then—the telegram that extinguished hope. And
the brave girl beside her had gone through it all
too. By those hours of mutual anguish they were
linked as vitally, almost, as by the child in Colleen's
arms. As for all she had lost in the sharing of
happier things, it was the penalty (she saw it now)

of an over-jealous devotion that unfailingly defeats its own ends. By keeping a wise restraint on it, how securely she had held her husband. With her boy she had too completely let herself go. And this——

Colleen had broken down at last. She was sobbing convulsively, fighting for self-control.

"My child—my child!" Clarissa cried in a sudden uprush of remorse, and gathered the two of them into her arms.

"If—if you *can't* love me . . if it's only him you want," Colleen lamented, and was summarily put to silence.

"My dear, don't misjudge me. Haven't I had punishment enough? You said—'Complete surrender.' I hold you to that!"

Sounds of arrival below stairs startled them apart.

"Godfrey!" Clarissa was on her feet hastily dabbing her eyes.

"Will he—be very angry?" Colleen murmured, quailing a little at thought of an unknown, unwilling father-in-law.

"Angry? No; one can't be angry with . . . the dead. But it will be difficult—making him understand. You wait here, you two, till I come back."

And she hurried out, leaving Colleen alone, shaken, yet uplifted; alone in the big friendly room, full of Derek's pictures, with his boy in her arms, and himself looking down at them from the mantelpiece. The living picture, it was. You could just catch the glimmer of a smile in his eyes.

"Derek asthore," she whispered, barely above her breath. "Is it content you are—now?"

1923.

TO
MARY

ESCAPE

ESCAPE

When a man and a woman are agreed, what can the Kaazi do?
INDIAN PROVERB.

I

DARKNESS brooded over Luliana—darkness, and the cold glimmer of paling stars. In the tortuous streets and mud-walled courtyards of the lone brown village,. life was already astir. Indian villagers rise with the sun; and they knew his coming was near at hand.

Already a herald brightness illumined the east. The pale stars quivered and went out. With incredible swiftness the veil of night was dissolved —and all the vast plain was golden with the unfiltered sunshine of a Punjab April morning.

The irregular cluster of mud huts, that was Luliana, boasted only here and there a more pretentious brick building. All around it lay ripe grain-fields, intersected with tree-bordered roads; and away to the north, beyond the river, beyond leagues of fertile cornland, the snow line of the Himalayas gleamed ghostly and unreal upon a sky of tenderest blue.

An invisible track through the grainfields led to the largest well on the borders of the village. Here, morning and evening, women and children flocked, like birds in autumn, with vessels of earthenware and brass, with jangle of jewellery, and clamour of high-pitched voices, to draw water for their daily needs.

But to-day the first flash of dawn revealed one solitary figure in the wide expanse of earth and sky—the figure of a woman swathed in a formless cotton garment, that drooped over her face and obscured it from prying eyes. On her well-poised head gleamed a brass *lotah* steadied by a circular pad. She walked with inimitable grace and freedom ; a swift elastic tread ; one olive-tinted hand resting on her hip, the other holding her *chuddah* across the lower half of her face. Her shapely arms were unadorned. No clink of anklets accompanied her as she moved.

The coarse cotton *chuddah*, the absence of trinkets, proclaimed her a Hindu widow—a thing of ill-omen, to be cursed by all, as a matter of duty, because of some unknown sin, in a former birth, that must have caused the untimely death of her husband. Punished by the gods, who had taken him, deprived by British law, of her only right—to die with him—nothing remained for her but a barren life of drudgery and prayers and penances, that might perchance win, for him, a better life-place in his next incarnation. They had taken her hair, they had taken her jewels ; no girlish vanities of silks and muslins for her any more. And she had just completed her eighteenth year.

Sixteen months only of honoured and honourable wifehood had been hers. Then her kindly young husband—the household god, on whose life hung all her hope of happiness—had fallen into a mysterious decline and died, leaving her a childless widow, in the house of an irate and injured mother-in-law, who accused her openly of having bewitched her son.

On the strength of this baseless accusation, Anunda had suffered more than the average widow's portion of drudgery and austerity. Her three sisters-in-law, uncomely full-blown damsels, dutifully followed the lead of their mother-in-law in the matter of petty tyrannies and the ' obligation to curse '——

Arrived at the well, she set her vessel on its low parapet, and sank down beside it: for she had walked fast. Her young figure fell into listless lines, that suggested utter weariness of spirit rather than bodily fatigue. For, on this golden April morning her young heart was dry as a handful of ashes; her power of endurance very nearly at an end.

And her time was brief. No rest for such as she. Too soon the jangling chattering line of water seekers would be threading their way through the corn—and she shrank from their light-hearted jests as a wounded wild thing shrinks from its unscathed fellows.

Reluctantly she rose at length, dropped the bucket into the darkness, and heard it kiss the water with a musical splash. It came up dripping and brimming. With a slow sigh she hoisted it on to the parapet. The water was crystal clear; and, as she bent above it, a dim reflection of her beautiful woe-begone face arrested her attention.

In a sudden impulse of vanity, she flung back her *chuddah*, and bending lower looked down at herself—at the comely features, at her swelling breasts and close-cropped head—till tears of self-pity filled her eyes. With shaking hands she dashed the water into her vessel, and stooped to pick up her cotton pad, that had fallen to the ground.

But she did not at once set it on her head.

There were days when it seemed beyond her

power to face the return journey; yet the sun climbed high and higher. How should he—the Great One, Slayer and Life-bringer—stay his march on account of one small, suffering woman? The accustomed path must be trodden, and that speedily, unless—— ?

Her eyes sought the well's wide mouth, and lingered there with fearful fascination. She leaned a tapering hand on the curb, and peered into the chill darkness. There lay the only other path, the only way of escape—swift and certain. One moment of courage, one sharp pang—and thereafter, oblivion, nothingness, peace. . . .

Anunda knew that this form of suicide was common enough among desperate young widows of her caste and creed: nor was it the first time she had been tempted to follow their example. But always, at the last, she had yielded to the incurably hopeful voice of youth within her, that urged her to wait . . . yet a little longer . . . for what?

No hope of release or change lightened the long years ahead: and innately she knew that the selfless spirit of martyrdom, of dedicated service —which alone glorifies the curse and the austerities of Hindu widowhood—was not in her.

Tales of such sainted ones she had heard from Big Mother—who, being old, would sometimes risk ill luck and give her a kind word or two, when none were by. Husbandless, they would serve all who were in sickness or need: childless, they would take into their hearts all the children of others. Of these it was sometimes said that, being too holy for life's commonplace, the Destroyer had set them free to pray. Yet even they—while held in sacred reverence, as beings apart—remained, inevitably, bringers of bad luck, not to be seen on auspicious occasions.

Though spurner and spurned alike be straws blown by the wind of Fate, this strange dissembling of love, this sanctifying of abuse, where love is not, are bitter bread for the young. And Anunda was no sainted heroine. She was simply woman, craving the worship of an actual husband, rather than the buying of spiritual benefits for one that was gone. Could she but return to her own mother, and fill the place of ' good home daughter,' her lot would be eased a little of its hardness: but the pitiless gods had taken her also.

Motherless, husbandless, childless—more and more the certainty grew upon her that Life had only one good gift for the giving—Death.

Lower and lower she leaned over into the merciful blackness. The breath of the hidden water struck a chill through her frame: but she mounted the well-curb, her desperate decision unshaken.

Straightening her slender figure, she flung out her arms, glanced quickly over the fields of wheat and sugar-cane, to make sure she was alone—and behold, her eyes that had willed to look on death, looked instead full into the eyes of a man.

Stricken with amazement he stood in the cane-field, not many paces away from her.

With a low cry, she let fall her arms and stepped back to earth. Her first impulse was to muffle her face in the discarded *chuddah*; her second, which she unhesitatingly obeyed, was to lower her lids demurely and remain unveiled. None witnessed her lack of modesty: and with throbbing pulses she awaited the outcome.

Swiftly it was upon her: a rustle among the

cane-stalks, a presence at her side, a man's hand gently touching her own.

Though the blood quickened in her veins, she neither moved nor looked up. She had no right; he had no right; save the common human right of his manhood and her womanhood. And once more gently touching her hand, he spoke:

"Maiden, thou art comelier than dawn upon the mountains. Why make haste to go down into the grave? Live, rather—and make glad the heart of a man."

Such words to her! With a pathetically eloquent gesture, she touched her bare arms and close-cropped head.

"Thou seest—I am a widow, and no woman. Dead already, though seemingly I live. Yea—and I *will* die. The gods themselves cannot rob me of death!"

Her voice quivered. She turned from him and would again have mounted the curb; but his hand closed tightly on her wrist.

Her beauty, her youth, and that pitiful quiver in her voice fired his manhood. For he, too, was young, and further emboldened by more than a smattering of enlightened ideas. He had never personally known one of these doomed, yet most sacred women of his race. Deeply stirred by the girl's beauty, and her tragic plight, he did not pause to reflect on after courses.

"Nay, but I will set my body between death and thee—and thou *shalt* hear me. Listen only—and I will give thee hope of life. I am not as these village pig-heads. I have read in strange books. I have seen men and cities. In mine eyes thou art *not* accurst——"

He broke off with a swift recoil. Faint yet

clear across the rustling cornfields came the shrill tinkle of women's laughter.

"Go—*go*———" cried Anunda, with startled eyes. "They come, the favoured ones, with their jests and their jewellery. Oh, begone!"

Hastily she gathered up her fallen *chuddah*.

"Not till thou hast sworn to wait———"

"I swear it."

"I must speak with thee again. Thou comest daily?"

"Daily.—Oh, begone!"

Two swift bounds carried him back among the cane-stalks: and Anunda stood alone with her gleaming *lotah*,[1] in the hot sunshine, like one newly awakened from an incredible dream.

The chattering throng drew nearer, the long line of lotah-crowned figures, gay with many-tinted muslins and armlets of glass, moved leisurely down the pathway that cleft the standing corn. Anunda cast one look toward the sugar-cane tufts. No sign of the madman—her preserver: and setting her *lotah* on its cotton pad, she sped homeward as one that trod on air.

II

Through the blazing hours of daylight she fulfilled her accustomed tasks—sweeping and cooking and sewing, with an uplifted heart.

To-day, for the first time, the 'obligation to curse,' so freely exercised by her frankly inimical mother-in-law, had no power to hurt. The astonishing words spoken at the well's mouth haunted her brain. "In mine eyes thou art not accurst— I must speak with thee again." What did he

[1] Brass vessel.

mean ? What could he possibly mean ? For such as she there could be no hope of marriage : but it was not unknown to her that here and there young widows, who were not of the sainted ones, sought distraction from the harsh decree of Fate in secret lapses from virtue. Could he believe her such an one ? Could she—even she— become such an one, because of the strange new ache within her and the quickened life in her veins ?

Her mind was too bewildered, too full of nameless hope and wonderment for sober speculation : only, as she set fine silver stitches in Moti's blue muslin *chuddah*, her heart kept repeating over and over, " Would the night were ended ! Would it were dawn ! "

The house of Anunda's father-in-law, Gunpat Rám—banker, grain-dealer, and a power in the isolated village—was a more imposing affair than those of the zemindars huddled around it on all sides. It boasted a second storey, and its mud walls were strengthened by a mixture of brick, a luxury almost unknown in Luliana. It boasted also a carved balcony, overlooking the narrow street, with its open shop fronts, its aimless flow of noisy life, its mingled odours of musk and spices, drains, and humanity.

Here Anunda worked and hoped and wondered throughout that interminable April day : and at sunset, during a brief half-hour of respite, she crept across to an adjoining housetop, to chew betel-nut with a kind little neighbour—a girl-wife, young as herself—and whisper into her ears the incredible story of the morning.

To the Oriental woman intrigue is the breath of life ; the one chance of excitement in the monotonous daily round of cooking and *pujah* and self-adornment. Though Toru counselled discretion with her lips, her eyes and the soft pressure of her hand counselled otherwise, to the great uplifting of Anunda's heart.

The first ray of sunlight stealing across the level land found her back at the well's mouth. Again her hand rested on the stone curb, again she peered down into the black depths that had tempted her to distraction twenty-four hours ago. To-day she smiled and shook her head, letting fall the bucket lazily; eyes and ears alert for his coming, who had sworn he must speak with her again.

No rustle; no movement; no sign of life in all the wide landscape. But the sun still rested on the utmost tree tops. In the same leisurely fashion she drew up the bucket and filled her *lotah*; then, resting one hand lightly on her hip, and one on the polished rim of her vessel, she stood and waited, her eyes turned resolutely away from the cane-field—waited, while the sun crept slowly, steadily up the bare blue sky.

Not a breath was stirring. In the vast expanse of cornland sounds were few. A noisy company of crows passed over her, winging their way from the plantation to the village. From afar came the wailing cry of a kite, and the mournful sound struck a chill into her heart. A broken sob escaped her. She turned to lift up her accustomed burden; and behold—the man himself stood before her.

With a low word of welcome, he drew nearer; and in sudden dread of her own boldness, she veiled her face and turned away her eyes.

But he would not have it so. Their manner of

coming together was, in itself, so entirely outside the pale of orthodox custom that conventional modesty seemed to him superfluous, however becoming.

"Dost so reward me?" he protested. "Mine eyes have hungered for thy beauty. It is not thus thou and I should speak together, my Bird. Not being, as those others, custom-ridden, why make pretence?" With gentle insistence he drew the coarse *chuddah* back a little from her face, from her shapely, close-cropped head; and again, as yesterday, her beauty fired him. "Of a truth," he told her simply, "thou art peerless among the daughters of men."

Such words, so spoken, the closing of his fingers upon her own, wakened all the repressed woman in her. Joy filled her heart to overflowing. Shyly she yielded to his insistence, without further question or misgiving.

Four times they met thus, undiscovered, by the well-curb at dawn. Ten minutes or so of shy talk: the touch of hands at parting: that was all. Yet it sufficed to carry Anunda, light-footed—light-headed almost—through the days' unchanging round, through home duties the most menial and irksome that could be devised by a stern mother-in-law, who saw her only as 'that luckless one,' indirect cause of her strong son's untimely death.

Though this cursing of widows be a matter of 'religious privilege,' there always remains human nature to be reckoned with. Too often, this left-handed fashion of helping the widowed to pay back her debt against the gods breeds personal animosity on the one hand, and on the other a morbid sense of being identified with the thing accursed. Only unshaken faith can combat this last; can 'falsify the curse' by a lifetime of selfless service. Let doubt enter in, and the foundations of courage are undermined.

Anunda—being neither heroine nor martyr—her faith in the spiritual commerce of gifts and cursings had been shaken all too readily by the strange new talk of That Other—Gopalu. She dared hardly 'take his name' even in thought. To her, it seemed, his knowledge of men and cities was beyond even the knowledge of priests. How then could she doubt him when he told her that, in very truth, she was not ill-omened, that her young husband's death had simply been caused by some natural disorder of diet or disease. Ardently she desired to believe him: and, in belief, as in other vital matters, the readiness is all. The touch of his hand at parting, the lightness of her own heart and body told her afresh every morning that she *was* no longer accursed. She was honourably beloved. It was enough.

Not so for the man, her lover, who had other ends in view. On the fifth morning he told her plainly, "We cannot continue this fashion of meeting, Anunda, Joy of my Heart. Others will come to know of it. There will be trouble."

"*Hai-mai*—trouble indeed!"

She shivered at the thought; but his voice and touch renewed her courage.

"Have no fear. I am thy man. And thou art my woman. Is it not so?"

She could only bow her head, silently admitting it.

"Hast never heard it said, 'When a man and a woman are agreed, what can the *Kaazi* do?'"

"But alas, I am no woman. There can be no marrying for such as I." Her voice broke. She sank down upon the well-curb shaken with weeping. "Would I had never spoken with thee—never risen from the dead."

Inexpressive as he was by race and habit, constrained by a sense of her sacredness, he could only draw a step nearer and venture a hand upon her bowed head.

"Stay thy weeping, my Bird. I have thought how this thing may be accomplished. Listen—and thou shalt hear. True it is that, amongst us of the Khatri caste, there is no lawful form of widow marriage. But there is a custom sanctioned by the Sikhs, the casting of a saffron dipped *chuddah* over the woman's head. For us, that will suffice —so thy courage fails not. We need only a single witness to make all complete. Hast knowledge of any woman thou canst trust to do this thing and to keep a still tongue in her head thereafter?"

"Yea, I know of one," came Anunda's tremulous answer. "But consider—— Has my lord no other women-folk, whose right is before this slave's?"

"Nay, I have neither wife nor mother. Both are dead these two years: and a man cannot live alone."

"But will not my lord lose caste by such unsanctified marriage? None will dare have dealings with him. They will go in fear of my father-in-law. He will seek me out. He will kill me. Nay—I cannot——"

"'Cannot' is a word for cowards," he persisted doggedly. "Thou art my woman. It is enough. We will fly north, to Rewāna, where none will know thy history—— Hark, they are already afield—the women-folk. Come again, before dawn to-morrow. And I will tell thee all."

III

Two o'clock of the morning, a full moon riding high in the heavens, and all Luliana sleeping unconcernedly beneath a windless sky. On the flat mud roofs, in the narrow streets, and open court-yards, the shrouded figures lay about in groups and rows, some on low string *charpoys*, some on the sun-baked earth—a veritable city of the dead.

Suddenly, in the courtyard of Gunpat Rám, a white figure moved stealthily from the sheltering shadow of the house, into the full glare of the moon. The fateful decision had been made, all details carefully planned by Gopalu himself: and Anunda—exalted yet fearful at her own daring—stood at last outside her father-in-law's house, equipped for flight.

The sum of her worldly possessions—a *resai*,[1] a cotton sheet, and her cherished *pān-dān*, stocked with *pān*[2] leaves and betel-nut—was tucked away in a neat roll under her left arm. With eyes strained to catch the least sign of movement on the adjoining housetop, she awaited the coming of Toru. Tender-hearted always, and fired with zeal for so brave an adventure, the girl-wife had consented to witness the curious Sikh ceremony, the nearest approach to lawful marriage that Gopalu could offer his bride.

Anunda's escape had been simplified by the fact that she was debarred from sleeping on the roof with the other women of the family. Through the suffocating nights of a Punjab summer, she must remain apart from the favoured ones, in a bare, windowless room on the ground floor. Here

[1] A quilt.   [2] Betel-nut.

she could make her modest preparations for departure without fear of disturbing those others, privileged to sleep under the stars.

Surely the gods themselves did not frown upon her desperate venture, since her very misfortune had made all things possible.

Once, only, while she waited, a whispered thought crept in of her young husband, of the spiritual gifts that she alone could buy for him through the prescribed cursings, the austerities, the penances on account of sins, unknown, in some former life, for which the gods had smitten her, here and now.

But, on this April night of stillness and stars, her youth, her budding womanhood were in open revolt against iron decrees of custom and priestly dominion. The cursings and penances were actual; the buying of gifts—as That Other had hinted— might be only a tale of the priests.

She was seriously concerned, just then, for one matter alone—would Toru succeed in slipping away undetected, from her husband's side?

Anunda held her breath in an agony of suspense, as the precious minutes slipped away—and no welcome figure appeared against the sky-line. Her neck ached with the strain of looking up. Her temples throbbed. Her eyeballs pricked and burned. What if the gods should prove inexorable, after all . . . ?

A light touch on her arm so startled her that she barely repressed a scream.

"Toru—thou? When didst leave the roof? I saw thee not."

"How shouldst thou, foolish one? Did I desire to be seen? There may be wakeful eyes to-night, other than thine. Come—favoured of

the gods. Thou wilt be a bride before morning.
Was ever such a wedding *tamasha* heard of in
Luliana ? "

" Oh, Toru-ji, I fear——"

" *Chut*! chicken-heart! Time for fear is past.
Give me thine hand—so."

Through the sleeping streets they sped, silently
as spirits; now lost in shadow, now emerging into
dangerous patches of moonlight; picking their
way, with breathless caution, among shrouded
forms lest they stumble over and arouse a possible
enemy.

Once Anunda's flying foot disturbed the dreams
of a half-starved pariah. The lank creature arose,
shook himself and ' woofed ' apprehensively. But
they only fled the faster, nor stayed to look behind.

Outside the village, though they breathed more
freely, they dared not slacken speed. Through
the wide, shadowless cornland, past the familiar
well, on which Anunda's eyes lingered, they flitted
still in silence, hand locked in hand. Even in
dreams, Anunda had never known anything half
so strange as this breathlessly amazing reality.

" Look, Toru-ji, look! It is the *ekka*! " she
whispered at last, as they came within sight of a
thatched shelter, adjoining the last of the fields.

Outside the shelter, the skeleton form of an *ekka*
showed ghostly in the moonlight, and a gaunt
white horse, tethered to a tree, was refreshing himself while opportunity offered.

Within, Gopalu awaited them. On his arm hung
the mysterious *chuddah*, its four corners dipped
in saffron—the *chuddah* that could change her from
ill-omened widow into loved and lawful wife.

There was neither time nor need for more than
the briefest words of greeting. No ceremony; no

endless chanting of prayers ; no feasting of insatiable priests. The strange bridal veil, with its yellow corners, was solemnly placed over Anunda's bowed head. Then, with a low cry, Gopalu lifted his wife bodily in his arms, and set her aloft in the *ekka*.

"Rest thou there," he whispered. "We shall be at Bijapur by dawn."

As the gaunt horse bounded forward, Anunda lifted a corner of her veil, and called softly down to her friend:

"Keep silence, Toru-ji, keep silence. May the gods send thee sons without number!"

Then the *ekka* rattled noisily down the wide white road: and one small shrouded figure sped back alone to the unsuspecting village.

At sunrise there was consternation and wrath in the household of Gunpat Rám. The ground-floor room was found to be empty ; and Mai Soontu perforce carried her own *lotah* to the well's mouth. Conjecture and gossip flowed freely. But Toru kept a still tongue in her head ; and let fall no hint of the truth.

IV

On the housetop of Nunda Rám, Zemindar of Rewāna, four women squatted in a circle ; four high-pitched voices discussed the latest item of village news, to the liquid gurgling of four hookahs. For the Indian village wife, her evening 'hubble-bubble' is as the pot of stewed tea to her Western counterpart

The August sun had set an hour since, leaving heat enough behind him, in the cramped streets and windowless houses, to last till his return, lest the brief respite of darkness should make men

forget the power of his might. An occasional
tepid breeze drifted up from the mile-wide river,
swollen with the Great Rains. The chatter of
cicadas shrilled loud in the trees; scarcely less loud,
upon the roof tops, shrilled the chatter of women.

"True talk, Mother," asserted a moon-faced
bride of sixteen with arched eyebrows and reddened
lips. "I had it from Jamuna, who had it from
Gunga Din. They say Anunda is no *pukka* wife,
but an ill-omened widow. Think of it—bare-faced
impostor! And these four months she has been
in Rewāna, as one of ourselves. Listen, sisters.
Thus I heard it. To Gunga Din's shop last night,
came one newly arrived from Luliana. He told
how the man, Gopalu, had fled from his village—
four months since—in company with a widow;
and none knew whither they had gone.

"*Ari, bibi-log*—a shameful tale!" The girl
applied her full red lips vigorously to the mouth-
piece of her hookah.

"*Tobah—tobah!*"[1] echoed Mai Munia—a lean
matron given to philosophising. "They be fools,
these men folk—fools all! Are there not virgins
enough and to spare—since daughters are multiplied
by the folly of the Sirkar—that a man must needs
defile himself through mating with a widow?
Now will he pay dearly for his folly. It will be
seen. To all good Khatris he must be '*Hookah-
panibund*,'[2] when *this* news spreads through the
village. His trade will fail. None will dare to
deal with him who is out of caste. And he, being
but man, will curse her in his heart as the cause of
his ill-fortune. How shall a fair face console any
man for loss of caste and loss of good rupees?"

"*Na—na*—it could never be."

[1] Shame—shame.   [2] Ostracised.

Their verdict was unanimous. With the callousness of the custom-ridden, they reverted to their *hukkas*. The unorthodox pair had sinned. The orthodox had pronounced judgment. What either might suffer was no concern of theirs: and the cicadas among the tree-tops chorused shrill approval.

To Anunda, walking homeward from the river— happy in the sanctity of honourable wifehood— the distant voices of woman and of cicadas were of no more account than all the other familiar sounds of the sunset hour. The possibility that either could disturb her new-found blessedness never entered her head.

On this stifling August evening, her limbs were heavy, her heart was light. That the gods had forgiven her, she had clear proof at last.

As Mai Munia had foretold, so it came to pass.

Next day all Rewāna buzzed with the news: and the village tradesmen—as orthodox Hindus— had no choice but to put Gopalu solemnly out of caste: which is to say that none might eat with him, smoke with him, or trade with him. In the event of discovery, he had known that so it must be: yet he could not see himself virtually condemned to social, religious, and commercial isolation without a secret sinking and bitterness of heart. And, as the burning August days dragged by, his desperate position was pitilessly brought home to him at every turn.

At the outset, being a man of spirit, he accepted his calamity with a brave face, doing all he could to hide from Anunda's eyes the despair at his heart. But in a very few weeks he was confronted by the fact that unless he left Rewāna, he would soon, in every sense, be a ruined man.

ESCAPE

Whither, then, should he go? Was the whole Punjab wide enough for escape from those who knew? Was the great world itself wide enough for escape from the anger of the gods? His brave veneer of enlightenment had by no means charmed away his inborn terror of the gods, and their mysterious machinations.

Anunda's devotion was unwearied. All that woman might do to ease the indignity and the desperate shifts of their impossible situation she did. Because he had looked on her face, ill-luck had befallen him. It was the bitterest thought of all. Try to hide it as she would—he knew. And his own pain exceeded hers: or so he believed, being a man. Though he cherished and desired her no less than at first, yet were there stifling, sleepless hours in the heart of the night, when he came very near cursing that April morning on which he had first beheld his wife's beautiful face.

So the August weeks dragged on—' passionate rain ' alternating with the deadly moist heat that melts the very bones and sinews. With the surreptitious help of certain friendly Mussulmans, they managed to procure food and drink: that was all. And the man began to ask himself—how long . . . ?

It was an evening of early September, a breathless twilight brooded over the land, when Gopalu at last acknowledged himself beaten in the battle against Fate.

He stood alone in the open courtyard behind the house, his eyes resting on a twist of pink paper that lay in the palm of his hand.

A man need only swallow that, and he could

not choose but sleep. Nay, if he willed it—he need never wake again.

Through three nights he had lain, wide-eyed and weary, vainly craving the respite of oblivion. With the approach of the fourth night, courage had failed him. He had gone out in secret, to the booth of one Ayub Khan, determined to win sleep at any price. And there, in his hand, lay the precious twist of opium—the blessed dream-compeller.

It was a strong dose. He had bought enough to last him several nights. And he intended to take it all, in a few hours' time. If he should chance to sleep so soundly, that no human skill could wake him—what of that? Such accidents happened occasionally—and he would be at peace.

Here on earth was no peace for such as he. Because desire came upon him, he had sinned: and the gods would set no blessing on his marriage. They would leave him to die sonless, a man doubly accursed and disgraced. Wherefore await their pitiless pleasure? Why not die at once—since he left no son on whom his wilful death would bring dishonour?

There would be none to mourn him, save her— his wife. And at thought of her his heart contracted. Twice left widowed—and so young. Gladly she would be *suttee*, burn with him on the same pyre. But the Sirkar [1]—strangely without understanding—would not permit——

Before he had time for further reflection, she was at his side.

With guilty haste he closed his hand over the twisted paper. But she had seen it; and his quick movement puzzled her.

"Lord of my life, thou lookest strangely," she

[1] Government

said, with a sudden swift premonition of evil.
" Art ill ? Has bought some medicine from the
good Ayub Khan ? "

He laughed, a short, uneasy laugh.

" True talk, wise one—some medicine. To-
morrow I shall be rid of all mine ills."

That laugh betrayed him. She was puzzled no
longer. She knew. As clearly as though her
eyes beheld it, she saw the hidden thing in her
husband's clenched hand.

Her heart jerked sharply ; her limbs trembled
under her. But here was no time for woman's
weakness. Her mind held one thought only—
this thing, this impending horror, must *not* happen.
She, who had brought him to this pass, alone had
the right to save him, even as he saved her at the
well's mouth. She, alone ? Nay, but she was,
now, no longer alone. A new power was astir
within her, a power strong to compel. Kneeling
before him she stooped low and took the dust of
his feet in wifely worship. Then, boldly, she
touched the offending hand and looked up searchingly into his troubled eyes.

" It is in the sleep of death thou seekest a cure
for thine ills. I have seen it—as if soul stood
naked to soul."

He was silent a moment, his eyes resting in
hers, the spell of her beauty and devotion strong
upon him. Then he laid his free hand upon her
dark head.

" Three nights I have not slept. My courage
deserted me. Thou hast guessed aright."

With a broken cry she slid to the ground, and
bowed her forehead again till it touched his feet.

" King of me, forgive ! It is I who have
brought this evil on thee—caused thee so to suffer

that death seems fairer than life. But—listen only——"

She knelt upright now, her shaking fingers interlocked.

"Beloved," she said. "I—alone—would not dare ask of thee to forgo this thing, to brave the scorn of gods and men. But I have a word to speak that may ease thee of thy strong desire for death. Lord of my life, we be no longer two—but three. In the name of him . . . that other, I make bold to bid thee *live*—and not die!"

Unclasping her hands, she held them towards him, the two pink palms upturned.

Without a word the man opened his clenched fingers, and let fall the twist of pink paper. She caught and imprisoned it in a corner of her yellow *chuddah*, tears of gladness raining unhindered down her cheeks.

Then Gopalu stooped and lifted her to her feet. "Truly the gods have forgiven us, Light of Mine Eyes, seeing they have blessed us after this fashion. We will be diligent in the matter of offerings and prayers, that he may be a son indeed. We will go south at once, to Lahore—a great city and a wide. Thither will Luliana mudheads never track us out. Dost fear to venture so far from thine own place?"

Quick and low her answer came to him.

"For me there is neither near nor far. I follow thee to the world's-end, my King."

So to the world's end they went: and in the swarming city of Lahore they rested at last from the tender mercies of the just. It seemed indeed that the high gods themselves had forgiven them, or forgotten them—which is perhaps more likely.

*TO
HELEN*

REQUITAL

REQUITAL

Love that hath us in the net,
Can he pass, and we forget?
Love the gift is Love the Debt:—
Even so.

TENNYSON.

PART ONE

THE GIFT

I

It was a late autumn evening. The stark white moon of the tropics lit up a narrow lane in the suburbs of Colombo. Down the lane a bullock-cart was jogging at an easy amble. Within the cart sat a female figure; and a few yards behind it, a young man on a restive horse was making desperate efforts to prevent the animal from breaking into a canter.

He could just see the girl's face, in silhouette. She had a good profile; and he enjoyed looking at it without embarrassing its possessor: but his pony, unconcerned with feminine profiles, had other ends in view.

By persistent disregard of his master's hands on the curb, he had just succeeded in edging alongside of the cart, when, with a sharp ting and whirr, a bicycle flashed past. The terrified animal, checked in his impulse to spring forward, swerved violently, and threw out his heels.

There was a crash, a scuffle, a shriek—and the pony, lightened of his load, went careering down the lane, while his rider stood making confused apologies to the profile in the cart.

One of the wheels had slipped into a ditch at the roadside; the pony's hoofs had smashed a shaft; and the bullock, though unhurt, was a good deal perturbed. The girl herself was inclined to be resentful in a dignified manner; but the gleam of a fair moustache, and the frank English voice, effectually disarmed her.

"I was more than a fool," he said, "trying to hold the beast in. I ought to have let him rip, but——" He was just young enough to blush uncomfortably at remembrance of the reason. "I'm really most awfully sorry. Can't I help you a bit?"

"Indeed, you are veree kind. I do not think anee great harm is done. We will soon see."

Her voice took unexpected cadences, rising where one expected it to fall. Her consonants were noticeably crisp; but these peculiarities conveyed nothing to the young man, who was new to the East.

Together they soothed the nervous bullock and examined the broken shaft; he casting furtive glances at her face whenever he fancied he could do so undetected. But women have an occult power of feeling a man's glances; and the girl felt suddenly glad that the shrouded light modified the dusky tint of her skin. Nor was she in any hurry to make an end of their mutual occupation.

"You must please let me get it repaired for you —Miss——?"

He hesitated, with questioning eyes.

REQUITAL

"De Somerez," she answered, with a smile. "Really we *cannot* let you do anee such thing."

"Well, anyway, I must see you safely home. Then you can send someone back to help the man with the cart."

The girl's heart pulsed excitedly.

"Thank you," she replied. "You are veree good."

Balthazar, the pony, having recovered his senses, was grazing at the roadside. The young man slung the bridle over his arm, detached one of the lanterns from the cart, and set out at her side.

From occasional glances under her lids, as she walked, the girl took in every detail of his spare, athletic figure and kindly face. Their talk was fitful and inconsequent, and freely sprinkled with pauses. Each was dimly aware of a growing interest in the other. Both were doing their best to conceal the fact.

By a painted gate in a low wall they came to a standstill.

"This is my house," said the girl. "Good-night. Thank you *veree* much."

"What!—for smashing your bullock-cart, and obliging you to walk home?"

She looked up and laughed. A very pretty laugh he thought it.

"Ah! But you have made *so* much atonement. It was for that I thanked you. Good-bye."

She held out her hand. He took it readily.

"*Au revoir*, I hope."

She was silent, but her heart echoed the hope.

"I shall have to come and ask after the cart, you know," he said casually. "Good-night."

"Good-night."

Bella De Somerez was the beauty of the neighbourhood. None among her girl friends disputed her claim to that honour ; and she herself accepted it with the unruffled calm of conscious superiority.

The neighbourhood in which she shone was the fashionable Eurasian quarter in Kolupitya, one of Colombo's most flourishing suburbs ; and her conscious superiority was based on a complexion several shades lighter than those of her black-haired, dark-eyed companions. She was even spoken of as the fair Miss de Somerez by simple and unenvious souls. Also she was undeniably handsome, with the full, ripe beauty of tropical latitudes.

" And she *can* dress—oo my, she *can* dress ! " little Miss Lobentz confided to her latest bosom friend, in a paroxysm of envy. " The English ladees in their carriages doan't look one half so grand."

Being a dark jewel, she affected brilliant colours. Her ribbons were always more varied, her flounces more elaborate, her hats more daring than those of her limply dressed and entirely eclipsed companions.

She lived with two sisters and a widowed mother, in a trim white house, with a red-tiled roof, and doors and shutters of a harsh uncompromising blue. The verandah pillars were adorned with broad stripes of the same tint. The little path leading to the road was of red laterite, flanked with vivid grass ; and above the low wall a row of clipped ' lettuce ' trees added their brilliant yellow-green to the glaring assortment of colours.

Such was Bella de Somerez's home. " And a veree prettee home too ! " she would declare with pardonable pride.

The de Somerez family considered themselves pure Dutch. As a matter of fact, they belonged to that mixed race known to Eastern Europeans as ' half-castes.' They had money enough to make a brave outward show, which was all they desired ; and their life behind the scenes was of the scrambling, slatternly order dear to their kind.

In the eyes of her neighbours, Bella de Somerez had every reason to be content with herself and her surroundings.

She lacked one thing only—a lover.

True, she might have chosen half a dozen from among the loosely built young men, with brown complexions and jauntily ill-fitting clothes, who composed the marriageable youth of Kolupitya. But she instinctively felt—and that not of pure arrogance—that she was worthy of better things.

So this proud beauty had gone on her way, scoring a succession of little triumphs, yet weary and discontented in the deep of her heart.

Now it seemed that her ambition was to be gratified, the desire of her life fulfilled. A golden moustache and a friendly English voice intermittently haunted her dreams that night.

II

" Oo my ! It is a wonder ! We *oll* may hold our heads higher after this. Onlee to think ! "

" But what for are you talking in riddles, Miss Lobentz. I would be glad of something more than ' onlee to think.' "

Miss Lobentz, chin in air, shot a contemptuous glance at her companion—a fat, comfortable-looking girl, with a waist under her armpits and eyes like restless beads.

"This great news doan't seem to please you veree much," the girl remarked, in all innocence.

"*Me!* What should *I* care? It is onlee that haughtee Miss de Somerez who has caught a lover with a white face, at *last*. And now perhaps the men will have sense to look at other girls. Oo, she is a wonderful beautee. But there *are* others. No doubt this English lover will make her throw up her nose more than ever."

The cushion-figured girl heaved a portentous sigh of envy and resignation, as Lolee Lobentz pursued the galling theme.

"Old Mrs. de Somerez can talk only of the wedding. *Oll* the rupees she keeps in the box under her bed will be thrown in the air for the young ladee's bride-clothes. Oo my! you should hear her! 'My dotter must have things becoming for the wife of an officer who wears the uniform of white-and-gold.'"

"A-ah!" sighed her listener, as she drank in, open-mouthed, these entrancing details; "they have got it all settled mightee quicklee."

"Yes, you may say so, my dear. That Miss Bella has more than two eyes in her head; she has the ring alreadee. Ah! but there may be a slip yet! Who knows? Nort that I should wish it. What matter to me? But it may be, for all that. I wonder if the other officers know about these doings?"

Her sharp face assumed a meditative look; and when she next spoke it was on a different subject.

In the small garden, behind the blue-and-white house, two other people were discussing the same theme from a somewhat different standpoint.

The slim young Englishman of the moonlight night sat on an iron seat under a tree. The girl, whose profile had so much to answer for, knelt at his side, her arms resting on his knee. The boldly cut features showed clear against a far-off background of green; and he was privileged to gaze at them as often as he choose.

He was looking at them now; but the look was changed. The feelings of that night, and of the days that followed, had died too soon—yet not soon enough. He was a man of impulse. He had acted on impulse: and here was the result.

For three weeks he had been secretly engaged to Bella de Somerez; and he was realising acutely that, before very long, he would probably find himself married to her.

"You have to go so *soon*, dearest?" she said, looking up at him. "Oh, how I wish you never had to leave me. You seem to drag the heart out of my bodee, and carree it away with you. But some day you will make me *oll* yours. And then . . . you will never leave me—will you?"

He smiled uneasily at the prospect and passed a hand over her hair.

"But, my dear girl," he rallied her, "even a married man must go to his work!"

"His work—oh yes. But after the work—he comes *home*. Every evening, Eric, I see in my heart how it will be."

Her dark eyes brimmed with a fervour of passion that awoke in her lover a sudden painful sense of responsibility. He had called up this sincere, if embarrassing, devotion from the hidden deeps of her nature; and he had only a little lukewarm scrap of sentiment to give her in return.

"Don't get weaving a fairy-tale out of it, Bella," he toned down her foretaste of rapture awkwardly enough.

"How can I help it? You *are*—my fairee Prince."

"Oh Lord, no. I'm only a very ordinary average sub in a line regiment. And when—we're married——"

The fatal word pulled him up short.

"*Soon?*" she pressed him.

"Oh yes—quite soon. But even then—as I was saying, I'll be just an ordinary average husband——"

"Not 'ordinary average' to me——"

"Oh well!" Her fervour oppressed him to the verge of impatience. "If you *will* make a fancy picture of me, that's your look-out. A fellow can't be—what he's not. We're just a pair of human beings—in love, my Bella. We'll both have to make allowances, one way and another. But I'll do my level best . . . to make you happy."

"Happee? *A-a-ah!*"

It was supreme content made audible; and her lover felt guiltier than ever.

"You will take me away in the great ship, won't you, darling? And show me that beautiful England I so wornt to see. And . . . you will love me . . . always, won't you, Eric? Sometimes, even now, I seem to feel you slipping away from me; as if I must hold you—hold you so tightlee . . . and never let you go."

She laid her hands on his, and gazed up at him with adoration, open and unashamed.

"My dearest girl," he reproached her tenderly.

REQUITAL

"You mustn't let such foolish fancies take hold of you. Haven't I shown I love you in every way a man can. Haven't I said . . . let's be married as soon as ever you like."

"Oo yes—you have said that . . . and manee things. But . . . if your heart was in the words, I would feel it . . . here." She took his hand and laid it against her breast; and he felt the mysterious, unceasing pulse of life within her throbbing heavily.

"That speaks to you, Eric, more than any words. I know I *ott* to be happy; onlee—inside, I am troubled."

If Lolee Lobentz could have seen her now! The haughty nature of the girl, who had never acknowledged a superior in her narrow circle of life, was utterly abased by this new imperious emotion that dominated her, body and soul. Seen against the glow and glory of it, the petty triumph she had craved looked like a tinsel crown in the light of the risen sun. And now, too soon, her brief ecstasy was dimmed by an encroaching shadow. With the terrible alertness of sense that goes with genuine love, she had been quick to feel the barely perceptible change in her lover's tone, in the look of his eyes: and her former pride served only to deepen her new-found humility.

It was this, the Eastern element in her love, that most troubled Eric Horsford, when first he realised how steadfast was the flame of her desire, how fitful his own. Unskilled in mere lip-service, yet genuinely anxious to shield her from unhappiness—he felt almost at his wits' end how to go through with the affair. Yet, go through with it he must—having done the damage.

He took leave of her with an embrace as fervent

as his native honesty could compass : and quit of
her searching eyes, at last, he breathed more
freely. Yet he was neither selfish, nor cold-
hearted. He was merely young : and he began
to see that he had wrecked his life for the gratifica-
tion of a passing desire.

Bella returned to the iron seat, and sank down
upon it exactly where her lover had been sitting
throughout their brief, momentous ten minutes
together. Her whole attitude expressed despon-
dency. No one, seeing her thus, would have
fancied her a bride elect ; nor did she feel much
like one, at that moment. Eric's parting kiss, his
renewed assurance of love were as little satisfying
to her passionate heart as a thimbleful of water to
a man dying of thirst.

The desire of her life, the triumph of her girlish
ambition, was accomplished at last : and to what
end ? She that held her head so high, knew now,
past question, that her heart lay trampled in the
dust—loving, yet unloved. What else could she
make of the change in him, this last week ? And
for all that—beloved or no—she craved this one
man with the unbridled fervour of a passionate
nature that wakes for the first time.

But pride was still strong in her ; though
love was strong also. And the two, in that hour,
measured their strength one against the other.

" He loves you a little, still : only keep him,
and he will grow to care more." It was the voice
of self-delusion, and the words were as pleasant
music to her ears.

" He does *not* love you. If you have any
strength of mind, you will give him up." That
was Pride : and the truth of it pierced her heart.

The sun fell low, and lower. His rays filtered through the 'lettuce' bushes, and played upon the girl's face and figure as she sat motionless, with clenched hands, distracted by the warring voices within her.

At last, very slowly, she rose and went into the house.

III

WHEN Eric Horsford entered the mess ante-room that evening the tail of a smile flickered on every face present.

"What's the joke, old chap?" he asked, seating himself by one of the senior subalterns.

"Mean to say you haven't heard? Well, I give you three guesses!"

He chuckled knowingly; the sort of chuckle that Eric—who went in dread of discovery—could least endure. For all his good nature the secret strain was affecting his temper and his nerves.

"Oh, you're a very funny chap," he retorted scathingly. "I'm not having any guesses, thanks. If you're death on keeping the joke to yourself, you're welcome."

"Can't be did. *You're* the joke, old man. That's the naked truth."

Horsford flushed all over his fair skin; and the senior subaltern laughed aloud.

"You've gone and got your head into a tight place, from all I hear," he went on, when his mirth had subsided. "The C.O.'s on the war-path. You'll smell sulphur, I tell you."

"But what *for*? What's the row?" Eric made a last futile effort to look innocent.

"That's a good one! You sit there, blushing like a maid, and you've the face to ask what for? You're safe for six months on detachment round the coast. Perhaps *that* piece of news'll enlighten you?"

"Damnation! But how did it get out?"

"How could it help getting out?"

Eric looked thoughtful; then he leaned nearer to his companion.

"To tell you the truth, Martin," he said in an undertone, "I *am* in rather a fix. Come into the verandah, there's a good chap. I'd like to tell you a thing or two. It's a quarter of an hour to mess yet."

They went out; and the smile on the faces of the other men deepened to a grin of unconcealed amusement. For most of them such incidents held no hint of tragic possibilities. They used them mainly as whetstones to sharpen the dulled edges of their wit.

Once outside, Eric Horsford gave his brother officer a brief outline of his story.

"God knows what possessed me to take the plunge in such a mortal hurry. But she is not so —so dark as the others: and she's awfully handsome—a real good sort."

"That's all very well. But the fact remains that you've made a blinking fool of yourself. And see what comes of it. You can't possibly carry the thing through."

Eric regarded his friend and counsellor with honest, startled eyes.

"But I'm bound in honour to carry it through. I can't go back on all my promises. That's what I *can't* do."

The older man, though still young, had already

allowed the keen edge of his moral sense to become a trifle blunted. He had a smile, half-envious, half-pitiful, for his comrade's singlemindedness. Yet he was resolved to dissuade him from his folly; and, as Horsford made it a point of honour, he decided to try another line of argument.

"What about your home people—eh?"

The thrust told.

"Oh, drop it. I feel bad enough as it is. I haven't written—since the affair was settled."

"But you'll have to one of these days, if you persist in this craziness."

Eric was silent a moment. Then, in his perplexity and distraction, he cried: "Good God! What a fool I've been!"

"Glad you admit that much. Better take steps to get out of your difficulty at once."

"What steps?"

He hated himself for the eagerness his words betrayed; but Martin noted it as a favourable symptom.

"Well, you'll be sent off to Trinco with the company's that leaving in a few days. Keep clear of the girl till then. Just before starting you can drop her a diplomatic little note—and the thing is done."

"*Done!* It sounds simply brutal. She trusts me—because I'm a Sahib. And I hate not playing fair with a woman."

"Lay this lesson to heart then; and don't let every passing impulse lead you by the nose in future. Impulse is the devil in disguise. That's sound wisdom, though it's I who speak it!"

As the lively notes of the mess bugle rang out, Martin turned and looked quizzically at his companion.

"Have I convinced you, old chap?"

"I don't know."

"Remember, it comes to this: whether you care more for the feelings of your own mother and sisters, or for those of this young lady whom you have known about a month."

"Oh, damn!" The ejaculation expressed pain. "If you put it *that* way there's only one answer."

"You'll drop it?"

"I must."

"Well, buck up, then. You look as guilty as if you had committed murder!"

"I feel it."

That night, when Horsford returned to his quarters, he found an envelope lying on his table; and the handwriting made him tingle all over.

"It's to name the day, I suppose," thought he. "I shall never write that letter—when it comes to the point."

The envelope was heavy when he picked it up—heavy with something which fell into one of the corners as he opened it.

"The ring she promised me. I'm done for! And, by the Lord, I deserve it."

He turned the thing over, and shook it before extracting the note. The ring fell out; perversely alighted on its side, and rolled off into some distant corner.

"Damn it all!" he swore aloud; and tossing the unread note on to the table, he set the lamp on the floor. He then proceeded to crawl round the room, moving his hands carefully over the dusty matting.

He made both them and his knees exceedingly dirty during this performance, besides working himself into a fever of moist heat. But the ring was not to be found.

"Under the chest of drawers—by all that's fiendish!" cried the distracted young man, as he knelt upright, mopping his damp face and brow.

Down he went again—flat on his chest this time—his outspread hand moving cautiously to and fro in the dark.

At last! He had found it this time. He drew it out and took it to the light. Then he started, and changed colour. It was not a man's ring. It was her own ring—returned.

If Horsford had felt guilty before, he felt trebly guilty now.

Replacing the lamp on the table, he opened Bella's note and read:

"Dearest Eric,

"You could not keep your secret, though you tried to very hard. I love you too much to make you unhappy. Here is your ring. Please don't answer this, or try to see me again.

"Bella."

Eric Horsford bent his head, and sat a long while motionless, with the open letter in his hand.

PART TWO

THE DEBT

On a breathless evening of March, Bella de Somerez walked by the winding margin of Colombo Lake—alone.

A low, fierce sun streaked the pale palm-stems with orange light, and set the water itself on fire. Earth and sky palpitated with colour. The red dust of the roads, and the splashes of deeper red among the trees—where the ' flamboyant ' blazed, rather than bloomed—seemed to exhale a heat of their own. Bella took no conscious note of these things. She merely preferred the Lake to the sea-front, which, on late March evenings, is parched, windless, unspeakably dreary.

It was Sunday, and her little world moved all about her in groups and couples. No other girl of her own age, or near it, walked unattended: though none among them excelled her in form or feature. Bella knew this, knew also that her ineffectual rivals were aware of her knowledge, and took a bitter pleasure in the thought.

Her lack of escort excited none of those backward glances and whispered comments which might reasonably be expected from such a community; for it was now three years since Bella de Somerez had been seen otherwise than alone on Sunday evenings: and the brief wonder of former days had died a natural death.

Prying minds had very soon discovered that she walked alone from choice, not from necessity.

REQUITAL

They discovered that one Andrew de Silva, assistant railway-traffic superintendent—a local Dives, whose shirt buttons were of blue moonstones, and his watch-chain of gilded silver—walked alone also, not from choice. It was whispered at tennis-gatherings and tea-drinkings that the proud beauty had been jilted by an English officer—a distinction which amply accounted for the fact that she moved among her chattering neighbours, a being apart.

Silent, and outwardly impassive, she lived over again and again those ardent, tremulous days before love's glory had vanished like the setting sun. She was but four-and-twenty now; and her cup of life held only dregs.

A shrill, familiar voice behind her dispersed her radiant dreams.

" Oo yess, she *was* a rare beauty then, in her *own* eyes, at anee rate. But she could nort keep her officer with the golden moustache, for oll that. She thott herself better than others. Now she sits in the lurch. It happens olways so to those who are so proud ! He ! he ! he ! "

It was Lolee Lobentz, regaling her latest admirer —a clerk from Kandy—with a staccato ripple of acrid comment on her neighbours. Bella had long been a thorn in her flesh, and she did not lower her voice in speaking. It is possible also, that the ' Europe ' hat with its cluster of red roses had a good deal to answer for.

" Old Mrs. de Somerez was readee to cut her throat with vexation," the penetrating voice went on. " Though she wornted us oll to believe that the break-off was Miss Bella's own doing. A likelee storee ! "

At this juncture Lolee tripped past her foe—a

small, pert figure, in pink print that crackled like paper, with cuffs, collar, and 'front' of magenta velvet.

"Good evening, Miss de Somerez," said she. "This is fine news I hear, that your little sister will soon be married. But you ott not to let her outstrip you. A double wedding would be veree prettee!"

And she passed on, leaving the thrust to rankle as it could scarcely fail to do, in the breast of a girl whose veins held three parts native blood.

Almost before the dull flush had left her cheek, Bella was accosted again. This time it was Andrew de Silva—lean, lank, and lugubrious—in a cotton tweed that hung limply about his thin shoulders and fleshless legs.

"Is it no use, Miss Bella, to ask if I may turn and walk with you a little—onlee this once?"

His lustreless eyes hung upon her face like the eyes of a hungry dog. She avoided them in self-defence.

"No. It is no use, Mr. de Silva," she said, quietly.

"Will it never bee *anee* use?" he persisted.

Lolee's taunt sounded mockingly in her ears; but she thrust it aside.

"Never, I am afraid."

A suspicion of weariness in her tone emboldened the man to further pleading; but Bella made a prompt forward movement.

"I must be going on now, Mr. de Silva," she said with polite decision. "Why talk of what cannot be changed? It pains us both, and makes me appear unkind, when I am reallee onlee most unhappee. Good-night."

He watched her comely figure, as she went,

with a new wonder in his eyes. Never before had she made open mention of her heartache ; and he, lover-like, had so far lavished all his concern upon himself.

Bella, rid of him, walked on alone, her eyes heavy with tears.

In fancy, as usual, she was back again with Eric Horsford, among the yellow lettuce trees behind the blue-and-white bungalow ; sunning herself in the light of his English blue eyes ; drawing in deep draughts of happiness with every breath.

But these tender memories stung like a whiplash, and engendered bitter thoughts. Why had she sent him away when her heart told her he had discovered his fatal mistake, but was too honourable to avow it. Why had she, with her own hand, dashed the cup of sweetness from her lips ? Why does a woman ever love a man better than her own soul ?

By what right, she asked herself, with wearisome iteration, had this debonair young Englishman possessed himself of her heart, and crippled her life ?

For Bella was no feminist, to glorify spinsterhood and independence. The blood of a nation of wives and mothers ran in her veins. For all her brave veneer of European culture and European clothes, wifehood and motherhood were, for her, the be-all and end-all of woman's earthly life. Yet —so strangely do East and West commingle—she could not, would not, accept a husband as a mere cloak for her own self-respect. Her small modicum of culture had at least taught her that love alone can hallow marriage. And love she had none to give.

In that black moment she tasted unalloyed the

bitterness of hate. Yet with it there came a great wave of pity for the man whose pain was so closely bound up with her own ; the patient lover, who gave so much and asked so little. If happiness were not for her, she still had it in her power to bestow a small portion on this one man. And why should she not do it, after all ? She would tear those cold northern blue eyes out of her heart —bright, dispassionate eyes, that came between her and the fullness of life. She would refuse to see them any more . . .

A quavering cry checked these valiant, if futile, resolves. Something snapped under her foot ; and looking down, Bella met the reproachful gaze of two liquid blue eyes, so strangely like those she had just banished from her memory, that the blood left her cheek.

The owner of the eyes was a pink-and-white baby, something less than two years old, whose tin treasure had been crushed under her heedless foot.

Instantly she was on her knees in the dust, regardless of Sunday flounces, soothing the injured baby, while her eyes devoured its enchanting curves of cheek and chin. The immature features revealed a shadowy something that set her pulses leaping, half in terror, half in hope.

" Whose child this ? What master's name ? " she asked of the plump Cingalese ayah in charge.

" Master's name Mr. Hossford : Engliss regiment."

" Latelee come back from England ? "

" Yiss, miss. Onlee back in Colombo two months."

" Baby little boy, or little girl ? "

" Little boy," replied the ayah, evidently resenting the possibility of doubt.

To her extreme astonishment, this very strange 'Miss' imprinted a passionate kiss upon the baby's smiling mouth—and withdrew without further speech.

II

THROUGHOUT the ensuing week Bella developed a strange predilection for morning and evening walks. Never in all her life had she taken so much steady exercise in so short a time; for the Eurasian does not count walking among the joys of life.

Twice only was she rewarded by a sight of the blue-eyed boy, radiant in baby finery of embroidery and lawn. On each occasion she spoke a few words to the ayah; and kissed the child, at parting, with the same unaccountable fervour.

Plump Anne Smith grew puzzled; turned the matter over in her shrewd, feminine mind; and finally spoke of it to her mistress. So the third time Bella met the child, and stooped as usual for a parting kiss, Anne Smith interposed.

"Ladee not liking strange Miss to kiss her Sonnee Boy," she said, with suave politeness.

Bella stared, speechless: then she passed on, crushed and tingling.

After that, the emptiness of life fell upon her soul once more. For a full week she scarcely left the house. Her mother buzzed about her with tactless questionings and shrill remonstrances, in vain.

At last—goaded by heart-hunger—she ventured out one early morning, to the Lake's edge; cherishing a nameless hope that consolation, in some sort, might be vouchsafed to her—as indeed it was, after a wholly unexpected fashion.

The sun's full power was not yet established, and the red roads were still mottled with cool patches of shade. In the east a wide belt of cocoanut palms showed black against a saffron sky. Ayahs, with their charges, sauntered chattering along the shadowed side of the way; an occasional early rider cantered past.

Something of the placid peacefulness of the hour stole into Bella's troubled heart, and eased its ache. It was not long, either, before she spied the small figure she sought trotting unsteadily along a shady strip of road, apparently unattended. A nearer view revealed Anne Smith—her charge forgotten—enjoying her morning flirtation over a neighbouring wall.

Bella's eyes clung to the restless white figure adventuring boldly on unpractised feet; now pursuing a bright celluloid ball, now chasing spasmodic squirrels, with shrieks of glee. Though pride would not let her draw nearer, love chained her to the spot. And as she stood thus, lost in wonder, gazing her fill, a rattle of wheels and thud of flying hoofs jerked her rudely back to reality —stark and terrifying.

Down the red road a rickety open *gharri* dashed towards her at a hand gallop. Its occupants were four sailors, well laden with bazaar liquor. A fifth, seated on the box by the abject *gharri-wallah*, brandished the stump of a driving whip, and shouted encouragement to the lank horse. Anne Smith— absorbed in her handsome *appu*[1]—had, as yet, noticed nothing; and out on the roadway, in the track of certain death, tottered Eric's child——

[1] Butler.

In a flash of impulse, too swift for thought, Bella flew to him . . .

Anne Smith turned, with a shriek of abject terror, as her small charge came rolling to her feet —a tearful bundle, smothered in red dust, but unharmed. And there in the road lay the strange 'Miss,' pale and motionless; an ugly stain, that was not dust, spreading slowly over her white skirt.

The *gharri* had pulled up. A couple of sailors, sobered by the catastrophe, were making clumsy attempts to staunch the slow stream of blood. Bella opened her eyes, and, with a low moan begged them not to trouble.

"Damn bad job, this, mate," remarked the Jehu, with a face full of rueful self-pity. "What in thunder——? 'Ere's a gent. P'raps 'e'll give us the tip."

An Englishman on a grey pony was trotting briskly towards them: an Englishman who, at sight of Anne Smith, called out angrily: "Hullo, ayah! What are *you* up to hanging about this beastly Lake road? Your mistress . . . Good God! An accident?"

Before either sailor had decided how to account for the girl, Anne Smith rattled off her own glib version of the affair.

"Yiss master, please master, I going quicklee, jus' now to seaside. Baba running in the road after ball; and this *gharree* coming much *too* quicklee round corner. So this ladee ran right across: save little master, and getting killed."

"Killed? . . . Out of the way, men? Hold my horse, one of you."

Hurriedly dismounting, he leaned over the unconscious girl—and found himself gazing at

Bella's face. *Bella*—and his boy! For a second the conjunction paralysed him: then he turned briskly to the stupefied group at his back.

"Don't stand staring, you fellows. There'll be a big fuss about this presently. Run into that house, one of you—Colonel Field's—and ask for water, brandy—something to carry this lady home on. Look sharp!"

Then, as the men rolled off in one direction, and the *gharri* vanished in another, Eric Horsford slung his bridle over his arm, kneeled in the dust and lifted Bella's limp brown hand.

Her lids parted at his touch. A gasping cry—half-anguish, half-ecstasy—escaped her.

"*Eric!* Is it reallee you? Is he . . . safe?"

A spasm of pain twitched her face, and his hand closed on her quivering fingers.

"Quite safe, Bella. Did you know he was . . . *mine*?"

"Oh, yes . . . I knew."

"God bless you, dear, for this!"

But her lids had dropped again: and he could only wait, in an agony of impatience, for help from the house.

III

At a late hour, that evening, Horsford stood once again on the familiar verandah steps of the blue-and-white bungalow, the scene of his brief, impetuous courting three years ago.

Mrs. de Somerez, tearful, voluble, and incoherent, had just made known to him the doctor's verdict on Bella's condition. Her spine was injured; one leg had been badly crushed, and she suffered terrible pain. She might linger, thus, for a week or ten days. But the end was inevitable—paralysis and death.

Eric Horsford mounted and rode very slowly back to Colombo Fort. The thought of his wife and child hurt him unaccountably at that moment; and he felt half reluctant to face them in the flesh.

Being by nature honest and impetuous, he was doomed to waste a large part of his life in repentance as fruitless as it was sincere; and, in the present case, he felt indirectly answerable for the fate of this brave girl, who had given her own life for a life he prized. How he and his wife were to express their gratitude was a minor question that sorely puzzled him. Even the most superficial acknowledgments would be a delicate matter—the two women being what they were.

Madge Horsford—orderly and spotless without and within—was a woman of sound common sense, strong prejudices, and narrow sympathies. Her knowledge of the East and its mysteries was negligible; and of all its queer products, the half-caste seemed to her the most despicable, the most intolerable. But she was pre-eminently a mother, in the first flush of possession; and the story of Bella's heroism stirred the most responsive chord in her well-regulated soul. Of course she must go and see the girl—do any little thing she could. So, presently, a dripping rickshaw coolie deposited Mrs. Horsford, laden with sick-room dainties, at Bella's garden-gate.

Through the tilted slats of her vivid blue window-shutters, Mrs. de Somerez watched her visitor's approach with mingled satisfaction and awe; satisfaction at sight of the numerous parcels; awe at a nearer view of the little lady's speckless white drill coat and skirt, her air of intimate acquaintance with soap and water—in respect of which Mrs. de Somerez practised a rigid economy.

She greeted her guest with fulsome politeness and relieved her eagerly of the parcels. Mrs. Horsford—chilled by this rude contact with reality—murmured correct commonplaces, with a sudden, distressing sense of their utter inadequacy. For this large, chocolate-coloured woman, with her oil-laden hair and her exuberant figure, innocent of stays, was human after all ; and in very deep trouble. The reddish-brown eyelids were swollen with weeping ; the high voice quavered as she spoke her daughter's name.

" If you will kindlee step through, I will introduce you to my dotter," she said, a shadow of the old pride in her tone ; and Madge followed her across the untidy living-room, her mind divided between genuine pity and an equally genuine desire to get away from it all as soon as she decently could.

The sick-room was long and narrow and oppressively hot : its white walls relieved here and there by Christmas-number supplements, in gilt frames ; and dismal, damp-flecked photographs shrined in varying shades of plush. On the dressing-table was a chaotic medley of toilet accessories and medicine bottles, unwashed spoons and tumblers. By the oval mirror stood a handsome frame of carved wood, with folding doors that hid that solitary photograph from view.

Could Madge Horsford have lifted one of those doors, she would have received a very unpleasant shock. As it was, her eyes sought only the girl on the bed—and rested there in unwilling admiration and surprise.

Bella, in a frilled pink jacket, her hair drawn loosely back from a low forehead, her cheeks bright with fever and suppressed excitement, was a vision of beauty and dignity for which this condescending little Englishwoman had been in no way prepared. Her neatly constructed speech of gratitude died on her lips.

"Mrs. Hossford . . . my dotter," Mrs. de Somerez, proudly punctilious, effected the introduction; and Madge held out her hand.

"Miss de Somerez, it is quite—quite impossible to try and thank you for what you have done," she said simply.

Bella did not answer at once. Her eyes were eagerly scanning the fresh-coloured face of Eric's wife. Suddenly she seemed to recollect herself; a deeper wave of colour crimsoned her cheeks and brow.

"Oh, it is nothing—nothing," she murmured. "Doan't try to thank me, please. I am onlee too happy I saved the child—onlee too happy."

Dreamy exaltation clouded her eyes, and she lay there silent, as if her visitor's presence were forgotten.

Mrs. de Somerez, standing at the foot of the bed, sniffed audibly once or twice, and retired behind a dun-coloured pocket-handkerchief. Madge, severely upright on her wooden chair—gloved hands folded, eyes fixed absently on a limp yellow jelly—sought in vain for some suitable remark to relieve the intolerable awkwardness of the situation.

The heat and the heavy odours of the sick-room oppressed her almost as painfully as the consciousness of the shattered, tortured body lying so strangely still under the bed-clothes. She was not an imaginative woman; but she felt very far removed from her familiar surface world of golf, and tea-parties, and Galle Face. The novel sensation robbed her of her accustomed self-possession.

It was Bella, after all, who broke the silence. She stirred uneasily, with a suppressed moan. Instantly Mrs. de Somerez was beside her; and Madge, as promptly, rose to her feet.

"I think I'd better not stay," said she, concern and relief mingled strangely in her tone. "Your daughter seems to be in pain. *Do* let her have a little more fresh air. And there is some really good jelly in the next room. She might fancy it presently. Keep it on ice." Then, with a last look at Bella's handsome face and closed eyes: "It's very, very sad," she murmured—and slipped out unheeded; devoutly thankful to have got it over.

For a full week Bella lay in her narrow, stifling bedroom, racked in body, strangely elated in mind. Her rapidly nearing death troubled her not at all. There were even moments when her soul seemed to be already released from earth; to be living, as it were, its own glorified life apart. For this, the last act of her life, had given her the keynote of all that went before, had revealed meaning and purpose where she had seen only senseless frustration. Though wifehood and motherhood had been denied her—the glory of giving a man-child to the world—a blessedness scarce less honourable was hers; the blessedness of saving the life of Eric's son. It was enough. At least she had not lived in vain.

To some extent, probably these ever-present thoughts were tinged with the exaltation of semi-delirium; but their power to strengthen and comfort Bella's soul was no less real than the torment of her body. Upborne by their mystical influence, she made light of her own physical agony; saw it simply as the price paid—and paid willingly—for the safety of Eric's child. Thoughts of his wife rarely troubled her now. With the detached mind of the dying, she lived in a blissful, shadowy Paradise of three.

It scarcely surprised her, therefore, when her sometime lover appeared one evening at her bedside, and, kneeling down, bowed his fair head over her hand.

The end was very near then; though she did not know it. Paralysis was gradually, mercifully numbing all sensation; and her mind, hampered no longer by the body's anguish, had become painfully clear.

"I couldn't keep away, Bella . . . I *couldn't*," the man murmured hoarsely, his face still hidden from view. "I feel a murderer when I see you lying there."

Her dry hot hand closed vehemently on his, and a sob broke in her throat. At his touch new life ran in her veins, and she felt that it was a bitter thing to die.

"Oh, Eric . . . Eric, doan't speak so," she pleaded. "I am onlee . . . so proud . . . I was able to do this thing. What is a woman's life worth but to give it . . . in some way, for . . . the man's? And I have given mine for . . . your son! I am not sad any more."

At that he raised his head. With a strange mingling of awe, admiration, and incredulity his blue eyes looked deep into hers.

"Bella—my dear—if only a few more women felt like that, how different we might be!"

She smiled, and shook her head.

"We don't wornt you different. We love you

as you are. And your boy will be a man, too, one day—so like you . . . so veree like you . . . Where is he now?"

"Up-country with . . . my wife."

He looked away from her, and a swift shadow crossed her face.

"Go to him, Eric," she said, a sudden weariness in her tone. "Go to . . . them, and be happee in their love. You ott not to be here."

"But you are not angry with me for coming?"

"Oh, Eric—— Can you *ask*? But you must go now . . . please."

He leaned to her with brimming eyes.

"Let me kiss you, Bella—just for the last 'good-bye.'"

The world and its warning voices were far from her, and death was very near. With closed eyes, and lips half-parted, she awaited her brief moment of bliss.

But at the touch of his lips on hers she fainted.

Mrs. de Somerez insisted on an elaborate funeral, followed by a gathering of the orthodox Eurasian type, throughout which she wept and wailed as befitted a bereaved mother; checking her woe—at intervals—to assure her guests that the wreaths and crosses had been more in number than they had known how to use.

Amongst them all was no rival to a magnificent cross of 'temple flowers,' with a card, bearing the initials E. H. Nor did the grief-stricken mother fail to note the presence in the churchyard of a single Englishman, who, throughout the service, stood apart with bowed head—and thereafter rode back to Colombo at a foot's pace.

1897.

TO
CONNIE

AS OTHERS SEE US
A Two-edged Comedy

AS OTHERS SEE US

A Two-edged Comedy

I

It was a mild, October morning in Colombo; and October is a pleasant month, as months go, in that overrated paradise of coco-nut palms, and very red dust and very yellow 'lettuce' bushes and assiduous insects, of every imaginable and unimaginable variety.

Jim and I were at breakfast in our airy bungalow, through which 'spicy breezes' from the Lake and the neighbouring bazaar and the Indian Ocean wandered at will. Over every door of every room —and Colombo houses bristle with doors—ran a two-feet strip of open carved woodwork: an admirable device for letting in air and letting out the occasional unguarded things better-left-unsaid that will crop up, now and then, even between well-regulated wives and husbands. For dwellers behind these perforated doors, to bicker or backbite is an indiscretion of the first magnitude. For your compound teems with birds of the air who will not fail to 'carry the matter!'

As it chanced, on this particular morning, we were models of discretion. Jim was placidly demolishing a dish of passion-fruit—queer-looking things, like shrivelled grey-green eggs—one of the real delights of the Island: while I—at the risk of getting less than my share—was exploring a certain mail-letter, in an unfamiliar handwriting, signed ' Jessica Morven.' Half a page of polite effusion, working up to a reminder that her ' dear Lavinia '—a former schoolfellow—' cherished affectionate memories, etc., etc.,' made me tremble for what might be coming over-leaf. And sure enough —it came.

The ' dear Lavinia '—wrote her mother—had from girlhood felt a strong spiritual yearning towards ' the teeming millions of our Great Dependency.' The ' dear Lavinia ' boasted a fanatical faith in the Equality of Races and the Brotherhood of Man. For years she had burned to take an active part in propagating her twin ideals: and now—her chance had come. In a week she was starting for Colombo to study the unsuspecting ' Cingalee ' among his native lettuce bushes and coco-nut palms, and to scatter sparks of her burning zeal among her own people on the spot; since their luke-warm attitude was disastrously delaying the Great Consummation. Jim and I, she felt convinced, would be ' different '; and in conclusion she fervently hoped that, for old sake's sake, we would do all in our power to help dear Lavinia to realise ' the dream of her youth.'

I read it all in a swift rush; half amused, half annoyed; and when at length I looked up, Jim was neatly beheading his thirteenth passion-fruit with practised skill.

Jim is a four-square, uncomplicated being: a better husband or soldier you couldn't wish to meet; but, regarded dispassionately, he did not strike me as cut out for the part of helping an ardent woman-of-one-idea to realise her dream.

As for myself—I am cruelly handicapped in the pursuit of Great Consummations and Supreme Ideals by an incurable sense of humour. I began to feel just a little sorry for 'dear Lavinia'; but a good deal sorrier for her hosts-to-be. I could see no way out of it. . . .

Suddenly Jim also looked up and caught the lurking gleam in my eye.

"You're suspiciously quiet, Molly," he remarked with his mouth full, "what's in the wind?"

"Listen," said I, reverting to my letter. "It's an occasion—a rather steep occasion. But we're going to rise to it, like—like Anglo-Indians!"

I may remark, in passing, that we were both incurable Anglo-Indians in the true historic sense of the word: and three years of Colombo had rather aggravated the symptoms, to the faintly aggrieved perplexity of our Ceylon friends.

With unmoved features, I read him every word of that astonishing farrago; and he greeted it with shouts of ribald laughter.

"You jolly well keep clear of her, Molly," he counselled sagely.

"But, my dear, she's the *Occasion*. I'm afraid—I'm very much afraid, we must have her here. In the circumstances, it's the least we can do."

His face fell. "The *most*—so far as I'm concerned. Did you know her well?"

"As well as twelve ever knows seventeen, at school. I chiefly remember her as a lanky girl, with a long neck, whom we impertinent juniors christened the Giraffe."

"Strikes me I'd better put in for leave and organise a 'shoot' up-country."

"You'll do nothing of the kind. You'll stand by your wife—and rise to the Occasion."

"Damned if I will!" was his husband-like rejoinder. But having been Mrs. Jim for ten years I was not dismayed.

II

In a week's time she arrived.

True to my resolve, I drove out to meet the steamer and proffered my invitation, which was accepted with alacrity. Evidently she and Mrs. Morven had also considered it the least I could do; and before we reached the bungalow I recognised ruefully that she bade fair to prove a very steep occasion indeed.

Picture an animated Maypole of a woman, in limp, disconnected grey garments: a woman whose intent, unsmiling eyes looked into you and through you; who talked in capitals and italics; who knocked you down with a volley of questions, and was miles away from the subject before you had even picked yourself up: and you will glean a faint idea of Miss Lavinia Morven.

She talked without ceasing all the way from the ship to the bungalow. She floated down from the dog-cart, face foremost, still talking; caught her foot in a trailing scarf and almost fell prone at Jim's feet. She tried to engage him in an argument, while he was giving the *sais* orders about grain. She followed me into the drawing-room—talking; and later on she preceded us into the dining-room —still talking.

Eating seemed as much of a side issue as her hat and her boots. She put sugar in her soup and helped herself to preserved ginger on my best silk d'oyley without—conversationally—turning a hair.

By the end of the evening our brains were

battered to a pulp ; our high resolve—like Bob Acre's courage—oozing away, out of the palms of our hands.

Later on, I had to reason with Jim and remind him that we were pledged to play up—like Anglo-Indians.

"All very well," he grunted ungraciously. "I suspect her family gave her the boot. It's beyond me how anyone could live with her for more than a week."

"The real miracle," I murmured pensively, "is—how she has managed to live with herself for close on forty years!"

Jim chuckled dutifully. He is impervious to random speculations that for me are the salt of life.

Our guest lost no opportunity of reminding us that we were Anglo-Indians—to quite another tune. She frankly informed us that—for all we had lived ten years in the East—we were abysmally ignorant of the true nature and aspirations of its peoples. This—one is led to believe, by those who know all about it and more also—is the hall-mark of the English in India.

"Your whole attitude to them is wrong—radically *wrong*," she informed us, with that uncompromising candour which is so disconcerting to those who cannot retaliate in kind. "They ask for bread and you give them a stone—for friendship, and you give them official condescension. Never, for a moment, do you regard them as brothers of one blood. Oh, I know, it's just Anglo-Saxon arrogance. And most of us are rather proud of it. In my opinion, we ought to be *ashamed* of it " (the descent of an emphatic fist set the wine-glasses shivering). "After all, the poor things only need a little real sympathy and understanding—the magic of the personal touch, if you know what I mean, to realise the error of their ways and become as clean and civilised as we are ourselves. You probably think I'm talking nonsense—but it's a *fact*."

Her long neck shot out, like the neck of an angry swan: but I was neither to be drawn nor browbeaten by facts with a capital F. I merely smiled the exasperating smile of the sceptic.

Jim—with the obtuseness of your plain, blunt man—fell into the trap and contradicted her outright. It was as if he had pulled the string of a shower-bath. Down it all came on his long-suffering head. For a solid fifteen minutes by the clock, she denounced us as apathetic, unbelieving, hide-bound Imperialists. Having eyes, we saw not. Having ears, we heard not. We sat there and sneered at the faith that was in her. But the fire of her zeal was not quenched. Her real hope lay elsewhere. All she asked was the chance of getting into direct touch with the people themselves. . . .

So we handed her over, with our blessing, to the people themselves; and shrugged our shoulders in the semi-privacy of our bedroom. Any comment louder than a shrug would have been heard all over the house.

Not till we were safely in our saddles next morning—miles away from the bungalow—did Jim vent his stifled wrath and threaten to bolt up-country in earnest, unless I manœuvred my ' infernal Giraffe ' out of the bungalow forthwith.

The woman who is fool enough to reason with an angry man will get what she deserves. But, when the atmosphere was calmer, I mildly pointed out that his demand was irrational and his threat—unsoldierly. If the Giraffe became more than impossible, I might manage to shift *her* up-country.

"Meantime, dear old boy," I urged persuasively, "we've got to see the humour of the thing! Wasn't it the immortal Mrs. Hawkesbee who said ' a sense of humour will support a woman when religion and home influences fail ' ? *I* am Mrs. Hawkesbee's very humble disciple. I foresee we are booked for a comedy ; and the management requests that the audience will keep their seats till the fall of the curtain ! "

My husband emitted something between a chuckle and a grunt.

" All very well to try and be funny——"

" I'm not trying to be funny," I retorted mendaciously. " I'm talking sense. Jim—if we take the Giraffe seriously—we're done for. If we have the patience to wait and the wisdom to smile and smile and hold our tongues—things will happen."

" What things ? " he asked hopefully.

" Keep your eyes open and your temper in hand —and you will see ! "

III

THE first thing that happened was Andrew de Silva—an amorphous, oily-tongued personage, whose verbs were all in the present participle and whose Heepian air of humility captured Lavinia's heart.

We returned from golf one afternoon to find him in possession : and on that solitary occasion, Jim did incontinently bolt from the field.

The stranger was presented to me as ' a most *interesting* Singalese gentleman ' of advanced views and progressive aspirations, who had offered his services as liaison officer—so to speak—between Lavinia and ' the people themselves.'

At this point he also made bold to offer me his hand. Just as I had sufficiently recovered my senses to respond, it was nervously withdrawn. He hesitated, blinking awkwardly—and the minute my hand fell, his shot out again. This time I fairly pounced on it—wondering if I had disgraced myself for ever in Lavinia's eyes.

After that I could only dispense tea—she had already invited him—and make such feeble amends as her cataract of conversation would permit.

Andrew de Silva had arrived at the amphibian stage of evolution; a stage that, in Ceylon, produces singular effects. Your genuine Singalese imprisons his legs in a seamless cotton garment, wrapped tightly round his hips—bath-towel fashion —and called a *comboy*. Now de Silva wore civilised trousers of checked cotton tweed, but had not as yet freed himself from the embrace of his cherished *comboy*. So he compromised by casing his hips in a length of the same tweed, that reached to his knees. His semicircular comb and womanish coil of hair would presently be eclipsed by a dusty black bowler much too small for his head. A tweed coat with blue moonstone buttons; a square moonstone ring and imposing silver watch-chain completed the attire of Miss Morven's self-constituted cicerone and ' friend.'

" He knows numbers of advanced Singalese families," she told me, when at last we were alone. " He is taking me to tea with one of them to-morrow. You won't mind his coming here—

will you, Molly ? We shall have such *oceans* to talk about. He is beautifully clean—isn't he ?—and so touchingly in earnest over it all. He has put himself and his time entirely at my disposal. He scorned the idea of accepting payment for his services——"

And so on and so forth—till I discreetly ' faded away,' having given my superfluous consent to the visits of her accomplice or disciple, whatever—in her perfervid blindness—she supposed him to be.

It was after this that things really began to move : and now—looking back on that strange episode—I am inclined to think that the Heepian amphibian one repaid us very inadequately for the wearisome odd half-hours we spent imprisoned in our small dining-room, cut off from merciful sea breezes, dabbing our moist foreheads, while that fiend of the oily tongue and the present participles lounged at ease among our cushions, discussing the prospects of the politically and nationally awakened East.

There were inglorious moments when rising annoyance at the woman's folly put a severe strain on our sustaining sense of humour. But on the whole we succeeded in keeping our tempers and holding our tongues, while the weeks grew into a month and the visits of de Silva became a matter of almost daily occurrence ; and I began to fear it might be my painful duty to speak to our ' dear Lavinia ' like a mother.

Mercifully, at that point, Fate took the whole affair out of my hands.

We had been out riding, and had finished up with half an hour in the stables. So it happened that we entered the dining-room from the back verandah. Voices warned us that, as usual, the drawing-room was occupied: but the voice of Lavinia was not as usual. And we exchanged hopeful glances as we took our seats.

It was hardly a case of listening. Thanks to our perforated doors we could not choose but hear.

Lavinia, the fervent apostle of Universal Brotherhood, was denouncing her guest in tones of shrill unguarded wrath.

"I'm amazed . . . I'm simply staggered by your presumption . . . your unheard-of impertinence!" (Could she possibly be addressing her whilom pattern of humility.) "I have honoured you with the privilege of my friendship—and I am subjected to—to *this!*"

De Silva's low, hurried expostulation escaped us —what there was of it.

"Go—*go*," Lavinia commanded imperiously. "I refuse to hear any more. I thought I was dealing with a *gentleman*. I never want to see you, or speak to you again!"

She seemed to be shepherding him to the door, whence he fired an inaudible parting shot, in tones from which all Heepian humility had entirely evaporated.

"What the devil has he done?" muttered Jim.

Before I could hazard a guess, Lavinia burst into the room—a changed Lavinia, pale and shaken by jarring contact with reality.

We sprang up, feeling vaguely guilty; and at sight of us she stopped dead. Her breath came in gasps, like dry sobs.

"My *dear*—what's wrong?" I asked with genuine concern.

AS OTHERS SEE US

"I've never been so insulted in my life!" She glanced at Jim's tactfully retreating form. It vanished: and she leaned down to me, lowering her voice.

"Oh, M-Molly—can you believe it?—he—he—he tried to k-kiss me! . . . He had the face to imagine I wanted to m-marry him. Naturally I ordered him out of the house and refused to see him again."

"Very right and proper—from our hide-bound point of view," I commended her gravely. "All the same, he's only human; and you must admit you've encouraged him to expect kinder treatment at your hands."

"*I*—encouraged him?"

She soared above me—five feet eleven of outraged, virginal integrity.

"My dear Lavinia, put white for brown—and what would you say yourself?"

A reddish tinge, that was almost a blush, crept into her face. But her dignity held.

"I suppose I'm dense. But I'm afraid I don't understand you, Molly. You seem to be taking his part. The man is *not* an Englishman. Can't you see that makes all the difference?"

"Naturally—*I've* seen it all along," I answered, speaking slowly that my words might take effect. "Perhaps I may be forgiven if I supposed that, in your eyes, the difference would be all in his favour. You *have* rather rubbed it in, you know—racial equality, Brothers in Blood and all that. And you have so thoroughly acted up to your views, that the man's impertinence is hardly surprising. Perhaps he sincerely wanted to help you in your great work? Narrow people would have been shocked, of course. The others would

have said you had the courage of your convictions.
Personally, I'm relieved to find that your convictions and your courage are still miles apart——"

For the first time, in my knowledge of her, language failed Lavinia Morven. She simply stood there, dazed and stupefied. I could see the fair edifice of her dignity crumbling, as it were, brick by brick.

Suddenly her face worked. She gulped convulsively—and fled vanquished from the field.

There were tears in my own eyes when I hurried to the study and told my tale. Jim—who was sheerly overjoyed—expressed surprise.

"I thought we booked our seats for a comedy, old girl? We'd got to see the humour of it, you know. And, by Jove, I *do* see it—now!"

"Yes—you would," I rejoined, blinking back my superfluous tears. "But still—it's more than a little pathetic when you come to think of it. Poor dear! That was probably her very first proposal!"

"And I'll go bail it's her last," he retorted unabashed. "She simply asked for it. And by the Lord she's got it!"

Had that been all. But it was not all.

Three mornings later, while we were enjoying our early tea, the 'house-boy' came to us with face aghast.

"Master come looking," he stammered. "One very big hole in dining-room. Very bad thief coming in, last night. Master's silver all taking away."

It was true.

Dressing-gowned, as we were, we hurried to the dining-room, and there—speechless with anger and dismay—surveyed our injured wall. Clearly the professional Colombo burglar had been at work on it; softening the clay and laterite with vinegar and cutting out a neat round hole large enough to admit the body of a man.

"So *this* is the last act of your comedy," Jim broke out when we were alone again. "And a pretty price we've paid for our seats! We shall never hear of that damned oily blackguard—*or* of our silver—again."

And we never did.

On this occasion it was the man who had the last word. Lavinia's dressing-table had also been assiduously tidied in the night—jewel-box and all.

She fled back to England, by the next homeward boat—an altered woman; chastened and strangely subdued: and we heard eventually of her safe arrival. Our correspondent added that it was now positively dangerous to talk of race equality or of universal brotherhood in her presence.

"Well, at any rate," said I, "we have the consolation of knowing that we helped to rid the world of one reformer-in-a-hurry. And they are the real stumbling blocks in the path of normal progress."

My mountain-top of philosophy failed to impress my husband. For answer, he gazed eloquently at our denuded sideboard.

Perhaps we did pay too heavily for our shred of consolation, after all.

*TO THE MEMORY
OF PITCHER*

PRIVATE PITCHER
A Tribute

PRIVATE PITCHER

A Tribute

*We aren't no thin red 'eroes, nor we aren't no blackguards too,
But single men in barricks, most remarkable like you.*
                                                    KIPLING.

Of the ways of the private soldier—of his pluck, his endurance, and his unquenchable cheerfulness—civilian England learnt a good deal during the splendid and terrible years of the Great War: but only to his officers and their wives is it given to know how he comports himself in the less heroic field of domestic service.

For the skilled duties of household life he receives no sort of training; yet any day he may be ' struck off duty ' to act as soldier-servant to one or other officer of his regiment. The hidden machinery that works a gentleman's house may be as little known to him as the Chinese alphabet: but he accepts his fate, in peace time, with the same smiling equanimity that he accepts the fortune of war.

In India, the soldier-servant is not. Out there, the least of us has—or used to have—a whole compound full of willing dependents at command. But there came a day when Jim's battalion completed its term of foreign service, dawdled across the ocean in a leisurely transport, sauntered at last into Southampton Docks: and we found ourselves, unbelievably, permanently at Home!

For the Anglo-Indian, Home (with a capital) spells England : not that particular corner of the land sacred to each individual, but the Home of the race.

The peculiar thrill of landing in England, after seven years of the East, the welcoming sense of familiar, yet unfamiliar, sights and sounds and smells, can only be conveyed to those who have known—and they need no telling.

To be Home ' on leave ' is pure rapture. To be Home for good, in a garrison town—on subaltern's pay and a trifle over—has its non-rapturous elements, as we very soon discovered.

India, if not a land of luxury, is a land of many ameliorations ; above all, of unlimited elbow room. The process of learning to live gracefully in a band-box takes time and strains the temper ; but it is the whole duty of the Army—men and officers and wives—to achieve the impossible with a minimum of fuss, and with no undue credit expected or received.

Before we had time to turn round in our band-box—a couple of very ill-furnished rooms—Jim was whisked off ' on detachment ' to Gravesend. A bachelor medical officer nobly lent us his ' quarters '—a small stucco-fronted house in an untilled patch of garden ; and we were grateful. If, on arrival, we felt more than a little dejected— well, India was obviously to blame.

Consider Gravesend—after Delhi ! Consider a six-roomed doll's house, after our spacious, if ramshackle, bungalow ; and in place of a dozen skilled Indian servants, one Gladys Jones—a condescending young lady of no particular capacity —and Private Pitcher, ' struck off duty ' for Jim's benefit—whose capacities remain to be revealed.

These two between them shared the various duties of cook, housemaid, parlourmaid, and valet. No sinecure that last, in the Army, if buttons, accoutrements, and boots for all occasions are to reflect proper credit on the wearer and, incidentally, on the regiment he adorns.

In the matter of buttons and boots, saucepans and floors, Pitcher was indefatigable, to the unconcealed amazement of Gladys, who made it a point of honour never to overtax her own elbow. Even if she knew the meaning of the verb, the state of being it indicates was far from her. She could cook—with a good many reservations. She could wash up—with a creditable tale of breakages. Beyond that, she would do no work that could by any device be evaded. It was Private Pitcher, who by virtue of sheer industry (the less said of competence, the better) became the backbone of our diminutive household—a sufficiently solid one, to judge by the build of him ; and a more than sufficiently willing one, if his honest eyes and capacious smile were a faithful index of his heart.

That they did not belie him, we very soon discovered.

Never was wholesomer, happier soul—so anxious to do the right thing, so certain to bungle it— disguised in clumsy tenement of clay. His zeal far outran discretion ; and for a beautiful good humour he had no match. He whistled and sang so lustily at his work that a lurking sympathy with his exuberant joy in life overruled our sense of domestic fitness : and we decided to suffer his carollings within a reasonable distance of our ears.

If boots and buttons suffered nothing at his hands, the same could not honestly be said of crockery and glass. His unlucky knack of doing the right thing in the wrong place involved a lengthening tale of minor tragedies, which we took far more philosophically than did the culprit himself.

Gladys being complacent, he had a weakness for doing his dressing-room work in the kitchen: and more than once, on such occasions—through the chronically open door—I overheard snatches of frankly bucolic love making, which I had not the moral courage to interrupt by ringing the bell. It was probably innocent, and Gladys struck me as a young lady very well able to look after herself: but the breakages that came of it could not always be so discreetly overlooked. Even had we willed to ignore them, Pitcher's native honesty would not have it so. Whether we were alone, or whether we had company, it was his duty to 'report a casualty' when it occurred. And if Pitcher never talked of duty, he never shirked it.

Take, as an instance, the violent death of my favourite blue-and-white jug.

It was tea-time. A couple of officers had dropped in. Jim had just rung for tea and crumpets, when a sturdy knock heralded the entrance of Pitcher, bearing—in place of the expected tray—the remnants of my treasure, the one presentable milk jug we possessed.

"If ye please, sir, this 'ere come in two jes' now," was his lucid statement; as he swayed from leg to leg in an agony of embarrassment.

"Without assistance?" Jim queried mildly: and Pitcher barely managed to repress an impermissible grin.

"Well, sir, not precisely. Ye see, I was a-brushin' of yer overalls . . ." A nervous pause. "On—on the kitching table; an' me brush come along a shade too quick an' . . . an' it split the jug right in two—an' I'm orf'ly sorry, sir."

In face of remorse so genuine, it were cruelty to try and ease him by treating the matter as a joke. Jim had rather a knack that way; but, to my relief, on that occasion, he toned it down.

"You've not ruined us this time, Pitcher," he reassured the culprit soothingly. "It might come a bit expensive, though, if you do too much of your valeting in the kitchen."

"Yes, sir—it might. I never give the matter a thought," Pitcher admitted, with a reproachful glance at the milk jug that had betrayed him. And he vanished forthwith.

It was Gladys—with cap awry and pursed lips—who brought in the tea-tray, glaringly disfigured by a plebeian substitute for my murdered treasure.

Never again, to my knowledge, did Pitcher brush Jim's overalls on the kitchen table; but in the demolishing of glass and crockery he continued to excel.

"My father was an 'orse-breaker. Seems like I'm a china-breaker!" I heard him confide ruefully to Gladys, on a day when he had smashed three breakfast cups in succession.

Nor could he rest content with such fragile spoils. There came an evening when he edged nervously into our presence through the half-open door, guilt written all over his broad face; and we knew—or thought we knew—from experience, what to expect.

"If yer please sir, I've—I've just bin an' knocked the 'andle out of a saucepan," he gravely informed us.

"Well played, *indeed*, man!"

Jim laughed outright, discarding all consideration for the culprit; while Pitcher stared hard at the carpet with twitching fingers and faintly twitching lips—for all his honest distress.

"How the devil did you manage it?"

"Well, y' see, sir, I was carryin' in the tray, an' I shoved a bit too near the range; an' the 'andle got caught in my pocket, sir, without me knowin'. An' before y' could say knife the 'ole concern went bang on the floor. An' the 'andle come out when it fell."

"Ah!" Jim glanced at me. "One of the hirelings, eh, Molly? Hirelings are the devil."

I ruefully agreed with him; but, for a subaltern in the British line, it is hirelings, hirelings all the way.

"If ye'd jus' step along and see, sir," Pitcher insinuated modestly—almost as anxious to show off his latest casualty as the country cottager to exhibit her sore leg.

"It might be as well," Jim agreed, collecting me with the tail of his eye.

Solemnly proceeded by Pitcher we stepped along to inspect the ruins—and were confronted by a flood. The kitchen floor was drenched with the greasy, miscellaneous contents of the slaughtered stock-pot; and from the vantage ground of her chronically untidy table Gladys surveyed the scene with delight unfeigned.

Serious reproof was beyond us. It was much that we managed to retire from the field with our dignity intact, leaving those two to clear up the mess in their own individual fashion. I hazard a guess that it was Pitcher who did all the clearing up, in the certain hope of ultimate reward.

But if the kitchen had its temptations and its pitfalls, these last were as nothing to the mysteries of his own particular region, technically known as 'the front of the house.'

PRIVATE PITCHER

In the rôle of parlourmaid Pitcher surpassed himself. Never, in all his five and twenty years, had he laid a gentleman's table or handed a dish or shown a visitor into a drawing-room. And we also endured our share in the ordeal of his initiation, during that first summer of English housekeeping under difficulties.

Imagine my feelings, on a certain afternoon, when our inimitable soldier-man flung open my drawing-room door, planted himself foursquare on the threshold, with outstretched fingers and twitching thumbs, and announced in a stentorian whisper: " If ye please, 'm—someone to see you."

Behind him towered a large woman—wife of a Gravesend magnate—gazing with injured amazement at his broad blue serge back. Before I could reprove him, he had executed a smart right-about turn, and vanished—leaving the burden of explanation to me.

On Jim's advent, he was summoned and solemnly ' put through his paces ' in the matter of front-door etiquette. Except for the poor fellow's visible anguish, I believe Jim rather enjoyed it: but his zeal to spare me further embarrassment was vain. When the next visitor appeared, Pitcher—in terror of his life—opened the door to her and fairly fled.

So much for the drawing-room: and in the dining-room also he exhibited a beautiful incompetence with undiminished zeal, and a concentrated earnestness that made criticism seem sheer barbarity.

He marched about our diminutive room to the tuneful accompaniment of ammunition boots; stood rigidly ' to attention ' behind Jim's chair ; and, at the end of each course, carried the laden tray jauntily down the passage, whistling as he went, shedding knives and forks and spoons at every second step.

Very tactfully, at last, Jim pointed out that the ideal waiter, like the ideal good little boy, should be seen and not heard. By way of encouragement, to his great delight, we gave him a pair of leather slippers: and ever after Pitcher—who could do nothing by halves—crept round the table with cat-like stealth, his shoulders bent, his good-humoured face set like a rock, till we dared scarcely exchange glances for fear of ignominious collapse.

Once outside the door, he was his own man again. To judge from the accompanying clink of glass and rattle of falling plate, he must have fairly danced from the dining-room to the kitchen door.

One might laugh at him, or swear at him—and we sinned very often in both respects: but when unexpected trouble came upon our doll's house, then was the hidden gold of Pitcher's nature radiantly revealed.

His own share of the trouble was simple and inevitable—he had fallen in love with Gladys. He may have fancied he concealed the fact from us; but capacity for concealment was not in him. It was written all over his shining face. And we looked for the equally inevitable result. But Gladys, it seemed, had a head on her shoulders, and a good conceit of herself, to boot. If she permitted a liberty here and there, it was all in the day's work. Beyond the day's work there were Sundays and 'evenings out'; and there were men of more exalted rank than a mere private— and a clumsy fellow at that—willing enough to take up with a personable young woman.

As August blazed towards an end, and work became a weariness and a burden, the incipient situation took a new turn. Gladys began to add wide and wider margins to those cherished evenings out, that kept Pitcher in a transparent state of strain : so transparent that merely to look at him or ask him a question gave one an awkward sense of intruding on the privacy of his distress. On each occasion Jim spoke sternly to the delinquent. On each occasion she wept and excused herself— and repeated the offence. And to Pitcher's visible distress was added a no less visible dread that Jim would at last lose patience and hurl his final thunderbolt—' a month's notice.'

But Gladys was woman enough to secure the last word.

There came a night when she returned not at all. Morning brought no sign of her. And Pitcher, tactfully questioned, staring very hard at nothing, confessed his own suspicion that a certain handsome corporal of ill-repute was responsible for all the trouble. To Jim he conveyed a delicate hint that perhaps the man had at last ' over-persuaded ' her—and she had not dared to come back.

Small loss for us ; but for Pitcher—who shall hazard a guess ? Was an idol shattered ? Or did he stolidly accept, as a matter of course, the facts of life and the way of a corporal with a maid, if she were foolish enough to put temptation in his path.

Inquiries, conducted by the hapless man himself, proved that his suspicion had been too well founded : and that Gladys—having exhausted her stock of washable excuses—had taken refuge with a married sister in the town. Pitcher had been privileged to see her. He explained the position with a brevity and frank simplicity that must have won

our hearts had they not been won already. And
later in the day, it was he who hoisted her shiny
black trunk on to a handcart and trundled it to
the married sister's address.

That done, he returned to barracks, looking a
few shades graver than usual, and announced his
willingness to take our entire doll's house on to
his own very broad shoulders, till the leave season
should bring our time on detachment to an end.

It was only a matter of five weeks; and he
would prefer it, he added, looking desperately
uncomfortable, to 'running in harness' with
another young woman—if we could put up with
him and his ways. We decided, without hesitation,
that we would sooner put up with our faithful
private and his ways than sample any temporary
'general' of them all. And the good fellow
beamed on us as if we were doing him a favour out
of all proportion to his own sporting offer.

If we secretly wondered how it would be, Pitcher,
I feel sure, would have forgiven us the doubt more
readily than we could forgive ourselves.

All that man might do, and a good deal more,
that indefatigable soldier did. From morning to
night, through those stifling August days, he
worked—without a shadow of grumbling or of
weariness—at every variety of household task,
ably hindered by myself. Cooking, alone, was
beyond him. He announced—with a brick-red
glow of pride—that he could fry chops and bacon
and boil potatoes; and on these, I am convinced,
he would fain have had us live, that the honour
and glory of serving us might be his alone. Since
we could not quite humour him to that extent,
we gratefully accepted the offer of the mess cook
to prepare our joints and puddings and speed them

across the blazing parade ground by the hand of our devoted soldier-servant.

In this amateur fashion we tided over the few weeks that remained till the opening of the leave season broke up our makeshift home; and Pitcher, the 'china-breaker,' Pitcher, our prince of servitors, returned to his niche in C Company ranks—and I saw his face no more.

A year later, however, we heard of him from his Company Commander, while we were away again, on winter leave.

"Your friend, Lance-Corporal Pitcher," he wrote, "has just added a wife to the strength of the regiment—an old flame, I believe."

"Gladys!" we exclaimed in one breath. And it was so.

Gladys, chastened by misfortune, hampered by an unfathered child, had attracted Pitcher, it seemed, even more strongly than the unblemished Gladys, with her maidenly nose in the air, of our doll's house days. What qualms, what jealousies, what delicate reluctances kept him from her for nearly a year, is a matter outside speculation. The man's heart was his biggest asset. It had triumphed over his moral sense. It had driven him to seek her out and persuade her to marry him.

It was more than she deserved: but that is life.

1915.

TO THE MEMORY OF
LORD ROBERTS

BOBS BAHÅDUR

BOBS BAHÁDUR

(SOME AFGHAN AND INDIAN REMINISCENCES)

After me cometh a builder. Tell him I, too, have known.
                                                KIPLING.

"NEVER say of me that I am dead!" wrote Robert Browning, shortly before the inexorable summons came to him:—the summons that for him spelt 'change and growth.' And it is a fact that there are certain men so transcendently alive that the conventional phrase 'He is dead' sounds like a mockery of the truth. Browning himself was one of these; and Lord Roberts was another. It still seems hardly believable that never again shall we see the small soldierly figure—erect and alert to the end—that filled so great a space in our national life.

> "Never again the war-wise face,
> The weighed and urgent word,
> That pleaded in the market-place
> Pleaded, and was not heard."

How deeply he felt that tacit refusal to hear his impassioned call to arms can be realised by his intimates alone: yet it may safely be said that he sorrowed, not for the slight to himself, but for England's peril—veiled from her eyes by a tissue of hypocrisies woven by masters of craft and guile.

It is said that he had fathomed the mind of the Kaiser and his military caste; but the Kaiser was always clever enough to make skilful use of his close connection with our Royal Family; and Lord Roberts, for obvious reasons, could not say publicly all that he knew. He could only exhort and plead and wear himself out with the strain of public speaking, of wrestling in vain with ignorance, indifference, and contempt. He could only spend himself to the utmost; and it still remains for England to prove that this his last—and perhaps his greatest—campaign was no failure after all.

In this matter of speaking to deaf ears, it is interesting to recall how, seventy-five years ago, General Abraham Roberts—clear-eyed and courageous as his son—was spending himself in the same thankless task that earned him nothing save unpopularity and loss of his post.

Brigadier Roberts was at that time serving with the Army of Occupation in Afghanistan; a conquered and friendly Afghanistan, according to the roseate conviction of Sir William Macnaghten, British Envoy at the Court of Shah Shuja ul Mulk. Roberts thought otherwise, and felt it his duty to say so plainly, like the honest man he was. He did not hesitate to denounce as ' most objectionable ' the site of those hapless cantonments on the plain, and he inveighed, more than once, against the folly of keeping all the Government treasure in Kabul city for the convenience of Sir Alexander Burnes. He did not believe in either a conquered or a friendly Afghanistan ; but Macnaghten had made up his mind on that subject, and did not choose that it should be unsettled by a pessimistic Brigadier.

It was in connection with his father's difficulties at Kabul that I began a correspondence with Lord Roberts—a correspondence valued by me on every count ; most of all, perhaps, because it brought home to me all that one had heard of his unfailing courtesy and kindliness and readiness to help, no matter what greater issues might be absorbing his time and energy.

That my subject had a special attraction for

him goes without saying. His father's share in the first Afghan War, his own greater share in the second one, and in the whole thorny problem of India's frontier policy, conspired to keep his interest in all that concerned Afghanistan fresh and keen. For this reason, among others, no excuse seems needed for quoting two of his letters of comment and reminiscence on a subject so near his heart:

" Your statement that Sir William Macnaghten manœuvred the removal of Roberts from Kabul, is quite correct," he wrote in August 1912. "For though my father did resign, his recall was inevitable after Macnaghten's letter of October 30 to Lord Auckland's private secretary.

" Two things I learnt from my father's experience : one, to insist on my having supreme political as well as military authority ; the other, to keep the troops, treasure, and supplies together. I was hard pressed by some of my senior officers to make the Bala Hissar my headquarters. I refused, because I found the accommodation was far too limited . . . Sherpur, the cantonment built by Sher Ali, was the only place that would suit. This was imperfectly defended and far too large, the perimeter being quite four miles. It had a good wall on the south side, partial walls on the east and west, and on the north were the Bemáru Heights—two low hills divided by a broad road.

"I was fortunate in having a clever Commanding Engineer, who filled up the gaps between the hills and fortified, as far as possible, the open spaces on the east and west. The Bemáru Heights were the key of the whole position, which was on the actual site (considerably more extended) of the ' folly on the plain,' the surrounding earthworks of which could be clearly traced. It was from

Bemáru that the Afghans began their attack on our troops in 1841 ; and I often wondered, during the ten months I was in Kabul, how any soldier could have decided to place troops on a plain without holding the only rising ground within musketry fire. That, no doubt, is what my father had in his mind when he pronounced the site to be ' most objectionable.' "

This personal description of his own position in 1879 has a special interest in connection with two stories of those critical days told by officers who were serving under him at the time—stories which strikingly bring out the qualities that made Lord Roberts beloved as a man and idolised as a leader by all the troops he commanded, whether in peace or war.

As is well known, the Kabul Field Force included those two magnificent regiments, the 72nd and the 92nd Highlanders ; and the story goes that on St. Andrew's Day, 1879, the 92nd distinguished themselves by an exploit probably unique of its kind.

On that great night of the year, Highland regiments are practically given a free hand : and by eleven o'clock the men had drunk themselves into that exalted condition in which all things are possible—though not expedient !

It was then that one—less bemused than his fellows—made the dire discovery that they had omitted to call on the General and wish him luck in the name of Scotland's patron saint. The 72nd had sent him a deputation earlier in the evening. It was unthinkable that the 92nd should be one whit behind their ' brither Scots ' in honouring the leader whom they would all have followed into Nebuchadnezzar's furnace, had it pleased him to give the word.

What was to be done ? Only an hour of the sacred day remained. Except for themselves and the sentries, the whole cantonment was abed and snoring. It would never do to let such a trifling consideration stand between the General and his luck. He might be needing every ounce of it before reinforcements arrived. The promptings of superstition and devotion were strong ; the promptings of whisky probably stronger still.

They hesitated no longer. There and then a deputation was formed.

Two hundred men, in varying stages of exaltation, briskly fell into line. A subaltern was commandeered to lead them and the band rose loyally to the occasion, each man playing his own tune in his own time with the full power of his lungs.

Already the snow lay thick on the ground ; and through it they tramped to the General's quarters—the swing of their kilts more than a little erratic here and there.

It transpired that Sir Frederick was in bed, probably asleep. Dared they wake him ? On consideration they decided to take the risk sooner than deprive him of his luck.

It was at this juncture that Captain Pole Carew (now General Sir Reginald Pole Carew, K.C.B.) was startled out of his first sleep to find Sergeant Macdonald (who afterwards became Sir Hector Macdonald) sitting on the edge of his bed.

Captain Pole Carew's hut adjoined the Chief's quarters ; and Macdonald—many degrees more sober than his comrades in adventure—implored the captain to get up and save the General from the tender mercies of two hundred uproarious and devoted Scots.

Needless to say that officer lost not a moment. Flinging on a garment or two, he reached Sir

Frederick's door simultaneously with two huge Highlanders, brimful of whisky and the courage that whisky gives.

"All right, men. I'll give the General your greeting," he said soothingly: and went in—leaving the two heroes not altogether content with the sudden change of programme.

Very soon he reappeared with a kindly message of thanks for their good wishes, adding: "As the General is very tired, he hopes you will excuse him from coming out to thank you in person."

This was not at all what they had bargained for. They had come, in full war paint, to give the greetings of the day to their adored Chief. Greet him they must—whatever!

Even while Captain Pole Carew reasoned with them, one strapping fellow managed to slip behind his back—and the thing was done.

In a very few moments the small, erect figure appeared on the threshold—and was received with rousing cheers.

'Bobs' took it all in admirable part; laughed heartily; wished them God-speed, and bade them get to bed as soon as possible.

This friendly command they condescended to obey and departed in a blare of triumphal discord, immensely satisfied with themselves and all the world.

Captain Pole Carew—annoyed at having failed to save his Chief from disturbance—spoke his mind when they were left alone: but annoyance was far from the heart of 'Bobs,' cold and sleepy though he was.

He understood. It was part of his genius that he could be counted on to understand; that he could see things through another man's eyes almost as clearly as through his own.

"Well, well, my dear fellow," he said, smiling at the other's concern. "One must make allowances on these occasions! They do such splendid work for me whenever I ask them, why shouldn't I do a little thing for them?"

Splendid work they did, only a week later—those of them that got safe home to bed that night. For the cantonment was intersected with many water-cuts, where the drifted snow lay so deep that all trace of them was lost. Into these several of the gallant two hundred fell, when stumbling back to their camp. And by the morning they were all dead men.

That hilarious St. Andrew's night was their last on earth.

Early in December—after months of surface calm, that had failed to deceive the 'pestilent *zabbardusti*[1] little General Sahib'—the storm broke in earnest. From every quarter the tribes were hurrying to Kabul; and Sir Frederick Roberts knew that he and his handful of picked regiments would soon be called upon to hold Sherpur against nothing less than a national uprising, with small hope of help either from the Khyber column or the force at Kandahar.

Sagaciously, he had forestalled the evil day by laying in an ample stock of provisions and strengthening his fortified cantonment to the best of his power. Now, with characteristic wisdom and daring, he took the initiative, and struck the first blow.

Five days of vigorous fighting against heavy odds culminated, on the 13th, in the capture of the Takt-i-Shah, a commanding hill above Kabul city; and it was the 92nd Highlanders, supported

[1] High-handed.

by the Guides, who achieved that brilliant feat of arms—to the glory of 'Bobs Bahádur' and the admiration of all beholders.

Not until the action was over did General Roberts realise the full significance of victory; for not till then did he learn that a great concerted attack on the British cantonment had been planned for that very night. As it was, a chastened enemy thought better of it; and the 14th opened with another fine exploit, the storming of the Asmai summit, a position of enormous natural strength close to Sherpur: the 72nd this time, with half a company of the 92nd—and once again the indomitable Guides.

Soon after daybreak the troops had marched out of the Western Gate, known as General Roberts' Gateway; and it was on the flat roof of this convenient look-out that the Chief himself paced to and fro, to and fro, while Captain Holdich, R.E. (now Sir Thomas Holdich, K.C.M.G.), with his telescope at his eye, observed and reported the progress of events.

Away towards Kabul, a Gurkha regiment held the Takt-i-Shah; on the Sher Darwaza heights, behind the city, were concentrated the troops of Macpherson's brigade. All the hills due west of the Gateway were held by the Afghans in force. What that force amounted to it was not yet possible to tell; the bulk of the enemy being in the Chardeh Valley, on the far side of the hills.

Restless standards, red and green, revealed his whereabouts to the watcher who reported while he watched.

The Highlanders' charge had driven those standards altogether from Asmai and there seemed good reason to hope for a general retreat before dusk. But it soon became evident that on a low peak to the right—known as the Conical Hill—

events of some importance were developing. The peak was held by four mountain guns and a party of infantry, with a picket of the 72nd thrown out upon a lesser rise between the battery and a farther hill, where standards flitted well out of harm's way.

Unluckily, for some reason, that outlying picket was withdrawn—a trifling move in itself, yet a prelude to disaster. The retreat proved to be merely a case of '*reculer pour mieux sauter*.' Over in the Chardeh Valley, unseen by the watcher on the Gateway, reinforcements were pouring in, and the tribes were rapidly re-forming for a counter-attack on the lost positions.

If the General, still pacing up and down, grew anxious or impatient, neither voice nor manner betrayed the fact. The whole man was concentrated on the work in hand. His very lack of inches seemed to intensify the effect of a concentration that no counterpull could divert a hair's breadth from the main issue.

And now the telescope revealed a fresh outcrop of red standards, that fluttered like poppies in a wind, not only on the farther hill, but on the ridge that linked it with the cone. The picket that might have checked them was gone. Nearer and higher the standards kept bobbing up, in defiance of a warm reception from the guns. Others appeared on the spur below Asmai and opened a cross fire on the Conical Hill. It was the signal for a determined attack from all points at once; and very soon Captain Holdich realised, with dismay, that things were not going well on the cone, that the guns were in danger of being swamped by the enemy.

He reported the horrid circumstance, which 'Bobs' stoutly refused to believe. Yet belief was forced on him before many minutes were out.

A helio-flash, from Macpherson above Kabul, told of ever more Afghans hurrying across the plain to the west of Asmai.

Back flashed the question: " Are they in great force ? "

The answer was conclusive: " The plain reminds me of Epsom Downs on Derby Day."

That settled matters. The worst confronted him.

" What struck me about him then," said Sir Thomas Holdich, who tells the story, " was the total absence of any strong expression of feeling ; the calmness with which he recognised that we were swamped by numbers and would have to face a siege."

It was then, also, that he revealed his remarkable capacity for adapting himself to a new position—a capacity that can scarcely be over-estimated as a main factor of success in war.

At that critical moment there were only two alternatives for his little army—annihilation or prompt retreat. Could they be recalled in time ? His aides-de-camp had all been dispersed, with orders to different units in the field. Captain Holdich alone remained.

Once again ' Bobs ' paced the length of the flat roof ; and in those few minutes all was decided.

Captain Holdich was dispatched to recall the cavalry, somewhere out on the snow-covered plain, with orders to collect messengers, as he went, to withdraw the rest of the scattered troops.

The force proved worthy of its leader. That sudden retreat—a move of supreme difficulty and danger—was finely carried out ; and by five o'clock the whole division, bringing in killed and wounded, was concentrated within the walls of Sherpur.

So ended December 14, that had opened with

the gallant storming of Asmai; and so began the ten days' siege, throughout which that undaunted garrison—now reduced to five thousand fighting men—more than held its own against overpowering numbers, that swelled steadily till, in the final assault, the Afghans were reckoned nearly a hundred thousand strong.

The tale of that siege has often been told. It is the sort of tale that will always bear repeating. A thumb-nail sketch telling how the final assault was converted into a brilliant victory has lately appeared in these pages [1] in connection with an Afghan incident entitled 'Light Marching Order.' I may add, in passing, that the inner history of that unique adventure was unknown to Lord Roberts till he read the tale in type; and he thoroughly enjoyed the joke against himself. "I was much amused," he wrote, "to learn the devices that had been resorted to in order to get that soda-water machine to Kabul!"

To return to greater matters in connection with that famous campaign: on no occasion was his magnetism as a leader, his power to get the last ounce out of the troops who worshipped him, more strikingly revealed than during the famous forced march from Kabul to Kandahar, under a scorching August sun.

Throughout those three unforgettable weeks he spared neither himself nor them—spared himself, indeed, least of all.

"At the end of every day's double march," writes an officer who shared in that achievement, "he used to get on to a fresh horse, late in the afternoon, and ride back all along the line, with a cheerful word of encouragement for any tired, footsore man who was straggling in; even for his

[1] *Cornhill.*

unfortunate rearguard officer, who brought up the extreme tail of his column."

Testimony of the same kind comes also from Dr. Joshua Duke.

"As one who actually *walked* the whole distance," he says, " I can honestly assert that it could not possibly have been done except under a General like Sir Frederick Roberts, who was believed in by all ranks, and who inspired a determination to fall down rather than give in."

Tales such as these, told by officers who knew him through the greater part of his service, give but a glimpse—though a welcome one—of a noble-hearted soldier, whose 'genius to be loved' rivalled that of Nelson himself. Like all great soldiers, he doubtless owed much to what the modern man calls 'luck,' and the early Victorian man called 'the hand of Providence.' It was George Eliot, I think, who said that the brave make their own luck; and certainly, in most cases, when a man is labelled lucky by his fellows, it would be safe to add the preliminary letter and write him down plucky.

In respect of this fundamental virtue—as in all else—' Bobs Bahádur ' was a soldier from his heart to his finger-tips. And he was something more. To the soldier qualities—that are the back-bone of all fine character—he added a rare serenity and lucidity of spirit; a faith in God and human nature that neither doubt nor disappointment could shake; and that indefinable something which can only be called personality. There were minor traits, also, equally endearing: the royal memory for all with whom he came in contact, the sympathy that was never merely superficial; above all, the thoughtful consideration for others—at all times and in any emergency—which, even more than the heroic virtues, makes a man beloved.

Stories illustrating this engaging trait are legion. One or two must suffice here.

A certain colonel had returned, victorious, from one of those difficult frontier expeditions which attract small notice at home. Summoned to the Chief's office he reported the result of his operations.

'Bobs,' being very busy at the moment, merely remarked, "I'm writing my dispatches. They are nearly done."

Before they were done he looked up again. "Well—how did the affair go off?"

The Colonel, in soldierly language, told his tale.

"Good—very good. Very well done," said 'Bobs,' adding, with his kindest smile, "Now, I'm sending a telegram to my wife. Wouldn't you like to send a word to yours? She will be anxious."

The Colonel's gratitude may be imagined—and the thing was done. There were more dispatches to write; but 'Bobs,' who could think of a wife's anxiety, could also think of the husband's immediate need.

"You've had a hard day of it," he said. "You must be pretty hungry. My dinner's waiting. Do sit down at once and help yourself."

Just a trifling act of courtesy at a busy moment; but it was typical of the man. No doubt 'Bobs' added another to his long list of devoted worshippers that evening.

Again: Some friends of mine were travelling in Scotland, with him and Lady Aileen, a few years ago. Before the train started, a poor old Irishman, hearing of his presence, fell into talk with my friend's husband, and poured forth his enthusiasm with Hibernian eloquence. If he could once shake hands with Lord Roberts, he declared, he would die happy.

The remark was inevitably repeated. At the very next station, out sprang Lord Roberts, made his friend find the old man, shook hands with him, wished him luck, and departed, leaving that amazed hero worshipper in a seventh-heaven of bliss.

My own experience of his unfailing readiness to help in every direction was naturally in connection with my two Afghan books. Some few months after *The Hero of Herat* came out, I was surprised —and something more—to get a note from Lord Roberts expressing a wish to know whether the book was being widely read, since he himself found it ' intensely life-like and interesting.'

Would anyone but ' Bobs,' one wonders—with the National Service Campaign in full swing— have troubled to make ' kind inquiries ' as to the sales of a mere book ?

Later on, when I wanted a picture of the Bala Hissar for *The Judgment of the Sword*, I again had occasion to write to him and one or two others who might possess sketches of the place. He was away motoring, at the time ; but he wrote at once suggesting that, if I had a camera, I should go over to Ascot and photograph a water-colour of Kabul, by Sir Thomas Holdich, that hung in his drawing-room. I had no camera: and in the end Sir Thomas Holdich lent me his own sepia sketch of the fortress for reproduction.

Naturally it did not occur to me to trouble Lord Roberts with any further mention of the subject : but very soon this kindest of men wrote again : " I am anxious to know whether you have succeeded in getting the picture for your book. If not, shall I have my Kabul water-colour photographed by

BOBS BAHÁDUR

the man here and send you a copy ? Don't trouble to answer unless I can be of any use."

It may be imagined whether I obeyed that last characteristic injunction.

The letter he wrote me after reading *The Judgment of the Sword* is the second of the two I have mentioned as worth quoting, on account of his frank comments on the men and events of that disastrous time.

"I cannot tell you in a letter how intensely interested I have been in *The Judgment of the Sword*. It appeals to me in a way that I cannot describe. The whole story brings back to my recollection what I had heard from my father, the Wallers, and others who were in Afghanistan during the first Afghan War; and what I myself saw of the cantonment site at Kabul—the Khurd-Kabul and Jagdallak Passes, the hills where the last stand was made near Gandamak, and Jellalabad, during the second war. It makes one's blood boil to think of the obstinacy and ignorance of Macnaghten, the want of nerve of poor Elphinstone, and the crass stupidity of Shelton; and I thank my stars that I insisted on being given supreme control when I was ordered to Kabul, to avenge the massacre of Cavagnari and his escort, in 1879.

"Sale's conduct has always been a mystery to me—why he left his wife behind ? Why he did not return to Kabul when he heard of the outbreak . . .

"Then I have never understood why Pottinger and others pressed for the occupation of the Bala Hissar, when the insurrection broke out and they must have known that Shah Shuja had no power.

"The occupation of the Bala Hissar would have ended in the Force being starved. Akbar Khan showed plainly that this would have happened.

"Shelton's behaviour was beneath contempt. How could any Court-martial have acquitted him? Lord Ellenborough's treatment of Pottinger, Mackenzie, and Lawrence was disgraceful. Poor Pottinger! What a sad career he had; everything against him; and what a splendid fellow he was!"

No tribute to Lord Roberts, however inadequate, would be complete without a passing comment on his special relationship to the Indian Army—the troops he loved as his own children, and who responded by almost deifying him, as they deified John Nicholson in Mutiny days. The story of that relationship alone would need an article to itself.

A glimpse of what that army feels for him we have lately had from the Indian trenches in France.

"He was not only our Colonel-in-Chief," said an Indian officer, hearing of his death. "He was our father—the pattern of the British officer we so gladly serve; brave, wise, and, above all, full of sympathy. Thank God, we saw him here at the last; and I, if I live, will be able to tell my children in the Punjab that he shook hands with me and spoke to me in my own language."

Thus one fighter, among hundreds. All were eager at once to perform some special feat of arms in honour of their 'father's' memory: which they did, with striking success.

"His memory and his example are priceless," wrote another. "There must yet be a great future for the land that can breed such men and inspire such devotion." When the future looks dark and confused, therein lies our one sure hope.

The spirit of a man like Lord Roberts may pass on: but a part of it will always remain with the country he loved and served—a heritage for ever.

December 1914.

'HE COMES!'

(IN MEMORIAM 'ROBERTS, F.M.')

A WORD sped through the trenches, like flame through summer grass,
Where Sikh, Pathan and Gurkha crouch in the mud and rain,
Where Rajput and Punjabi cheer at the shells that pass,
Reckless of death or danger, eager to smite again.
' Never a war like this war,' a thousand bullets sing :
' Great are the guns of the foemen ; greater the British King.'

A word sped through the trenches, ' Our *Jung-i-Látsahib* '[1] comes !
He, that was ' Bobs *Bahádur* ' of Kabul and Kandahar—
Unforgetting and unforgotten of us in our Indian homes—
Soldier, he greets his soldiers in thunder and flame of war—
His the will and the courage no burden of years can bend,
Victor in the beginning ; victor unto the end.

' Can we forget, who knew him in the noontide of his fame—
Worthy avenger of heroes, little and wise and bold—
When Hindostan was ringing with the glory of his name,
And we that had seen bore witness wherever the tale was told ?
Lo, neither fame, nor honours, nor years can wean his heart
From the warrior sons of India. Hail to our *Jung-i-Lát* ! '

He came—and their eyes beheld him : changed, yet himself indeed ;
Still the face of their leader, though frosted with age and frail ;
Still the imperial spirit, supreme in the hour of need :
He came—and they gave him greeting : Roberts ' *Bahádur*, hail !
Conqueror, loved and honoured, from Comorin to Tibet,
Your trophy—the heart of India. Shall India ever forget ? '

Enough that he had their greeting ; enough that he saw and heard
The cannon lighten and thunder, the flash and crash of the fight ;
Enough that the guns of England should speak the parting word
As he passed beyond their voices into the Greater Light :
Enough that an Empire acclaims him—soldier, patriot, friend ;
Victor in the beginning ; victor unto the end.

MAUD DIVER.

[1] Lord of War.